PRAISE FOR ERIC B

"*Necropath* was a real success for me:
the depth of the characterisation; a very alien,
yet deeply sympathetic life-form; the authenticity
which Brown gives to the society on Bengal Station.
This is a place that you can see, hear and virtually smell."
SF Crow's Nest

"The writing is studded with phrases I had to
stop and reread because I liked them so much."
Fantasy

"Eric Brown's *Helix* is a classic concept – a built world to
dwarf Rama and Ringworld – a setting for a hugely imaginative
adventure. *Helix* is the very DNA of true SF. This is the
rediscovery of wonder."
Stephen Baxter

"*Helix* is essentially a romp – a gloriously old-fashioned
slice of science fiction... What gives the novel a unique spin
is its intertwining parallel plots. It's smart, fun, page-turning
stuff, with an engaging cast and plenty of twists...
A hugely entertaining read."
SFX

"He is a masterful storyteller. Eric Brown is often lauded as the
next big thing in science fiction and you can see why..."
Strange Horizons

"SF infused with a cosmopolitan and literary sensibility...
accomplished and affecting."
Paul J. McAuley

BINARY SYSTEM

ERIC BROWN

ALSO BY ERIC BROWN

Novels

Murder Take Three
Jani and the Great Pursuit
Jani and the Greater Game
Murder at the Loch
Murder at the Chase
Salvage
Satan's Reach
The Serene Invasion
Murder by the Book
Starship Seasons
Helix Wars
The Devil's Nebula
The Kings of Eternity
Guardians of the Phoenix
Cosmopath
Xenopath
Necropath
Kéthani
Helix
New York Dreams
New York Blues
New York Nights
Penumbra
Engineman
Meridian Days

Novellas

Exalted on Bellatrix I
Reunion on Alpha Reticuli II
Sacrifice on Spica III
Famadihana on Fomalhaut IV
Starship Spring
Starship Winter
Gilbert and Edgar on Mars
Starship Fall
Revenge
Starship Summer
The Extraordinary Voyage of
Jules Verne
Approaching Omega
A Writer's Life

Collections

Microcosms
(with Tony Ballantyne)
Rites of Passage
Strange Visitors
The Angels of Life and Death
Ghostwriting
Threshold Shift
The Fall of Tartarus
Deep Future
Parallax View
(with Keith Brooke)
Blue Shifting
The Time-Lapsed Man

BINARY SYSTEM

SOLARIS

First published 2017 by Solaris
an imprint of Rebellion Publishing Ltd,
Riverside House, Osney Mead,
Oxford, OX2 0ES, UK

www.solarisbooks.com

ISBN: 978 1 78108 551 6

10 9 8 7 6 5 4 3 2 1

A CIP catalogue record for this book is available from the
British Library.

Designed & typeset by Rebellion Publishing

Printed in Denmark by Nørhaven

To Ian Whates

and

Helen Sansum

CHAPTER ONE

THE PRIDE OF *Amsterdam* was transiting the Lunar wormhole when the explosion ripped through the starship's fusion core.

One second the *Amsterdam* was a billion-tonne, city-sized exploration-and-terraforming vessel embarking on a routine mission to 61 Cygni A; the next, a broken-backed wreck torn apart by an expanding fireball of superheated plasma. Two thousand crew members perished in the merciless vacuum of space as the stern of the ship fell away in beautiful silence, tumbling end over end towards the cratered regolith of the moon far below. Another hundred spacers died when the front end of the *Amsterdam* was shunted light years through the wormhole into an uncharted region of the galaxy.

The only thing that saved Cordelia Kemp was her stubborn insistence that she would see out the jump in the gym, rather than cocoon herself in a transition pod at the rear of the ship. Delia had suffered her fair share of shunt malaise in her time, but during her las few missions had elected to battle through the sickness. Anaerobic exercise occupied her metabolism and took her mind off the transit.

In the event she misjudged the starship's transition. In her haste to leave the gym to meet Timothy for coffee in one of the observation nacelles, she stepped into the corridor a minute before the shunt. She was feeling fit and energised, and looked forward to seeing Tim Greene again. They'd met at a mission briefing in Paris a month ago – it was to be his first extra-Solar tour of duty – and she'd felt an immediate attraction to the tall, softly-spoken xeno-biologist.

Their first date had gone well and they'd dined a few times before embarkation. Tim had been full of the wonder of the neophyte, and Delia comfortable in her role as the wise older woman blessing the young Englishman with her experience of interstellar travel. Not *that* much older, she told herself; she was thirty-five, Tim twenty-seven. In her last communication to her parents in Ontario, she'd even told them about Tim, surprising herself. She had hardly thought she was so serious about him until that moment.

She took a lateral slideway that ran alongside the outer skin of the *Amsterdam*; there was no one else in sight, fore or aft. Soon, with the shunt over, the ship would be swarming with crew members going about their duties. She touched the implant at her temple – relinquishing the silence she enjoyed while working out – and sub-vocalised, *Timothy?*

A small voice spoke in her head: *Mmm...*

She laughed: *Blitzed?*

A little whisky before climbing into my pod, he replied.

Well, make sure to take a sober-tab before we meet, hm?

Yes, Doctor Kemp. A hesitation, then: *Delia...*

Yes?

I love you.

That stopped her in her tracks. She'd been walking along the slideway, to hasten her progress; but now she allowed the slide to carry her past a long, curving viewscreen. She stared out at the pewter face of the moon, a million kilometres to starboard.

Is that the alcohol talking, Tim?

I've been meaning to tell you for a while. That last meal in Paris... Remember the moon? I said I couldn't believe that soon I'd be up there, making the transition... and you took my hand and told me not to be afraid. You understood, Del, you saw through all the bravado and knew I was scared.

I'm trained to...

Anyway, he cut in, *that's when I realised you mean a hell of a lot to me.*

She spoke softly: *Thank you.*

He cut the connection and Delia walked on, feeling as if she were being carried along on a cloud.

She muted the mind-noise of her Imp: the restaurant where she and Tim had last dined was beaming a farewell message – *Bon voyage aux astres, Dr Kemp et Dr Greene!* – and offering a fifteen-per-cent discount on their next meal. A sub-program was reminding the *Amsterdam*'s crew of the safety procedures to be observed during the shunt. Zeena Al Haq, a friend in Engineering, squirted her an invitation to the 61 Cygni A rendezvous party twenty-four hours from now. Delia accepted, on the condition that she could bring someone.

She glanced through the viewscreen. The vacuum ahead of the starship pulsed with the lapis lazuli effulgence of the quantum lattice. Her Imp told her that transition would commence in thirty seconds.

She stepped from the slideway and found a handhold on the bulkhead. She braced herself for the wave of nausea, staring along the curving wall to the raised outline of a lifeboat hatch. The frame was coloured a garish red and yellow, the only splash of colour in the silver-grey corridor. All the easier to locate in an emergency.

Her Imp said: *Transition in ten, nine, eight...*

She opened a channel to Tim and whispered, *Love you, too...* and immediately cut the connection before he had time to reply.

The blue light of the lattice consumed the ship and Delia hung her head as a queasy heat passed through her body. She felt as if she were going to be sick. She swallowed, riding the nausea.

The ship bucked, throwing her off her feet. The transition had evidently affected the artificial gravity, and only her hand-hold kept her where she was. She floated, thinking that this was the worst shunt she had ever experienced.

Then the *Amsterdam* bucked again and she cried out with the knowledge that something was very wrong.

She accessed the data-stream via her Imp, wanting the reassurance that all was well. All she heard, through a firestorm of static, were a thousand screams and a computerised voice issuing status reports, a techno-babble meaningless to her.

She heard the rending screech of metal on metal as the ship up-ended. She held on, crying out.

Her Imp said, *Delia, the emergency lifeboat.*

She looked along the corridor. The hatch was now beneath her. She pushed off towards it, at the same time trying to summon Tim.

Tim, Tim... for chrissake, answer me!

All she heard was a hail of static, punctuated by screams.

She grabbed hold of the hatch's lever and pulled. The door gave with a pressurised *whump* and swung inwards, pulling her inside. She slammed the hatch shut after her and experienced a sudden, profound mind-silence. Normally, even when commanded to silence, her Imp updated her every few seconds, a background noise so ubiquitous she was hardly ever aware of the mind-chatter. Now she experienced absolute silence, and it was shocking.

Imp! she called. *Why the...?*

Systemic communications failure, Delia.

What's happening? She was turning end over end in the confines of the life-raft. She found a handhold and steadied herself. *Imp?*

Assessing data input.

A second later it resumed: *Initial detonation in reactor core.*

Secondary explosions in decks A and C.

What? she cried, stunned.

A hundred life-rafts dotted the carapace of the starship, positioned close to the banked transition pods. Chances were, she told herself, that Tim had managed to make it to a raft...

Her Imp said, *Move to the control console. Initiate jettison manoeuvre.*

But what about...?

Her Imp anticipated her: *There are no more survivors in this section of the ship. Move to the control console and initiate jettison manoeuvre.*

She looked around her, saw the console and pushed herself towards it. She grabbed the edge of the console and palmed the initiation plate, then strapped herself to the wall and waited.

The life-raft jerked as it ejected itself from the wreckage of the *Amsterdam.* She imagined the tiny craft spinning away, turning over and over like a leaf in a gale.

Tim! she called.

Comprehensive communications failure, her Imp said in its maddeningly neutral masculine voice. *Intra-crew communications impossible.*

As the life-raft had stabilised its flight from the starship, she looked down. At first she thought she'd wet herself in panic; then she saw a spread of transparent gel ooze across her thighs and down her legs. Her abdomen spasmed as the gel caressed her like a lover's hand, then spread upwards to cover her chest. It stopped at her throat, thankfully, leaving just her head free and the rest of her body cocooned in a warm, gelid mass.

Imp, the ship's reactor core... How close was it to the crew's transition pods?

Precisely three thousand metres distant.

So... that's a long way, yeah? I mean, the blast...

She stopped herself. She was babbling, clutching at straws.

There is a ninety-nine-point-seven–per cent likelihood that the crew's transition pods were consumed in the initial blast within a time-frame of between one point three and four point five seconds.

She had the irrational impulse, then, to shout at her Imp, rail at its smartware for being so inhuman and emotionless.

Tim...

Nevertheless, she could not believe that Tim had perished. Surely he'd managed to scramble to a life-raft... The initial blast might not have destroyed the pod sector.

She shut her mind to any other possibility and considered her own survival.

How long before I can expect to be picked up?

After a delay of a second, her Imp responded, *Unable to assess.*

Can you calculate how many other survivors there might be?

That is impossible to determine without access to the Amsterdam's *core AI.*

She snapped: *You can't guess?*

Her Imp ignored the question. Smartware did not guess.

She imagined the raft floating like a tiny seedpod around the moon, soon to be rescued by one of the Lunar teams. A matter of hours, she told herself.

The Imp might not be able to tell her precisely how long it might take to be rescued, but surely it could give her some indication of her present position.

She asked.

Unable to determine, her Imp responded.

She swore. *Chrissake, why not! Do a calculation. How far away were we from the moon when the blow-out happened? What direction did the life-raft take when we jettisoned? Work it out, damn you!*

That is impossible, Delia, it said.

Impossible? Why impossible?

Because the Amsterdam *was in the process of transition when the explosion occurred.*

An icy hand gripped her innards. *But... but the shunt hadn't completed –*

The fore section of the Amsterdam *was negotiating the lattice when the detonation occurred.*

She nodded, telling herself to be calm. *I see. I understand. So... that's okay, that's fine, isn't it? We made the transition, right, so we're somewhere in Cygni space right now? We'll be picked up by an extra-Solar team, right?*

Delia, her Imp said, *the explosion aboard the* Amsterdam *resulted in a translation failure.*

She nodded again, swallowed. She felt terribly constrained by the gel cocooning her body. She wanted to be free to move around, work off her fear. *So okay... And what* exactly *does that mean? 'Translation failure'?*

The lattice was damaged in the explosion. In the nano-seconds before transition, I received information that the fore section of the Amsterdam *was shunted at least ten thousand light years through space, perhaps as far as fifteen thousand light years.*

"At least ten thousand..." she murmured to herself.

In humankind's expansion, the furthest they had ever explored was two hundred light years from Earth.

So, where are we?

That is impossible to determine, Delia. All that I can state with any degree of certainty is that we are in an unexplored sector of space.

Panic gripped her. She struggled, but the safety gel gripped her as rigidly as any straitjacket.

Delia, said her Imp, *for your own good I am about to sedate you.*

And within seconds her fear subsided and she slipped into blessed oblivion.

CHAPTER TWO

DELIA.

Mmm...?

I am bringing you round.

I think I'd rather sleep, thanks all the same.

I have been monitoring your metabolism. You should eat.

She blinked her eyes open and stared around the cramped confines of the life-raft. *How long have I been out?*

A little under twenty-four hours.

She relived the explosion. *Tim!*

She moved, finding that she was no longer constricted by the safety gel. She floated across the raft, came to the curving wall and gripped a hand-hold.

You will find a container of supplies in the unit marked Three. Food and water.

I don't want to eat.

For your wellbeing, Delia, you should eat and drink.

Why?

For your wellbeing, her Imp repeated.

I mean, why should I bother? I'm stranded in uninhabited, unexplored space, at least ten thousand light years from Earth...

That is no reason not to eat.

Typical machine logic, she thought.

What are the chances of ESO sending out a rescue mission? she asked.

That is impossible, Delia.

That fist again, ice cold and gripping her heart. *Why?*

Because the Amsterdam *was shunted on a random trajectory through space.*

Wonderful. The furthest we've ever shunted before is, what? Two hundred and ten light years?

Correct.

And now I'm at least ten thousand light years from the nearest human... and you want me to eat?

For your well –

...For my wellbeing. Yes, I know. She closed her eyes and tried not to scream. *How much food and water is there?*

Sufficient to last four people six days.

So... do the math for me, Imp, I don't feel up to it... How long will the supplies last me?

If you eat and drink sparingly, the supplies will last for approximately sixty days.

Great. And then?

And then the supplies will run out.

Sixty days, and then no more food and drink.

She paused.

And then? She wanted to push her Imp to state the cold hard facts; to hear it admit the obvious.

And then you will have exhausted the life-raft's supplies.

And what will happen to me then, Imp?

If no other source of sustenance is discovered, then you will begin to starve.

She nodded. *In other words, I will die.*

Yes.

And you?

Refine your question, Delia.

What will become of you, when I die?

I will have reached a state of redundancy, and will commence a closedown procedure.

And what do you think of that?

Closedown is not an optimum state of existence. I am, after all, programmed to serve you and ensure your continued wellbeing.

Delia sighed. *And I appreciate that, Imp.*

She pushed herself over to the unit marked Three and pulled it open. Six canisters of water and a package of shrink-wrapped supplies.

She took a long drink of water and chewed on an energy bar.

And what are the chances of our discovering another 'source of sustenance'? Not much foodstuff between the stars, Imp.

I am investigating the viability of the closest star system, Delia.

A star system? She was unable to suppress a small surge of hope.

Affirmative.

There's a star system nearby?

It is approximately one hundred astronomical units distant.

Delia found a web and fastened herself in.

And you're taking us there now?

Yes.

How long before we reach this star system?

Approximately two days until we reach the system's heliopause.

Delia felt despair grip her by the throat. *And what are the chances, Imp, of finding a planet that won't be inimical to a carbon based life-form like me?*

The reply came a fraction of a second later: *Between one hundred thousand to one, and three point seven million to one.*

"Great odds," Delia grunted to herself.

She pressed her palms to her eyes and wept.

CHAPTER THREE

Imp.

Yes, Delia?

Where's the medi-kit?

Unit Four.

She pushed herself from the web, swam across to the unit, and hauled it open. She found the medi-kit and what she was looking for: a hypoject and a small ampoule of chemical opiate – sufficient to kill her painlessly in seconds.

Imp, will you project my mother and father, please?

She blinked through her tears as they appeared before her, as solid and lifelike as if they were with her in the life-raft. They were smiling at each other, chatting away at some commonplace of life in far away Ontario.

Three missions ago she had had her Imp record her parents and set up an interactive paradigm, so that, far away from home as she worked amongst the stars, she could access her parents' avatars and assuage her loneliness.

And oddly enough, surprising herself, after only her second meeting with Timothy Greene, back in Paris, she had had her Imp do the same so that she could be with him even when he wasn't with her. She had done it with other prospective lovers, years ago; her friend Zeena had said it was her way of vetting them without their knowledge.

She said, "Mom, Dad, how's things?"

They looked up and smiled at her. "Just fine, Cordelia," her mother replied. "We're well. Your father's arthritis is playing up a little."

"But nothing serious," he put in.

"And you, Cordelia? Tell us all about where you are now."

She began to say, "Far, far away..." but the words caught in her throat and she commanded her Imp to cease the projection.

Her parents vanished and she was alone again in the life-raft.

She worked to keep her breathing steady, then said, *Now Tim. Project Tim.*

Timothy Greene appeared before her, reading a softscreen. He looked up and smiled, and grief cut through her heart.

"I just wanted to say goodbye, Tim," she said in a tiny voice.

"Goodbye?"

"I just wanted to see you one more time, to remind me of how beautiful you are. And you are, Tim."

Imp, cease the projection. She closed her eyes before it did so, and when she opened them again, Tim was gone.

She returned to the webbing, carrying the medical case, and stuck it to the bulkhead next to her.

Imp, you said that in sixty days, when the supplies run out, I will die.

Affirmative.

Very well... But I've chosen not to wait for that inevitability. I'll take an overdose immediately, understood? And I don't want you to take countermeasures which might keep me alive.

You wish to enact Protocol 21? Imp asked.

Affirmative.

Very well. However...

Yes?

I think it would be wise to wait until we have reached the star system and I have evaluated the possibility of its harbouring a life-sustaining world.

But you said the chances of that were millions to one.

To be precise, between one hundred thousand to one, and three point seven million to one.

In that case, I see no reason...

But Imp persisted with its implacable machine logic. *Delia, I advise circumspection. Wait until we have reached the star system. I suggest that I sedate you once again for the duration of the journey, some twenty-two hours...*

Why postpone the inevitable, she thought. *Very well, Imp, sedate me.*

CHAPTER FOUR

SHE WOKE AND said, *Well?*

We are entering the heliopause of the star system.

And? No signs of life, right?

It is too early to tell.

She thought of her mother and father and the grief they would be suffering now, having heard the news about the *Pride of Amsterdam*. She thought of Tim and Zeena, and all her other friends...

She felt physically ill.

She reached for the medical package adhering to the wall beside her, then stopped.

How many planets are there in this system? she asked.

Seven, her Imp responded. *From the outermost to the innermost, two micro worlds, four gas giants, and one approximately Earth-sized planet.*

And is the latter in the Goldilocks zone?

Why am I doing this? she asked herself. I'm prolonging the agony. Of course there won't be an Earth-like planet down there.

I think not, though that is difficult to ascertain –

I don't see why it should be, she interrupted.

Because the Earth-sized planet describes a highly elliptical orbit around its primary.

How elliptical?

The answer came a second later: *At the furthest point from its primary, it is ten astronomical units away; at its closest, less than half an AU. The planet describes an orbit that, in Terran years, takes almost ten years to complete. Nine years of harsh winter, and one of summer.*

Intense winter, she said, *then a brief, blistering summer.*

Yes.

So... the chances of the world sustaining life are... zero.

Her Imp corrected: *Life as we* know *it.*

Quite. Life as we know it.

I might as well inject myself now and get it over with, she thought. Curiosity, however, got the better of her.

Imp, can you bring up a visual of the star system?

Affirmative. Please allow five seconds.

She would look upon this distant star system, the first and only human in history to do so. Perhaps, one day, the life-raft would be discovered by human explorers; they would find her lifeless corpse and maybe even name the planet down there after her: Kemp's World.

Delia, visuals coming through.

She was quite unprepared for the beauty of the scene that washed the far wall of the life-raft. The interior was lit up by two suns, one a great ruddy ball, the other a much smaller white light. Around the red primary gyred seven worlds: four huge barrelling gas giants, striated with an artist's palette of colour; then the two tiny specks of the micro worlds, so small that her Imp had resorted to indicating them with haloes – and, finally, the Earth-sized world.

Something caught in her throat and she leaned forward.

Imp, are those clouds?

She stared upon the pale, chiffon-scarved planet, hardly daring to hope.

Affirmative. The planet does possess cloud formations, and an extremely active weather system.

Clouds... she murmured. *That means water. The possibility of life!*

We need to get closer for me to ascertain the likelihood of the planet's sustaining life, Imp said.

Sedate me, Delia ordered, *and wake me when we're closer.*

DELIA...

She woke instantly and tried to make sense of the scene splashed across the far wall.

The life-raft was vibrating madly, rattling her. Only the web she was strapped into saved her from being thrown around the raft like a pea in a drum.

The scene on the viewscreen was yawing, an icy horizon tilting like a see-saw.

How long have I been unconscious?

Fourteen hours.

What's happening?

We're coming down.

I gathered that, she said. If her Imp had decided to land, that must mean...

I brought the raft in low because I detected what might be cities, Imp said.

Her heart thumped. *Cities?*

We were coming in low, well south of the planet's equator. I was running atmospheric content tests when the life-raft was hit.

Hit? You mean, we hit some debris...?

We were hit by either a laser or a missile.

A succession of emotions chased each other through her head: fear of crash-landing, exhilaration that there might be cities down there, wonder as it came to her that she just might be experiencing the first ever human-sentient alien contact in the history of her race.

A laser or a missile? You sure? You mean, something fired in anger, by... by...

By extraterrestrials – yes, Delia. It clipped our dorsal fin, hence our instability.

"Sentient aliens... " she said to herself.

She leaned forward in the web, staring at the viewscreen. They were racing low over a vast icy plain like striated glass. In the distance, on the horizon, she made out an enfilade of mountains like a thousand rearing stalagmites. She could see no sign of civilisation down there.

Imp, can you bring us down safely?

I can achieve a landing without compromising the structural integrity of the life-raft.

I'm glad to hear that.

Of course, a safe landing would mean nothing if she were unable to breathe the atmosphere of the ice-bound world.

Imp, did you manage to find out if the atmosphere is breathable?

I am working on it, Delia.

But even if the atmosphere were breathable, what were the chances of the planet yielding foodstuffs that a human metabolism could process? And the cold? It looked pretty hostile out there – and what about when the planet swung towards its primary? The brief, intense summer? She would be frozen stiff and roasted by turn. And then, of course, there was the attention of the hostile ETs to take into consideration.

Delia, hold on tight. Landing in thirty seconds.

She tightened the webbing around her, pulling down a head-rest and cushioning her neck against the impact.

The ice plain sped beneath the ship in a blur.

Ten, nine, eight...

Despite her best intentions to watch the final few seconds of the landing, she involuntarily closed her eyes as the ice rushed up to meet the ship.

She had expected a jarring impact, the rending of metal, even an explosion. But the life-raft hit the ice like a flat stone skimming across the surface of a lake: a glancing impact, a bounce, then a second impact, and another and another. Then the raft was spinning like a puck and Delia knew they had landed safely.

Well done, Imp. Damage?

Minor abrasions to the shell as well as the original damage to the dorsal fin.

But we could still use the raft, yes? It'll still fly?

We would have to repair the dorsal fin. And we have limited reserves of fuel. Of course, we could never achieve escape velocity in a craft this small...

Of course.

She released herself from the web and fell to the floor. The gravity was less than Earth norm; she felt buoyant. She picked herself up and approached the viewscreen.

The life-raft had ploughed up a bow wave of shaved ice; the view through the bottom half of the viewscreen was obscured by melting slush. Above it, all she could see was a plain of grey ice and the jagged mountains on the horizon. Straight ahead the ruddy sun – a huge globe filling a quarter of the sky – hung like a glaring eye. The small white sun was a tiny point far to the right.

Delia, I have the results of the atmospheric analysis...

She closed her eyes. *Tell me.*

The atmosphere is sufficiently Earth-like to sustain human life.

Exhilaration swelled in her chest.

So I'll be able to breathe the air?

Yes.

She stared out across the ice plain. *What's the outside temperature?*

Twenty-three below zero, Imp replied.

But I'll never survive that!

The raft is equipped with thermal suits. I suggest you find one and put it on. Unit Seven.

She opened the unit and hauled out a suit, a crimson one-piece that shrunk to fit her as she hauled it on over her grey uniform. She drew up a hood like a balaclava; the suit was even equipped with a face-mask, which she hung around her neck in readiness.

Of course, if there's nothing to eat out there...

Delia, the fact that this planet sustains sentient life-forms suggests that there is a food supply. Whether it would sustain you, of course, is another matter.

She wondered at the chances of her being able to eat the food – whether she would be able to metabolise the proteins and carbohydrates she might find on this world.

And then there was the small matter of unknown pathogens.

Imp, what about the threat of disease?

The face-mask should filter and purify the air; of course, I am unable to ascertain its efficacy. Also, at present I am unable to analyse the threat of potential pathogens.

She would fill her mind, she told herself, with the small questions of minute-by-minute survival. Because to look upon the larger picture – that she was all alone on an inimical alien world – was just too much to contemplate without inviting madness.

Imp, does the life-raft carry a supply of weapons?

Negative.

Great. If the extraterrestrials who brought us down are hostile, I'll need something to defend myself with.

Delia...

Her Imp paused.

Go on.

I have detected movement outside.

Right... She swallowed, her heart hammering.

Activity approximately three kilometres straight ahead. I will magnify the image.

The screen went blank. Delia felt a moment of irrational, claustrophobic panic. If there were hostile ETs out there, she wanted to see them.

Then the screen flickered back into life. The mountains were closer now, and on the plain of ice she detected movement: a column of small, dark... *creatures*... like a line of ants, but too far away for her to make them out individually.

They're heading this way?

Affirmative.

Coming for their spoils...

Delia, take the food supplies and the medical package and place them in the backpack you will find in Unit One.

She hurried around the raft, collected the packages and slipped them into the backpack, shrugging it onto her back. Earth's greater gravity would have made the weight a burden; here it was as if she were carrying nothing at all.

Don't forget the charger, Delia.

The charger! *There is one aboard the raft?*

Affirmative. Her Imp told her where to find it, and she slipped the silver disc into the hip pocket of her thermal suit.

Once a month she placed a charger beneath her pillow as she slept, and in the morning her Imp was refuelled. Without it, her Imp would have sufficient power for a month before shutting down.

The thought of being without the comforting presence of her Imp – quite apart from its life-saving assistance – did not bear contemplating.

She stared through the viewscreen, and what she saw took her breath away.

The extraterrestrial column had advanced towards the life-raft, resolving itself into a dozen or more discernible creatures as they marched across the ice.

Delia braced her arms against the viewscreen to control her shaking.

They were perhaps half a kilometre away now, but huge even at this distance. Three metres high, four? They resembled spiders, or perhaps crabs, jet black creatures with multiple legs on either side of oval, chitinous carapaces.

And there I was, hoping to be greeted by beautiful, angelic humanoids.

The likelihood of that... her Imp began.

I was joking, Delia said. "They look... fearsome," she murmured to herself.

Delia, the larger creatures are not, I surmise, the dominant species.

What do you mean, the 'larger'?

Observe, mounted upon the backs of the spider-crabs.

The riders, six to each creature, resembled locusts: thin, attenuated beings, as silver-grey as the surrounding ice, their long legs drawn up and jutting out on either side of almost equine heads.

What... what should I do, Imp?

It is imperative that you are not perceived as a threat by these creatures. Their actions in bringing down the life-raft might have been hostile, but their dominant motivating factor now might just be curiosity. Of course, that would be ascribing anthropocentric tendencies to the aliens.

Should I exit the raft and greet them?

No. Allow me to assess their intentions, if that is possible.

The caravan of spider-crabs came to a halt a hundred metres from the life-raft. Delia stared out, her stomach tight with apprehension.

As she watched, the insect riders on the first spider-crab dismounted, and Delia gasped in astonishment.

One second, the locusts were seated one behind the other on their mount – and the next they were standing on the ice beside one of its great hairy forelegs. There had been no noticeable transition. They had moved so fast that it was as if the creatures had teleported themselves from the back of the spider-crab.

A heartbeat later they had crossed the intervening hundred metres and were standing very still and staring at the life-raft. This time, Delia had detected a blur of movement, a sheen of silver-grey as the locusts moved, lightning-fast, across the ice.

Involuntarily, she took a step back from the viewscreen, although she knew the aliens could not see through the wall of the craft.

Behind the first six locusts, more of them dismounted, vanishing instantly from atop their mounts and appearing beside their compatriots, their long heads and bulging, microphone eyes directed at the life-raft.

Delia took a step forward to better examine the aliens.

Their arms and legs were long and perilously thin, osseous spars jutting from skeletal shoulders and concave pelvic flanges. They looked as if a light tap might send them skittling.

Their heads moved from side to side as they examined the shell of the vessel, their mandibles opening and shutting in silence.

She turned in alarm as something clanged against the side of the life-raft. A vibration conducted itself through the carapace.

What...?

I think they are cutting their way into the life-raft, Delia. Activate your thermal suit and pull on the face-mask.

Delia did as instructed and turned to the source of the noise. Something appeared through a slit in the padding of the life-raft's ceiling, a hooked blade that slowly worked its way down the curving bulkhead like an antique can-opener.

I should be able to see the funny side of this, Imp, she said. *But to be honest...*

Remember, do nothing that might be perceived as a threat. I suggest that they will be as fearful of you as you are of them. You are, after all, a member of a technologically superior race, going on what I have observed to date.

She was heating up in the thermal suit. A wind like a razor blade slashed through the gap, freezing her hands. The sleeves of her suit incorporated gloves, and she lost no time in pulling the material over her hands.

The blade had reached the extent of its vertical incision. It withdrew, to appear a moment later at the top of the slash, cutting horizontally.

Delia glanced at the viewscreen, but all the aliens had moved around the raft to view the opening.

The blade was now slicing another vertical gash in the wall. She expected them to make another lateral cut at the bottom, forming a square, and stood back to avoid the section of the wall falling in upon her, but they took another approach.

As she watched, the flange of metal bowed inwards – pressed downwards, she saw, by the great hirsute foreleg of one of the spider-crabs. A freezing wind filled the raft, and despite her thermal suit Delia shivered. When the flap of metal was folded down all the way to form an ad hoc ramp, the monstrous leg was withdrawn.

A dozen insect heads appeared around the edge of the gap, staring in at her. She stood erect, matching their inscrutable gazes.

She wondered what they made of her, this puny scrap of humanity cast up so far away from home.

Four aliens were beside her in the life-raft. She didn't see them enter; they simply winked into existence at her side.

She backed away.

Their long heads jutted forward, moving from side to side as they examined her, their mandibles clacking like a cacophony of castanets.

Remain calm, Delia, her Imp counselled. *They have shown, so far, no inclination towards hostility.*

She saw a flicker of movement to her right as one of the aliens plucked the charger from her hip pocket. The creature passed the silver disc to its neighbour, who held it at arm's length, as if testing whether or not it might be a weapon. Another alien took the charger, turning it over and over. They looked at each other, jaws working.

Delia watched them, willing them to replace the charger in her pocket.

She should be so lucky. The alien to her right completed its examination of the device, then dropped it to the floor.

Before she could work out how to retrieve the charger, she felt something wrap itself tightly around her arms, legs and torso. She was bound by a tight silver thread, and it was all she could do to remain on her feet.

Then she was borne aloft and carried at incredible speed from the life-raft and across the ice. She felt claws digging painfully into her arms and legs.

The charger, she thought...

Remain calm, her Imp said. *Don't struggle. They have shown no desire to do you harm.*

Yet, she said.

It is my assessment that they are more curious than hostile.

She was carried at dizzying speed across the ice towards one of the huge spider-crabs, everything a blur around her. Her vision adjusted as she was lifted up onto the back of the creature. Two aliens tied her, again with loops of silver thread, to the dome of the spider-crab's body above its antennae'd head. To either side of her, a forest of thick black hairs sprouted from osseous follicles. She was joined by two guards who settled themselves beside her, their femurs folding up alongside them. Another alien climbed onto the creature's head and gripped its antennae.

The spider-crab moved, and Delia felt a plate of chitin shift beneath her. To her right and left, the spider's great legs rose and fell like pistons.

She looked down and saw her life-raft. A group of aliens was attaching thick silver ropes to the vessel and slinging them around the haunches of one of the spider-crabs. The creature took the strain and the life-raft moved across the ice like a sled. She thought of the charger on the floor of the raft, and wondered at the chances of her getting it back again. At least they weren't leaving the life-raft out on the plain.

The procession moved across the ice, heading in the direction of the distant mountains.

Where was she being taken?

She sub-vocced the question to her Imp.

No doubt to the nearest extraterrestrial city, it replied. *Remain calm.*

She smiled. *There's little else I can do.*

You are warm enough?

Toasty, thank you.

I think it would be wise to sedate you, until journey's end.

Very well, but I don't want to miss anything. Wake me if anything interesting happens.

Imp released sedative into her system, and Delia slipped into unconsciousness.

CHAPTER FIVE

SHE WOKE FROM a dream of dining with Timothy in Paris.

The reality of where she was and what had happened came crashing down on her. *The dream I had been enjoying should be the reality*, she told herself – *and this the dream... or nightmare.*

They were no longer on the ice plain.

From her position above the head of the spider-crab, Delia looked across a vista of folded foothills, falling away like buckled steel, scintillating with silver frost. She turned her head to look to the rear; hers was the leading beast. A dozen more followed slowly along a narrow road that climbed into the mountains. The same mountains, she realised, that she had seen on the distant horizon.

Imp, how long have I been out?

Almost one day, Terran, Delia.

One day...

How long does a day last on this world?

Approximately twenty Terran hours.

The guards crouched on either side of her, their bulging eyes staring ahead at the falling foothills. Four other aliens squatted behind her on the dome of the spider-crab's body.

From time to time the guards conversed in an incomprehensible rattle of mandibles.

She had a thought.

Imp, can you translate what they're saying?

For the past twenty-four hours, since our capture, I have been running a logic analysis on their language. I estimate that I might have a rudimentary understanding of their spoken language within six hours.

She looked ahead, up the winding length of the road into the mountains. She made out rearing silver peaks, more attenuated and spire-like than natural rock formations on Earth. It was as if they were sculpted, joined one to the other by scooped ice walls. Above the peaks the great red sun bathed the scene in its bloody light.

Imp, are we heading into winter or towards summer?

The planet is moving towards its primary, Delia. I calculate that in approximately one Terran week, a great thaw will take hold of the planet, presaging the brief summer.

Things must change dramatically, she said.

The ice will vanish, the landscape will be reformed. I suspect that dormant seeds will take advantage of the sunlight and bloom, briefly, before dying back as another long, hostile winter commences.

What a world... and yet sentient life has evolved.

Life that has adapted itself to extremes of great cold and punishing heat.

Timothy could only have dreamed of experiencing this world. As a xeno-biologist, he would have found the strange, inimical planet fascinating, a case study that would have occupied him for years.

She shut her mind to Timothy and his fate and concentrated on the here and now.

Imp?

Yes.

Even if I survive, if I'm allowed my freedom by these... these creatures... even then, what are the chances of my ever leaving this world – of getting back to Earth?

The reply was what she expected: consoling, avuncular, wise. *We are in no position to make such evaluations at present, Delia. We are not in full possession of all the facts. In time, maybe, when we have assessed the level of technology possessed by the extraterrestrials, then we might be able to determine our chances of escape. Until then I counsel calm, caution, and vigilance.*

The road ahead turned around a projecting knuckle of ice-covered rock, and an archway through a wall of ice hove into view. The caravan of spider-crabs plodded on. Delia was lulled by the back and forth motion of the great beast. She was warm in her thermal suit, and she guessed that her Imp was releasing tiny quantities of sedative into her system. By all that was right and proper, she should be grieving her lover, and her homeworld. Instead she felt only a dull fear, tempered by curiosity

But if she could not retrieve the charger, then in time she would be without Imp.

The thought roused her and she said, *Imp.*

Delia?

I can't recall... when was the last time I used the charger, back on Earth?

Almost twenty days ago.

She felt a pit of despair open up within her. *But that means in ten days...*

Be calm. Don't dwell on eventualities that might never occur. Ten days is, after all, a long time. I will work to retrieve the charger.

She nodded. *Thank you, Imp.*

CHAPTER SIX

FIVE HOURS LATER they left the plain of ice in their wake and took a track that wound further into the foothills, and an hour after that they rounded a pinnacle of rock and came upon a remarkable sight.

It's... it's beautiful.

The mountain fastness of the natives, Imp said.

On the far side of a yawning chasm, which she guessed was a kilometre or two wide, was an ethereal city of spires that mimicked the soaring peaks strung out to either side. The towering buildings, accessed by broad sweeping steps and cantilevered walkways, glowed in the bloody light of the sun. She looked for any sign of mechanised traffic, but saw none, and this absence lent the city a quietude that matched its grandeur.

The high, narrow road curved around the chasm to the city. A keening wind whistled through the peaks; Delia was grateful for her thermal suit.

She wondered what awaited her in the city of the locusts.

Imp, have you managed to work out their language yet?

I am working on it.

How long until...?

Soon, now.

The caravan clanked along the roadway around the chasm. They passed from the shade and Delia felt the warmth of the sun on her head. Halfway along the great curving roadway, she looked back and saw the last spider-crab, hauling her life-raft. The vessel filled the width of the road, and the locusts in charge of the creature were urging it forward little by little.

She looked away, fearing it might slip into the chasm and be lost forever, the precious charger with it.

Seconds later the locust mounted on the headpiece of her spider-crab pulled on its antennae and brought the beast to a halt. The guards became excited; they chattered to each other, then called out in a string of clacking, ringing notes to the steersman.

She became aware of a sweet, acrid stench, faint at first but growing stronger. She heard shouted commands along the length of the caravan. The alien to her right prodded her, and pointed into the chasm. They evidently wanted her to take note of something.

What is it? she asked her Imp.

It appears to be some form of graveyard. Look...

The stench rising from the chasm made her gag, even through the facemask.

She peered down.

The vast oval of the chasm was half-filled with what looked like discarded sections of sable chitin, great cowls and domes of shell stretching away to form an oddly beautiful osseous landscape. Here and there, blackened body-parts protruded through the chitin and high into the air, stark shanks and vaulting ribcages. Nearby a timber jetty extended into the chasm, raised on pillars above the sea of bones.

As she watched, a spider-crab was removed from the caravan by its erstwhile riders and goaded along the jetty. The creature, perhaps sensing its fate, appeared reluctant to advance; the locusts prodded it with staffs, working them into the gaps between its jointed legs and twisting savagely.

What are they doing?

The question was rhetorical, but her Imp answered anyway. *It would appear that this is some form of sacrifice, perhaps a ritual appeasement or offering.*

She glanced at her guards, and at the other aliens mounted on the spider-crabs. All were silent, intent on what was taking place on the jetty as the hapless creature was goaded forward little by little.

Then the dozen aliens drew long, scimitar-shaped swords from scabbards and proceeded to rend the spider-crab limb from limb. The locusts moved in a blur; Delia watched in appalled fascination, seeing not the movement of the beast's tormentors but the effects of their handiwork as limbs appeared to fall away, one by one, by their own volition. The air was rent with high-pitched squeals as the beast tottered on its remaining limbs.

The creature toppled and hit the timbers with a crack, a limbless torso leaking ichor across the boards of the pier, its severed limbs scattered like so many jackstraws.

A great clacking cheer went up from the gallery of watching aliens, and the creature's executioners proceeded to discard the limbs and eye-stalks from the pier, the body parts rattling down into the grave pit.

Then, working in concert, the locusts heaved the dripping body and tipped it into the chasm. It fell in a spray of ejected body fluid and hit the sea of shell-fragments with a ripe, cartilaginous crack.

Delia glanced at her guards; their mandibles moved, but in silence, and she wondered if they were intoning silent prayers to whatever alien god they worshipped.

The caravan started up again and they proceeded along the roadway to the city.

They're savages! she said.

It would be a mistake to fall back on anthropocentric prejudices when considering an alien race, Delia. They might be a highly civilised, learned people, for all we know, with abstruse philosophies and strict moral and ethical codes. None of that would be inconsistent with what he have observed.

You're right, she allowed, *but even so...*

She stared ahead at the city rising from the escarpment. The soaring towers and minarets were ethereal, and so bright that she thought, at first, that they had been carved from ice. The caravan approached the city and proceeded along a wide boulevard. The buildings on either side were fashioned from scintillating stone, long blocks placed end to end, with high, narrow openings – windows and doors – carved with fluted embrasures and arches.

The most striking thing about the city, she noted, was that it appeared entirely deserted. Not a single citizen moved along the boulevard or the narrow alleys running off it between the towering minarets. An eerie silence prevailed, broken only by the sound of the spider-crabs' ringing footfalls on the vast slabbed paving of the boulevard.

They passed between two high buildings, as grand as Terran cathedrals, and came into a great square – and here at last Delia saw movement.

She blinked in surprise at the figures gathered at the far end of the square. They were not the locust creatures, but small beings which resembled thin, long-limbed Terran apes, though with fur coloured a striking iridescent blue.

A hundred of the creatures hauled slabs of stone across the square; others worked on the stones with chisels and saws.

As the caravan emerged from between the buildings, the blue creatures ceased work and stared across the square.

Delia said, awed, *Another sentient race?*

So it would appear... Though the probability of two sentient species emerging on a single planet is very low, based on current evolutionary models.

They can't be related, the locust and these... these primates?

Obviously not. A client species, or...

Yes?

Or a slave species.

They left the square and passed down an alley between tall buildings, entering cold shadow. She made out an archway ahead, hewn from natural rock. The steersman of her spider-crab urged it on, ducking when they came to the arch. They passed into a tunnel and Delia pitched forward against the ties that bound her as they began to descend.

Darkness fell, alleviated once in a while by flaming sconces set into the wall. She made out chiselled stone, occasional branching passageways.

At last the spider-crab came to a halt and Delia felt herself being untied. She was carried off again at speed, horizontally, along shadowy passages. She lay on her back, aware of a dozen points of pain where the locusts' claws dug into her arms, legs and torso.

Light appeared up ahead and she passed through a low archway into a dim chamber, where she was lowered to the floor. She looked around; her captors had retreated in a blink, pulling shut a stone slab door behind them.

They had also, she saw, released her from the silver cords that had bound her arms and legs. She was free to move for the first time in hours. She stood up, rubbing her arms, and examined her twilight prison.

She was in a large room with walls like white marble, in the centre of which was what looked like a circular pit. On closer inspection she saw that the pit was filled with a single huge cushion, evidently an alien bed. The walls were without decoration or ornamentation. At the far end of the chamber, her eye was drawn to a high arched window.

She removed the pack from her back, placed it next to the bed-pit, then moved to the window. A dozen slabs of thick glass were set in a heavy metal frame. She looked for a means of opening the window, then pressed her palms against the frame. It was solid, immovable. She pressed her forehead against the glass and peered out.

The chamber overlooked the grave pit, and as she peered down she was overcome with a sickening vertigo that made her want to drop to the floor. The bloody sun glowered between two distant mountain peaks, a symbol of how utterly removed she was from all she had ever known.

Delia, perhaps some music? her Imp suggested.

Music? She almost laughed at the idea. Her Imp held a cache of a hundred thousand music files in all genres and styles – as well as films, holo-dramas, plays...

I could play one of your favourites: Ravel?

No! It's the last thing I need, just now. Music, to remind me of everything I've lost...

Feeling despair rise in her like nausea, she returned to the bed-pit and threw herself down, ordering her Imp to administer a sedative that would remove her from all that was alien and threatening.

CHAPTER SEVEN

WHEN SHE AWOKE, the room was in darkness.

How long did I sleep?

For more than twelve hours.

I feel a little better.

The thermal suit had kept her warm, but as she rolled from the bed-pit she noticed a patina of frost on the tiles beside the cushions, evidently where her breath had frozen while she slept.

She moved to the arched window at the far end of the room and stood with one hand touching the embrasure. Massed stars were spread across the heavens above the jagged mountain peaks. They were so closely packed they resembled the fused radiance of a nebula, a gauzy gold and cerise incandescence. She wondered where Earth lay, and felt a stab of anguish at the thought.

What am I going to do, Imp?

You're alive, Delia. There is hope. Before we landed here, there was not even that.

It's odd, but I feel more despair now than I did when I thought my fate hopeless.

Without warning a source of light sprang into being at her back. She turned. The door at the far end of the room swung open and a burning orange flame flew towards her.

It halted in midair, borne atop a long staff carried by one of three locust creatures. They appeared before her suddenly, their long mandibles working.

A series of meaningless clicks reached her ears.

Do you know what they're saying?

I can apprehend the occasional word. They are asking who you are, where you came from. They... want something from you.

Want something? The idea alarmed her. *What do they want?*

I can't decipher their request. The ideas are too abstract. They want your help with something...

She stared from one to the other of the aliens. They appeared identical, skeletal beings towering over her by almost a metre. Their heads, like their bodies, were the dead grey of bleached bones. They stared at her with jet black eyes that caught the highlights of the flickering flame.

Their jaws worked, clicking at her.

When she had met foreigners on Earth, whose language she could not speak, her Imp had translated their words. Then she had simply replied to them in English, Imp translating in an approximation of her voice.

Can you translate my words from English? she asked.

In theory. But it would be unwise to let them know you understand them, for the time being. They want something from you, Delia; they want your help, and it is in their interest to ensure your well-being until they get it.

But if they don't get it, if I play dumb, then they might think I'm useless to their cause and... and dispatch me as they did the spider-crab.

Until we know what it is they want from you, it will be wise to remain silent.

Very well.

One of the aliens lifted an arm. She felt something touch her chin. Her face-mask was raised, exposing her to the sudden cold and a machine-oil stench she identified as the body odour of the locusts.

The aliens leaned forward, their bulging eyes ogling her revealed face. Their mandibles worked as they discussed her.

Imp?

They wonder if they have removed a layer of your skin, Imp replied. *They cannot work out why you have not reacted.*

Should I?

I think not. Perhaps it is better to remain impassive.

She stared at the aliens, her face growing numb with cold. The flame seemed to radiate not the slightest heat, merely light. She longed to replace her face-mask and wished the aliens gone.

The locust in the middle clacked its mandibles again.

It said they will bring someone who... who will be able to communicate with you.

The light fled, and with it the aliens, blinking out of existence before her. She heard the slab door ring shut at the far end of the room.

She replaced her mask and felt it warm her face.

She crossed to the bed-pit, opened her pack, and ate an energy bar, washing it down with drafts of icy water.

What I'd give now for a strong, hot coffee, she told Imp.

Ration yourself to one bar. We still don't know whether the foodstuff here will be viable.

She closed the pack, despite wanting to gorge on another bar.

She walked around the room, examining the walls in the wash of starlight that fell through the arched window. The walls were smooth and featureless, without a hint of decoration. She wondered if the room was hewn from the stuff of the mountain, or if the marmoreal surface had been inlaid.

Her thoughts were interrupted by the reappearance of the flickering flame.

This time two locusts appeared before her – and between them, a third of their height, was one of the blue ape-like creatures.

Its fur was long on its arms and legs, and short on its small, compact torso. Its head was domed, without much of a neck. It had the regular complement of facial features: a wide, lipless mouth, a snub nose and two huge, flat brown eyes.

Delia received the odd impression that the tiny alien was abasing itself before her. It appeared abject, its shoulders slumped, its humanoid eyes staring not at her face but down at her feet.

One of the aliens clacked, and the blue creature responded, lifting its head slightly and speaking in a softer, much slower approximation of the locusts' language.

Delia asked her Imp, *Can you...?*

It is much easier to understand, Imp said. *The blue creature says, 'My Masters wish to learn: what is your name and from where did you come?'*

Should I respond?

Before Imp could reply, one of the locusts moved. It did so slowly – and Delia knew why: it wanted her to witness its actions.

It reached out a claw and gripped the back of the blue primate's neck. At the same time it drew a crescent-shaped blade from a bandolier slung over its bony shoulders and pressed it to the primate's forehead, as if threatening to scalp the creature.

The primate spoke, a string of urgent glottal stops, and Imp translated: *'My Masters wish to know your name and from where you came, and will eliminate me if you do not respond.'*

I must, Imp!

Very well.

She stared at the locust with the blade and spoke: "My name is Cordelia Kemp, and I come from a world called Earth, many light years distant."

A second after she spoke, she heard a clatter issue from the speaker at her temple in an odd approximation of her own voice.

The locusts prodded the primate, who relayed her words in the speeded up version of the locusts' lingo.

The alien with the knife released the blue creature and spoke again. The primate relayed its words, and in due course Imp told her: *He said: 'My masters want your help. They have the vessel in which you arrived. They wish to know how it works. You will tell them.'*

Delia... her Imp said, *the creature implores you* not *to tell the Skelt – its name for the master species – how the life-raft operates.*

Hell, Imp, what should I say?

We should play along with the Skelt, and request that you should be taken to the vessel. But I'll reassure the primate – his people are called the Fahran – that you will tell them nothing of importance about its operation.

Very well. Tell him this.

Imp spoke, and for the first time the Fahran looked up and established eye contact with Delia, and she wondered if it really was an expression of gratitude she saw in its huge brown eyes.

The Fahran turned to its captors and spoke, and the locusts moved their heads together and conferred. They spoke to the Fahran, and the primate looked up at Delia and relayed their words.

Imp translated. *They said they'll take you immediately to where they are holding the vessel. They will have engineers on hand, and scientists.*

Very well, she sub-vocced. *I hope we can play this to our advantage, and tell them just enough to keep them satisfied without really telling them anything. At the same time, you must question the Fahran about the set up here, and if there might be any means of escaping the Skelt.*

Affirmative.

And the charger! she went on. *We might be able to get our hands on the charger.*

In this, Imp said, *the Fahran might be able to assist us.*

The flame swept away from her as one of the locusts moved to the door with the Fahran. Another Skelt gripped Delia's upper arm and she was escorted across the room, through the door and down a long corridor.

At length they emerged into the star-speckled, freezing night, crossed a square to yet another building that resembled a Terran cathedral, and passed inside.

CHAPTER EIGHT

SKELT TORCH-BEARERS STOOD in the four corners of the huge chamber, their flames casting a flickering illumination over an odd scene: in the ancient, marble-floored room stood the sleek, tear-drop shape of the life-raft, its scarlet shell a jarring splash of colour. Delia felt nostalgic as she gazed across at the vessel: a link to Earth and to all that was familiar, out here thousands of light years from home.

She and the Fahran were escorted across to the vessel, and they were joined by other Skelt, appearing as if by magic. She counted a dozen of the skeletal, insectoid creatures.

Imp said, *Allow me to conduct the dialogue, Delia. I will keep you informed.*

A tall, stooped Skelt stepped forward and addressed her. Beside it, the tiny figure of the Fahran relayed its words.

It wishes to know what powers the life-raft. Without knowing the technological capabilities of the Skelt, it is hard to judge a response. I am sure that they are ignorant of ion drive technology. Whatever I tell them will be beyond their comprehension.

You must be careful –

Of course. If they think they can elicit nothing from us, then you will be in danger. If I tell them too much, I contravene the Fahran's plea.

I'm glad you're doing the parleying.

While her Imp was conducting this interior dialogue, it was also responding to the Skelt's question via the transmitter embedded in Delia's temple. The Fahran then relayed Imp's words to its masters.

Delia found herself effectively redundant, a puppet reduced to miming a role while the speaking part was conducted by another. From time to time her Imp instructed her to move around the vessel and indicate various vents and cowls.

The dozen Skelt specialists crowded around her, eager to ask their own questions. The creatures were almost identical, varying only in height and in the degree of stoop; Delia surmised that the more bent were the oldest, although nothing else seemed to indicate their age.

The back and forth of questions and answers went on for an hour, Delia moving slowly around the ship, eager to get inside and locate the charger.

While her Imp spoke to Fahran, it said to Delia, *The Skelt are an ancient race, and according to the Fahran they once possessed the capacity for star flight.*

What happened?

I would like to know that. Unfortunately, the opportunity to ask the Fahran pertinent questions is limited.

Do they understand what you're telling them about the drive?

I thought it wise to tell them nothing of ion drive technology. They would have little comprehension of the theory behind the concept.

So what have you told them?

That the vessel utilises jet propulsion.

And they understand the concept?

One or two of their number seem to grasp the idea.

They had rounded the vessel and arrived at the flank where the Skelt had cut through the fuselage, the rectangular gap revealing the shadowy interior.

Three Skelt bent over her and the cowering Fahran, firing off questions in their loose-jawed, clacking language. Her Imp responded at length. Delia wondered how she would have fared without her implant. The thought sent a shiver down her spine.

Between answering the Skelt, Imp said at one point, *I am questioning the Fahran about his people and their 'masters.' Contrary to my first assumptions, the Skelt are not native to this world – which the Fahran call Valinda. The Skelt invaded a thousand Valindan years ago, which corresponds approximately to ten thousand Terran years. They came in a fleet of starships and colonised the world, subjugating the Fahran and the Vo.*

The Vo?

The giant spider-crab creatures. The Vo are sentient, according to the Fahran, and exist in other parts of Valinda as free, autonomous beings – though some of their tribes are hostile and feared by the Fahran.

So the Fahran and the Vo are the true natives of Valinda.

Correct. The Fahran are an ancient race; they are known as scholars, poets, philosophers.

And the Skelt? If they came in starships, they evidently devolved in the ten thousand years they've lorded it on Valinda.

Just so. The Vo put up a stiff resistance to their invasion, and the Skelt's limited forces were hard pressed merely to survive the onslaught of the suicidal spider-crabs. Without aid from their homeworld, over the centuries they lost their technological wherewithal. Now they retain a dim knowledge of the halcyon days, and would like to regain their former glory.

Hence the Fahran's desire that they should know as little as possible.

She stared at the towering, insectile Skelt crowding about her. *I wonder where they hailed from, Imp.*

Perhaps from further along the spiral arm, 'beyond' Valinda in relation to Earth, which is why we have yet to come across them.

She shivered, despite her thermal suit. *The thought of a technologically-advanced, space-faring race like the barbarous Skelt...*

Precisely. Not a prospect to consider with equanimity.

Imp fielded another question from a Skelt scientist, then said to Delia, *Gesture towards the opening. I will suggest we go inside.*

Delia moved a hand towards the opening. The pair of Skelt beside her vanished, reappearing a fraction of a second later within the ship. They evidently called for illumination, as a torch-bearer swooped past her.

Delia felt a prod in her lower back and stepped up and into the ship, joined by the Fahran.

As covertly as possible, she glanced across the floor of the life-raft. Her heart jumped when she saw the charger. During the journey to the city, it had fetched up against the far bulkhead.

There, she said.

I see it, Imp replied, at the same time conversing with a Skelt via the Fahran.

Now move around the vessel, clockwise. I am describing the raft's control system. I have said nothing about the fact that it is not in itself capable of flight between the stars. I suspect they know nothing of the vast distances involved, anyway.

As instructed, she moved around the vessel, indicating the various consoles when Imp gave the word.

Imp said, *The difficulty will be in diverting the Skelt's attention while either you or the Fahran retrieves the charger.*

You could always say you need it as part of the process of repairing the ship.

I considered such a dissimulation, Delia. But that runs the risk of arousing the Skelt's suspicion. Better to obtain it surreptitiously.

At least there are only three of the creatures in here, she said.

With others outside, looking in. That should not be a problem, as their view will be obscured.

While this dialogue was going on, her Imp was conversing with their captors. The attendant Skelt were so tall that they had to stoop to accommodate themselves in the life-raft. They shuffled back and forth with difficulty, and this would be to her advantage.

Imp said, *In thirty seconds I will give the Fahran a long spiel to relay to the Skelt. For perhaps as long again, their attention should be on him. Judge the situation, and utilise this time to obtain the charger. I suggest you sit down against the bulkhead. I will claim tiredness...*

Very well.

Imp spoke to the Fahran in the Skelt's glottal language, and the creature turned to the Skelt pair and addressed them.

Casually Delia moved towards the bulkhead, watching the Skelt. When she judged that their attention was solely on the tiny blue alien, she leaned against the padded wall.

Imp said, *Now*, and she slid down on to her haunches.

She felt her heart thumping in her ribcage. She slid further down the bulkhead and felt the charger pressing against the small of her back, hard and cold. A Skelt turned its long head to regard her, then looked back at the speaking Fahran. She glanced across the vessel to the *ad hoc* entrance; three Skelt peered in, though obscured by the attenuated shanks of their fellows.

You are unobserved now, Delia.

Here goes...

Heart thumping, her mouth suddenly dry, she moved her right hand down by her side and felt the ice cold disc of the charger through her thermal glove. She grasped the device and, while the Skelts' attention was still on the Fahran, slipped it under the elasticised band on her thermal jacket, the frozen metal against her skin making her gasp involuntarily.

Well done, Imp said.

She rose to her feet and leaned against the bulkhead.

The Fahran came to the end of its spiel, and in due course they exited the life-raft and stood in the cavernous hall, regarding the craft.

A Skelt turned to her, its mandibles working.

Imp responded, and Fahran relayed its words.

The Skelt says that we have given it much to contemplate, Imp told her. *They claim to understand the principle of jet technology, and wish to take the vessel apart. Evidently they are cognizant of the concept of reverse engineering. It informed me that they will transport the vessel to one of their machine shops. Then they wish you to be on hand to assist in the process. That, at least, should buy us time.*

A second Skelt appeared before her, bending so that its bony face was centimetres from hers. Its mandibles worked, its words high-pitched clicks. She took a step back, intimidated, but a second later the alien vanished.

What did it say? she asked, alarmed.

It issued a warning, Delia. It suspects you are dissimulating – holding back your knowledge.

And...?

It threatened you.

Tell me.

If you don't divulge the secret of the life-raft's technology, then it will have you put to death.

The light-bearers moved, the flaming torch swooping like a comet across the chamber towards the double-doors. Guards appeared suddenly to either side of Delia, and she felt a peremptory jab in the small of her back. Before they left the chamber, the Fahran looked up into her eyes and lifted a hand in what might have been a farewell gesture.

One of the Skelt addressed her again, and Imp said, *They will come for us at dawn and take us to the machine shop.*

Dawn?

Approximately four hours from now.

She felt another prod, and the guards escorted her at speed from the chamber, across the square and back to her quarters.

CHAPTER NINE

ON HER RETURN she found a tray of food beside the bed-pit.

She ignored the meal and turned her attention to the charger, pulling the disc from under her tunic with elation and activating it. Normally she would have slipped the device under her pillow so that her Imp would recharge it while she slept, but she was too wide-awake to sleep now. Instead, she slid it under the hood of her thermal suit, pulling the elastic tight around her face and securing the charger in place at the nape of her neck.

She sat down and stared at the food: a grey-green mush and a strip of what might have been overcooked meat. Next to the thick pottery plate stood a goblet full of what looked like water.

She picked up the plate and sniffed the food. While it didn't look too appetising, it didn't smell bad. The liquid had no odour.

What do you suggest? she asked.

Take a small sip of water, a morsel of the mash and the merest taste of the meat-analogue. I'll run an analysis.

She hesitated. If I can't metabolise this... she thought.

If her Imp's analysis on the food and water found that the foodstuffs of this planet were inedible, inimical to her metabolism, then she was as good as dead. And it would be a slow, unpleasant, lingering death of starvation and dehydration. Better, she thought, for a swift end at the hands of the Skelt.

She considered the irony of her situation: she had overcome vast odds on her way here. She had survived a starship blow-out; then her Imp had located a nearby world; the atmosphere of that world had proved amenable to human life, and she had survived a crash landing... all for nothing, if she was unable to metabolise the food of this strange planet.

She picked up an eating implement like a square-ended spoon, dipped it in the mush and took a tiny taste. It wasn't as vile as it appeared; in fact it was quite palatable; a strong, iron-rich vegetable, she suspected. The meat tasted like well-done beef. She took a sip of tasteless water.

She paced the length of the chamber, from the slab of the door to the high, arched window and back.

You should rest.

I'm too nervous to rest.

She approached the slab of the door and pushed experimentally; it swung outwards on gimbals. Through the gap she made out a guard with its back to her. She pulled the door shut and moved away.

She could always, she thought, attack the Skelt as it turned and paced away from the door. In the medi-pack was a laser scalpel with an extendable ten-centimetre blade... But even if she managed to overcome the lightning-fast guard, the chances of her escaping from the city were scant – and to what end? She had no idea how she might contact the Fahran, or what she might do then. She was trapped on an ice-bound, alien world moving from inimical winter to a hellish summer.

She came to the window, suddenly stupefied with despair at the enormity of her plight.

She recalled the Skelt's threat: that if she failed to divulge the secret of the life-raft's technology, then she would be put to death.

Imp...

Go on.

I was wondering, how long you might be able to string the Skelt along, before they realise –

Imp interrupted: *Judging by the scant Skelt technology I have witnessed so far, I think that they do not possess the means of manufacturing a jet engine. Thus I will offer to assist them in developing an engine from the ground up, so buying you even more time.*

Time for what, exactly? I'm stranded here! Look, even if I could get off-planet there's no way I can get back to Earth, let's face it.

You are looking too far ahead. First we must consider your immediate survival. When we have secured that, then we consider how to evade the Skelt.

And then?

And then it would be a wise move to establish contact, and relations, with the opponents of the Skelt, the Fahran.

To what end, she wanted to ask? She was stranded here, ten thousand light years from the nearest of her kind, with no hope of ever returning...

She raised a hand and stared at the massed stars above the distant mountain range. *And if I can't even digest the damned food on this hellish world?* she raged.

Imp did not respond.

Imp, I said...

I heard you, but on that score I have some news.

She swallowed, suddenly tense. *Go on.*

My analysis of the constituents of the food you sampled shows that you can metabolise the nutrients of this world. In other words, Delia, you can survive.

In spite of herself, she felt a quick stab of pleasure. *That's something, at least.*

It is the first step along the road to gaining your freedom. The Skelt want something from you, and despite elements within their ranks threatening you with death, I suggest that the scientists and technologists of this world will be eager to keep you alive until we have divulged all the secrets we have to offer. This of course is to our advantage – and buys us considerable time and leverage.

To what end?

Fortunately, all negotiations with the Skelt go through the agency of the Fahran translator. The advantage of this is that I can question him on all aspects of the Skelt and their domination. Perhaps, with the assistance of the Fahran, we might be able to escape the Skelt.

And go where? she asked. *If the Skelt rule much of this world, and have the other sentient life-forms in their power... I'm sorry. I'm being pessimistic. It's just...*

I understand.

You do?

You are far from home. You are alone. The chances of your ever returning to the ones you love are vanishingly small. Of course it is natural to feel despair.

And you don't?

I am a self-aware artificial intelligence, with advanced cognitive and computational capabilities, but without emotion. I think logically. Your welfare is my priority. My aim is to ensure your survival, and hence my own.

And yet you understand that it's natural for me to feel despair.

I understand the psychological system that engenders such a state – I understand, but cannot empathise.

You see emotions as a weakness, then?

In some situations, certain emotions can lead to impaired judgement. However, in others, for humans the ability to think emotionally, to empathise, is an advantage to the attainment of certain desired conditions.

She leaned against the embrasure of the window and stared out at the midnight pit. *You can have no comprehension, Imp, of how much I miss my parents, Timothy, my friends...*

That is correct. I have no comprehension.

She felt the need to weep. She fought the urge, and ordered Imp to summon the images of her parents.

She turned so that they could be projected into the room.

They appeared before her, standing beside the bed, as solid-looking and lifelike as if they had been whisked light years through space in order to ease her loneliness.

"It's good to see you again, Mom, Dad..."

"And how is our favourite spacer?" her mother said. "What adventures have you been having lately?"

Delia felt a catch in her throat as she replied, "Oh, I'm far away on an alien world, an ice-bound planet soon to undergo a fearsome summer." And I'll never, ever, see you again...

She was overcome with the thought that her parents would be going through hell at this very moment. In their timber-built villa on the shores of a lake thousands of light years away, they would be grieving the loss of their only child in the catastrophic starship blow-out – the worst accident in the history of spaceflight.

If only there were some way of telling them that she had survived; that, at least – even if she was denied ever seeing them again – would be some small measure of comfort and relief.

"And what are you doing now?" she asked.

"Oh, Ed's just about to drive down to the store for some nails," her mother said, smiling at her. "The porch needs fixing again. And later the Taylors are coming over for dinner."

All a lie, of course, a simulation created in the memory banks of her Imp – but a comforting lie, nevertheless.

"I miss you," Delia said.

"And we miss you, too, Cordelia," her father said, his watery grey eyes full of love.

End, she commanded – and the homely images winked out of existence.

She considered summoning the image of Timothy, but the sight of him would be too much to bear right now.

Delia, Imp said now, *you should rest. In three hours the Skelt will summon you, and who knows how long we will be required to remain in their machine shop. You need to sleep.*

She shook her head. *I can't sleep now.*

I will sedate you.

She would welcome the oblivion if she did sleep, but then her next encounter with the aliens would come all the sooner. She had no desire to be awoken and whisked off to do the bidding of the fascistic locusts.

No. I'll sleep later, naturally, when I'm tired.

Then at least finish the food, Delia.

She crossed to the bed-pit, sat down and took up the plate. She almost enjoyed the vegetable mush, but she had to force herself to eat the meat. It was slimy and tasteless; she tried not to consider the type of animal from which it came.

She finished the meal and drank the accompanying water, but was still hungry. She opened her pack and ate an energy bar, finding its familiarity reassuring – a tablet of cereal, fruit and sugar, manufactured on planet Earth!

She lay in the bed-pit and, despite her earlier decision, was about to instruct Imp to sedate her when she heard a sound. At first she thought it was the guard, come for her prematurely. She sat up, staring across at the door – but the sound was coming from the other end of the chamber, near the window.

She moved from the bed-pit and, cautiously, crossed the room.

She heard a sound, and another, like ice cracking underfoot. Then the lowest pane of glass in the tall window shattered across the marble tiles, and the small figure of a Fahran squeezed through the gap and climbed to its feet before her, a length of black bone griped like a club in its small left hand.

CHAPTER TEN

THE ALIEN SPOKE in an urgent whisper.

Imp translated: "You are in danger."

She asked why, and Imp relayed the question. As it did so, Imp told her, *It is the translator we met earlier. His name is Ahntan an Mahn. Mahn for short.*

The Fahran spoke, and Imp translated: "My friend works for the Skelt Council. She was present at their last meeting, just two hours ago, and overheard the Skelt discuss your fate. My masters are divided, with the scientists on one side and the military on the other. The latter do not trust you, and petitioned for your immediate execution. The scientists said that there was much to be learned from you – much that might aid the Skelt oppression of the Fahran and the Vo – but the military were adamant."

Delia felt something tighten in her stomach; gut fear.

The Fahran went on, and Imp relayed its words. "The military outnumber the scientists on the Council, and the Council leader – who in theory is neutral – favours the military. They voted, and a decision to order your execution was passed."

"When will they...?" she began, her heart pounding as she awaited the alien's reply.

"They will come at dawn, three guards and a judge, and put you to the sword."

She said, "What can I do? I have no suitable weapon. If you could supply me with..."

At this, the alien reached out its abnormally long hand and Delia felt its warm fingers enclose her wrist. Its liquid brown eyes looked into hers as it spoke.

Imp translated: "You would stand no chance against the Skelt. They move at great speed, and their skin is resistant to the blade. The only way is to run."

She tried not to laugh. "Run?"

"I have come to take you from Alkellion –" *That's the Fahran name for this city,* Imp supplied. "We will head south from here, over the mountains towards the equator. The journey will be long, and dangerous, but it is the only way."

She wanted to hug the alien to her. "But how? The chamber is guarded."

Even as she asked the question, she feared the reply.

As she expected, the small blue alien gestured to the window. "We will descend into the chasm."

"Is that possible?"

"I came that way. In darkness, we will not be observed. We will be away from here before the Skelt discover your disappearance."

She nodded, despite her fear of what might lie ahead. "You put yourself in danger to help a stranger."

"The risk is balanced against the trouble it will occasion our enemy."

"One moment. I have supplies I must take with me."

She fetched the medi-pack and the pack containing food and water, then considered the charger. It was far from secure, lodged where it was in the hood of her thermal suit. She removed the disc and slipped it into the medical pack.

The Fahran was crouching beside the broken window pane, peering down into the darkness. More than ever Delia was reminded, in his hunkered, ape-like posture, of a chimpanzee. Then the creature turned his long, narrow head towards her and the fact that he was an alien reasserted itself: nothing born of Earth had eyes so huge in a face so narrow, and nothing, she told herself, possessed such iridescent lapis lazuli fur.

His thin lips moved, hissing an urgent sibilance. Imp translated: "You must follow me. Care is imperative. Think not of speed at this time. Move slowly, considering every hand- and foot-hold."

She nodded, then was aware that the gesture would mean nothing to the alien, and added, "Very well. I understand. However..." She examined the opening through which the alien, Mahn, had entered. "I don't think I'll fit through there."

She saw the bone with which Mahn had broken the glass, and picked it up from the floor where he'd left it.

She slipped the length of bone through the gap between the lower frame and the window sill and pushed it forward. The metal spar resisted her pressure at first, and she pushed harder, until the spar buckled and the glass shattered. Her heart racing, Delia looked over her shoulder at the door. Seconds elapsed. The guard had not been aroused.

Heartened, she applied more pressure, and the metal frame twisted, leaving a space which, she judged, she'd be able to squeeze through.

The alien slipped through the gap; it was as if the creature became suddenly boneless, his pelt flowing from the chamber like poured ink. On hands and knees Delia poked her head through the opening and peered down.

Now she saw how Mahn had scaled the sheer precipice. A fine capillary network of what looked like ivy vines branched out across the stonework, faint in the starlight. Here and there she saw gaps in the mesh where it had broken off under the weight of the Fahran, and she feared that the root system would be unable to bear her weight.

Already Mahn was three metres further down the precipice, staring up at her with his huge eyes.

Taking a breath, she pushed her pack onto the window ledge, then turned onto her stomach and eased herself through the gap feet-first. Her left foot found a precarious hold on a vine, and biting her lip in apprehension she allowed it to take her full weight. She retrieved her pack and slipped it onto her back. Still clutching the sill, she lowered her right foot until she encountered another vine, then let herself down little by little.

The lighted archway above her head was but one of a hundred such windows in the cliff; above and below her, light spilled into the night. Her heart raced. If a Skelt moved to one of those windows and peered out...

She shut her mind to the thought and concentrated on climbing hand over hand, down the sheer face. As she descended, the vines became thicker and her descent a little easier; ice coated the vines, and she knew that, without her thermal suit, she would have suffered frostbite within minutes. Even with the insulating layers of her suit, an uncomfortable chill penetrated to her hands and feet.

You're doing well, Imp reassured her.

The thought of being butchered at dawn by alien locusts does wonders for your survival instinct.

She paused to regain her breath, staring at the lattice-work before her eyes; she made out tiny creatures like silver lice scuttling for cover as her hot breath plumed towards them.

How cold is it? she asked as she resumed her descent.

Minus thirty, Imp told her.

She swore.

But it's warming up, Imp went on.

It is?

Valinda is moving from winter to summer, remember. Five Terran years ago, in the depth of winter, when the planet was as far from its primary as it gets, I estimate the temperature for the duration of a Valindan day was minus one hundred.

But how do the Fahran and the Skelt manage to survive?

Earlier, while we were in the life-raft, Mahn told me that the Fahran migrate underground. They have vast cavern cities far below the surface, where they spend nine years at a time, coming out only for approximately ten Terran months during summer. I am speaking of the free Fahran, of course – those who dwell beyond the mountains south of here.

And the Fahran enslaved by the Skelt?

They must endure the winter above ground, in cities such as Alkellion. Many do not survive the rigours of winter, or the sadism of their masters.

And the Skelt? They can endure the winters?

Yes. They live in the cities to the north, and in the far south, all the long winter – seeking shelter below ground only when the searing summer approaches.

They descended, and Delia wondered when the climb might end.

The Skelt see the Fahran as an inferior species, Imp went on, *hardly sentient, and therefore fair game. They work the Fahran to death building cities and extending roads across the face of Valinda, and they do not baulk at eating the creatures when their use for labour has ceased.*

Now I understand why the Fahran are loath for advanced technology to fall into the hands of the locusts.

She paused in her descent to regain her breath. She looked left and right, then above her head. They had covered two hundred metres, though it was hard to judge precisely which of the many lighted archways above her had been her chamber. She pushed herself a little way from the wall and peered down the length of her body, beyond her feet, to Mahn. She had expected to see him far below by now, and was surprised that the tiny creature was no longer descending, but climbing towards her.

He reached out, touched her ankle, and whispered something.

Imp translated: *He says you are approaching a chamber inhabited by the Skelt. You must proceed with extreme caution.*

"Understood," she whispered.

She peered down, beyond the Fahran. Three metres below Mahn, and slightly to his left, was an archway spilling yellow light into the abyss. With the light came sound: the abrasive clicking of the Skelt language and something else, a high-pitched chirruping that reminded her of the stridulation of cicadas.

Mahn had slowed his descent so that he was at her side as they approached the opening. The high, whining note, not dissimilar to a violin played by a madman, filled the night, interposed with Skelt voices.

The Fahran moved his head close to Delia's and whispered. Imp relayed what Mahn had said. "A Skelt garrison. What you hear is their music. A battle song. They boast of defeating the massed ranks of a Vo battalion, and sing of how they will rid the world of new-born spiders when summer has passed."

They were alongside the opening now and the sound of the roistering Skelt was deafening. She imagined a drunken locust – did they allow themselves alcohol, she wondered? – leaning from the opening and beholding her and Mahn clinging to the wall like flies.

Bile rose in her throat as her stomach rebelled. She swallowed, fighting her fear, and lowering her feet one after the other with extreme care. She was cheered by the thought that any noise they made would be drowned out by the vaunting revelry of the Skelt militia.

They passed the opening and descended more quickly. When she next looked down, Mahn was five metres below her. She looked up. Something sailed from the opening – a bone or rind, she guessed, tossed into the night by a negligent reveller.

She tried to see beyond the Fahran to the foot of the vertical drop, curious how far they might have to descend. All she could make out was an impenetrable, inky darkness, unrelieved by any illumination.

Judging by the uneven surface before her, they had dropped below the foundations of the city and were descending the face of the mountain upon which Alkellion stood.

Something else indicated that they had almost finished their descent: she was assailed by a sudden stench of putrefaction from the Vo grave pit.

She looked down. Mahn had disappeared. She increased the speed of her descent, fearful that the Fahran had lost his footing and fallen. She was telling herself it was unlikely when the vine beneath her right foot gave way with a sharp crack and she pitched sideways. Her left hand slipped, and it was all she could do to hold on to the vine with her right hand. She swung like a pendulum, the vine tearing away from the cliff-face. She seemed to fall forever – though it could only have been for seconds – before something stopped her descent and gripped her midriff. Mahn steadied her, then eased her down the rest of the way until she was standing on stony ground. She arched her back and rubbed the muscles of her arms, craning her neck to make out the sheer cliff-face and the spread of stars high overhead.

Mahn indicated the line of the mountains far to the west, where the sky glowed with the coming dawn.

His thin lips worked and Imp translated: "We must hurry. Soon the Skelt will come for you and find your room empty."

He gestured ahead, and in the dim light Delia made out the scattered expanse of Vo chitin.

"But won't they simply follow us through the pit?"

Mahn reached out long fingers and touched her wrist. "The Skelt will not dare to follow us through the grave pit of the Vo. They are a superstitious race. They fear that the pit is haunted by the ghosts of the slaughtered Vo."

A hundred metres to her left she made out the pier projecting into the pit, and admitted that the scene possessed a certain stark grandeur, at once alien and grotesque. This close up she saw the activity on the surface of the pit; small animals like multi-legged rats skittered amongst the debris, ducking in and out through follicles and nacelles in the chitin. She gagged on the smell and baulked at the thought of making her escape through the noxious pit.

Mahn spoke, and Imp translated: "This way."

They advanced into the pit, ducking beneath bleached archways and descending through the obstacle course of bones. Overhead, the light of dawn filtered down through the crazed tesserae of spider-crab shells. Delia was surprised to find that, even though she was drawing deep breaths in exertion, she had already become so accustomed to the stench that it was hardly noticeable.

She followed Mahn as he climbed down through the stacked chitin, locating her footholds with care.

Once she slipped and fell, losing her grip on a bone and tumbling painfully a few metres, narrowly missing Mahn. She came to rest on her back, a jarring pain in her shoulder, and stared up through a network of spars and struts. Above her, Mahn's head appeared over a lip of cartilage, peering down at her.

She looked right and left, wary of moving lest she fall again, but found herself sitting in the bowl of what might have been a spider-crab's abdomen. She sat up slowly, massaging her shoulder. Mahn picked his way down on a makeshift ladder of bones and seated himself cross-legged before her.

His lips moved, issuing a series of soft, plosive sounds.

"We can rest now for a short time, if you wish."

"That'll be good. I need a breather."

She pulled off her backpack and withdrew a canister of water. She took a drink; it was icy cold and refreshing. She considered passing it to Mahn, then consulted Imp on the advisability of sharing the water.

I think not. There might be contaminants that an alien metabolism would be unable to cope with.

"I'd share," she told the Fahran, "but it might make you sick."

The alien blinked at her. His lips moved, the clicks echoing amongst the bones.

"I understand," Imp translated. "I will drink later, when we reach the mountains."

Delia took another mouthful of water then stowed the canister in her pack.

After a silence, Mahn said, "You are all alone on this planet."

"That's right. All alone."

"Why did you come to our world?"

"It was an accident. The vessel I was travelling on... there was an explosion. Most of my colleagues died in the blast. I... as far as I know, I am the only survivor."

"But the vessel you came to Valinda in, the small craft?"

"When the explosion destroyed my starship, I managed to board the life-raft, the small vessel, and come to Valinda that way."

The alien blinked. "I understand," he said, and added, "It is an honour to be able to help you."

She took his hand and squeezed. "It is an honour to be helped. Without you, I would be dead by now."

"And without you... I would never have had the courage to flee my masters and leave Alkellion, even though I dreamed of doing so."

"How long have you been there, working for the Skelt?"

"I was captured by Skelt militia just after the last Brightening..." *Approximately ten Terran years ago,* Imp supplied. "I was in my village, instructing novices, when the raiding party came and took me and six others. We were transported to Alkellion and given duties. With my facility for languages, I was ordered to translate for my masters."

"What will you do now, Mahn?"

He gestured with an upturned hand. "I will return to my village. I must attend to the grave tree of my mate. You see, she was killed by the Skelt in the raid. I... I saw it happen, but I was powerless to..." He stopped, staring into space.

Delia said, "I'm sorry..."

"When I have tended the tree beneath which she sleeps for eternity, I will embark upon a Brightening pilgrimage in memory of Ahntan an Mareen, my mate."

"Tell me about the pilgrimage," she murmured.

"Once in a lifetime, a Fahran must make the long trek to the valley of Mahkanda, to pay respects to Chalto."

"Chalto?"

"My god. Oh, for these long years I have looked ahead to this Brightening and wondered if I had the courage to escape from Alkellion and make the pilgrimage. You see, the Brightening is a special time, when Chalto rises from his sleep and appears before his disciples. And soon he will Rise and Appear, and I will do my best to reach the valley of Mahkanda and witness this miracle."

She smiled. "I hope you achieve this, Mahn. How far from here is the valley of Mahkanda?"

The alien looked about him, reached out to a spar of bone like a twig and snapped it off. He tried to score a circle in the dust on a plaque of chitin between them, but failed.

Imp said, *Delia, I will project a schematic of Valinda.*

Do that.

While Mahn was still attempting to sketch a circle in the dust, a full-colour image of Valinda appeared in the air before him. He sat back suddenly, alarmed.

Delia said, "It's okay. I'm doing this. It's your world, Valinda."

Mahn stared at the projection. "But how...?" he began.

"I have a device, a tiny machine, up here..." She tapped her forehead. "I'm projecting the image."

Mahn walked around the floating world, staring at the projection in wonder.

"Now just point to where we are on the globe," Delia said, "and where the valley of Mahkanda is situated."

Tentatively Mahn reached out with a long, thin finger and pointed to the globe above the equator. "This is Alkellion. We are here." He traced a straight line between the city and a point south of the equator. "The valley of Mahkanda is as far south of the equator as Alkellion is north of it."

"And how far is it from here to the valley of Mahkanda?"

"Almost two thousand kilometres."

"And how long will it take you?" she asked.

The alien regarded her impassively. "From here to here," he said, gesturing to the equator, "perhaps a week, and the same again from the equator to Mahkanda."

"Two weeks? But that's impossible! You will travel two thousand kilometres in just two weeks?"

He turned his palm. "I *must* do this, you see. Soon the Brightening will be well underway, and Chalto will Rise and Appear. And I *must* be there, do you understand?"

She ordered her Imp to cease the projection, and the image of Valinda disappeared. "I understand," she said. "And, Mahn, I will do all I can to help you on your pilgrimage."

"You will?"

"As a small gesture of thanks for your helping me escape the Skelt," she said. "For saving my life."

"You will be the first alien being to witness Chalto Rise and Appear!" the Fahran carolled.

"I will be honoured," she said. "I look forward to that. And your god, Chalto? Is he in the image of the Fahran?"

"Only the Vehren know that," Mahn said, "those who have successfully completed the pilgrimage and returned. They do not speak of Chalto, for it is written that it is forbidden to depict images of our god, or describe his likeness. It is enough to look upon him and hear his wise words, and for evermore bask in the privilege and honour, knowing what few others know."

An interesting belief, Delia said to Imp. *I'm more than a little curious to see Chalto myself.*

A little later Mahn suggested that they continue on their way. He pointed to a complex structure of bones that wound down into the shadows like a tortured ladder. "We will climb to the bottom of the pit, where it will be easier to walk towards the mountains."

Delia shouldered her backpack and followed the alien as he descended.

CHAPTER ELEVEN

IT WAS LIKE climbing through a grotesque adventure playground, she thought, with the vista constantly changing as they dropped. Over the years the spider-crabs' skeletons had come apart, and individual bones and shields of chitin had found their own precarious resting place. Below her, Mahn tested each strut and spar for stability before continuing. Delia was careful to follow his example.

The climb was considerably easier than the descent from the chamber; there was not the immediate fear of capture to concentrate her mind, for one thing, and the chitin offered more hand- and foot-holds than had the vines.

As they descended, the dawn light became ever fainter, casting bizarre shadows through the stacked bones. Occasional pillars of red light struck through the mass, contrasting with the shadows, and here and there the thinner bones and plaques glowed pink with transmuted light. From time to time her elbow or hip displaced a loose bone, which went rattling off into the depths of the pit.

A little later she said, *Imp*.

Yes.

I've been thinking about the Skelt. They're a star-faring race.

Their ancestors were, Delia. The Skelt who inhabit Valinda are but a sorry remnant.

It's perhaps as well that we've never encountered them in our travels among the stars.

Fortuitous, yes, but understandable. We are thousands of light years from Earth, and humankind has not explored this sector of the spiral arm.

She concentrated on lodging her foot on the upper spar of a rib-cage and lowering herself rung by rung.

She asked: *Do you think that the star-faring Skelt were as... as bellicose as those of Valinda?*

The likelihood is high that this is so.

In that case... it would be well if the authorities on Earth were aware of the potential threat.

Correct. However...

I know, I know. You're going to point out, with incontrovertible machine logic, that we are in no position to alert them. Am I right?

You paraphrase my thoughts succinctly.

She smiled to herself. Down below, Mahn was hanging onto a cross-strut and staring up at her through the gloaming. When she caught up with him, he continued his descent.

But if there was some way of escaping Valinda, and getting word back to Earth...

In that case, if it were possible, we would do so. However, I advise you to concentrate your thoughts on more attainable goals, both for your peace of mind and for your more immediate welfare. There will be travails ahead which will tax your mental and physical endurance, and it is to these that we should be addressing ourselves.

Mahn called up to her. Imp relayed his words: "We have almost reached the bottom of the pit."

A little later the tiny Fahran jumped the last metre, and turned to watch Delia negotiate the final bone-ladder and step down to join him. She looked around, and then up, in wonder. Dim shafts and beams of sunlight penetrated the confusion of spars at odd angles, reflected and refracted through the osseous canopy. A strange, aqueous light prevailed at this depth. The ground underfoot was smooth and jade green, shot through with glowing seams of silver. An intense, freezing cold struck up through the soles of her boots.

"What is it?" she asked, indicating the ground.

"Over the decades," Mahn said, "the ichor and body fluid from the Vo has dripped to the bottom of the pit. In winter it freezes solid and forms this bed. In summer, when the sun is at its hottest, all this melts to form a terrible, disease-filled lake of putrefaction."

He indicated ahead, and they walked side by side through the maze of bone and chitin.

Delia wondered how many Vo had come to their end here.

"On my way to Alkellion," she said, "we stopped on the roadway overlooking the grave pit. A team of Skelt led their Vo along a timber pier, then hacked it to death and pitched its bones into the pit. Why do they do this – why *have* they been doing this, apparently, for a long, long time?"

"When the Skelt invaded Valinda, they fought a long war against the Vo, for though the Vo possessed only rudimentary technology and weapons, they were numerous and fearsome in battle. They fought desperately, and were an implacable enemy. In time, however, the Skelt prevailed, and the Vo retreated to the equatorial deserts. The Skelt first used the captive prisoners as cattle, for their meat, and then bred them as a means of transport. The Skelt are highly superstitious, and worship a vengeful god which demands sacrifices. After every outing with their mounts, a patrol of Skelt militia must put to the sword the Vo they consider the weakest of their stable. This is the barbarity you witnessed upon your arrival at Alkellion."

"And the Vo? You said they're sentient."

Mahn turned his hand. "Indeed; they are an ancient race. They have a language, and songs and stories, though no written language unlike we Fahran. Their hatred of the Skelt knows no bounds, and rightly so."

"And the Fahran's relationship with the Vo?"

"We maintained an uneasy peace with the Vo, in times gone by. In ancient times, our scholars tell of great wars raging between our peoples, and to this day there are skirmishes when territorial misunderstandings arise, though the Vo reserve the major part of their enmity for the Skelt."

"The Skelt are truly..." she began, searching for a word to amply describe the aliens.

Mahn said, "The Skelt are *vheer*."

"Vheer?"

"It means," the Fahran said, "a combination of 'ignorant of others,' 'concerned only for their own welfare,' 'wholly convinced that only they know the truth,' and 'blood-thirsty.' This is a lethal combination. Many times in the past, our elders have attempted to parley with the Skelt; we have tried to reason with them, to seek common ground. We have extended a hand of peace, only to have that hand – literally and metaphorically – struck from the body. The Skelt are implacable, and cannot be reasoned with."

Delia nodded. "Once, a few centuries ago, the civilised world on our planet was faced with an enemy, of our own kind, driven by twisted religious fundamentalism. They too thought only themselves in the right, and killed whoever opposed them ideologically. They were, indeed, *vheer*."

"And what became of these people?" Mahn asked.

"Opinion was divided amongst their opponents. Some wanted to annihilate them utterly, to wipe them from the face of the planet – but how can one defeat an ideology by military force? Over decades a more liberal schism of their own ideology prevailed, and in time the fundamentalism of the radicals was diluted, and they were accepted back into the fold of civilised, humane discourse."

Mahn ducked under a flange of chitin, and Delia followed him. "It would be pleasing to think that the same might be true of the Skelt," he said. "But, you see, amongst the Skelt there are no liberal voices. They are of one mind, implacable, *vheer...*"

"So... how do you see the future between your races, Mahn?"

He turned his hand. "The future will be much like the past. The Fahran will exist in peace in the equatorial regions, suffering occasional raids; many of my kind will be enslaved by the Skelt, and the Skelt will rule with merciless sadism, as ever."

"I hope you're wrong," she murmured.

Imp said: *It was unfortunate that the life-raft came down in territory occupied by the Skelt. A few hundred kilometres to the south and we would have found ourselves welcomed by the Fahran.*

Something occurred to her. *The level of Skelt technology is relatively primitive, yes?*

By our standards, that is so.

So... I wonder how they had the wherewithal to bring down the life-raft.

The anomaly occurred to me, too. Based on the technology I have seen so far, I would have said the Skelt do not have the capability to manufacture such weaponry. But the very fact that we were brought down suggests otherwise.

She asked Mahn about Skelt weaponry.

"Their militia are armed with crossbows. And every Skelt carries a sword – the curved blade with which they threatened me yesterday."

"But weapons capable of bringing down my vessel?"

"I have never heard of the Skelt possessing such a weapon."

"Then could it have been fired by the Vo?"

"The Vo? Impossible! The Vo have no technology, not even knives and swords."

"So we were brought down by something that could only have been fired by the Skelt..."

"A mystery," said the alien, and fell silent.

A mystery indeed, Imp said.

A little later, Delia said, "By now they'll know I've escaped. They'll know I've headed through the grave pit – but will they be awaiting us on the other side?"

"They will have rounded the pit to search for us," he said. "We will emerge with caution, and use the cover of farze bushes to evade their attention. Soon we will be in the foothills and away from the Skelt."

"And then? We're surrounded by mountains; presumably we must cross them at some point?"

"There are many low passes through the range. We will take one of these. On the other side, we will be high up, looking down on a great plain many kilometres below us. This is hostile land, and stretches for two hundred kilometres, patrolled by wild beasts and poisonous creatures."

She stared at the alien. "And we will traverse this land on foot?"

"Among the many animals there is one which will assist us. Soon, then, we will have covered this plain."

"Help us? How?"

Mahn gestured. "You will see. It is hard to describe, without... without alarming you."

"Very well," she said, unsure. "And then?"

"And then we will enter the lands of the Vo," Mahn told her. "And careful negotiation will be required for our safe passage."

"It would appear," she said, "that interesting times lie ahead."

"Interesting indeed," Mahn agreed.

Delia followed the alien through the forest of chitin.

CHAPTER TWELVE

ONE HOUR LATER they left the plain of frozen ichor as the ground began to slope upwards. They climbed the increasingly steep incline, pulling themselves along with the aid of bones embedded in the ground. The air lightened as they approached the edge of the pit, and soon Delia made out the foothills of the mountains, their folded slopes covered in the silver-grey shrub that Mahn had called farze.

He gestured for her to remain in the cover of a domed Vo shell while he scouted ahead. She sat in the scooped, ribbed carapace and watched the Fahran disappear through the thicket of bones.

And if the Skelt are swarming around the pit in their hundreds? she asked Imp.

I would surmise, in that event, Mahn would suggest waiting until nightfall to leave the pit.

How long until sunset?

Eighteen hours.

Great. She looked around her. *I don't see anywhere comfortable to bed down.*

Are you tired?

Surprisingly, no. I'm too wound up to sleep.

She heard a noise from further up the incline. Mahn hurried back through the bones and dropped into a crouch before her.

"The Skelt have discovered your escape and deployed militia around the pit. Also, they have wir with them."

"Wir? That's bad?"

"Wir are animals with a very powerful sense of smell," Mahn explained. "The Skelt use them to track their prey. They are small but very long, with brown segmented shells and a thousand legs."

"So... what do you suggest? We could always wait until nightfall."

Mahn considered the idea. "That is one option. Darkness would assist us, but by then there would be more Skelt deployed, and their wir."

He turned and stared through the chitin to the filigree tangle of undergrowth coating the hillside. "I think it would be wise to make for the foothills now," he said. "The Skelt have deployed their guards at intervals around the pit. The nearest wir is perhaps fifty metres away."

She stood, heart hammering, and followed Mahn.

The Fahran dropped into a stealthy crouch as they approached the edge of the grave pit, then ducked behind a disembodied leg and peered out. Crouching behind him, Delia peered over his head. The red sun hung above the mountains, casting its light over the Skelt militia stationed around the circumference of the pit. To her right, the nearest alien was, as Mahn had said, perhaps fifty metres away; to her left, a guard was positioned a little further away. They stood with their crossbows poised, staring vigilantly into the grave pit. Beyond the Skelt to the right, a column of guards marched around the pit, restraining wir beasts on long leashes. They resembled giant centipedes.

Ahead, the cover of the nearest undergrowth was ten metres away – not far, but far enough when time came to make the crossing.

The silver shrubbery covered the hillside for about a kilometre, then gave way to a growth of crimson-leafed trees with low, spreading branches.

"We'll never cross the gap without being seen by at least one of them," she said.

Mahn looked at her. "What do you suggest?"

Imp, she sub-vocced, *I have an idea.*

Go on.

Project my holo-image five metres from our present position, moving away from us to the right, along the edge of the pit towards the nearest Skelt guard. And then have the image retreat into the pit, well away from Mahn and myself. Understood?

Affirmative. You will have to manoeuvre yourself to the edge of the pit so that you have a line of sight towards the guard.

Very well. Tell Mahn what we're doing, explain about the projection, and tell him to follow me when I give the word.

Imp relayed Delia's instructions. Mahn stared at her, his huge eyes growing wider. At last he turned his hand in what she took as an affirmative gesture.

She crept forward and peered along the rim of the pit, her heart thumping. All it would take, she realised, was for a guard to glance into the tangle of bones and glimpse her crimson thermal suit.

She turned towards the guard to her right, positioning herself on her haunches for a quick getaway.

She levelled her gaze along the rim, then said to Imp, *Go ahead. Project.*

Five metres from where she crouched, the holographic projection sprang into ersatz life, running along in the margin of the pit. She held her head very still to prevent any destabilisation to the image that might give away the fact that it was not a real flesh and blood person.

The avatar hurried along the incline, towards the closest guard, lifelike but for the fact that its feet failed to scuff the scree.

Delia held her breath, willing the guard to look up and notice the image. The wait was almost unbearable. The sooner its attention was drawn to the decoy and the firing began, the sooner she could take flight with Mahn.

It worked. The guard moved in a blur of motion, levelling its crossbow and calling out in a castanet rattle, and seconds later it was joined by a dozen others. They raised their weapons and fired, the bolts passing through the projection and kicking up spurts of earth. The projection ran on unscathed, then turned towards the pit and vanished into the chitin. The guards gave chase. Delia looked to her left, relieved to see that the closest guards had hurried into the pit as well.

"Now!" she hissed to Mahn. She burst from cover and sprinted up the incline, slipping on the loose earth, and expected to feel the impact of a crossbow bolt at any second. She reached the cover of the silvery shrub and turned to pull the Fahran in after her. Despite the icy air, she was sweating. She peered out along the lip of the pit, right and left. The Skelt had vanished into the pit in pursuit of the non-existent quarry.

"This way," Mahn said, taking her hand and pulling her up the slope through the undergrowth.

Delia maintained an even pace and controlled her breathing.

The cover of the undergrowth petered out after a hundred metres, and they came to the forest of low, crimson-leafed trees. They ran up the hillside, Mahn easing out in front of her in an almost negligent, loose-limbed lope. She knew, from the fluidity of his movements, that he too had plenty in reserve and could increase his pace if need be.

After five hundred metres Mahn slowed down, approached a tree and swarmed up it in seconds. He clung to the trunk like a koala and peered down the incline.

His eyes widened at what he saw. "The wir have our scent," he reported. "One creature and its keeper are racing to where we emerged from the pit."

He leapt down, grabbed her hand and dragged her up the slope. She ran, panic lending her flight a new urgency.

Ahead and to their right, a notch in the jagged line of the mountains suggested a cutting, and Mahn altered their course and headed towards it.

She wondered if the wir could move as swiftly as their keepers; if so, then all was lost. If not, there was hope. She and the Fahran may yet pass through the cutting and find the creature that, according to Mahn, would assist them in their onward passage.

But could it outrun the Skelt, she wondered?

What had Mahn said about the animal? That he would not describe it for fear of alarming her? At the moment, she would accept a ride on a man-eating tiger if it meant escaping the Skelt.

They passed into the steeply-sided cutting, the trees on either side changing, becoming even smaller and more contorted, like alien bonsai. The terrain changed too, from being relatively smooth underfoot to being strewn with mossy boulders which hampered their flight.

At one point Mahn leapt onto a huge rock and peered back the way they had come. Driven by curiosity, Delia joined him and peered down the hillside to the distant grave pit.

The sight took her breath away with its alien beauty. In the distance, ranged along the horizon against the glow of the bloody sun, the city of Alkellion rose and fell in a fairytale profusion of stark towers and obelisks. Before it, the grave pit was a sea of frozen bones, something gothic and nightmarish in its osseous architecture. On the near side of the pit, the Skelt platoons were a blur of activity.

She saw several wir-handlers arrive where she and Mahn had left the pit, and she knew for certain now that the creatures had their scent. The Skelt hurried towards the foothills, following the path through the undergrowth towards the pass.

She wondered how long it might be before the first Skelt had them in its sight.

Mahn leapt from the boulder and pulled Delia after him.

The cutting was perhaps ten metres wide. On either side, the bare stone rose sheer to a height of more than a kilometre. Silver-leafed trees dotted the narrow path but provided little in the way of cover. The crest of the rise was perhaps half a kilometre away, and Delia wondered what awaited them on the other side.

Mahn pulled her to the right, so that they were running through the scant cover of the trees. She risked a quick glance behind her, but saw nothing of the pursuing Skelt.

It came to her that, if they were caught, then she could expect to be incarcerated again and questioned about the life-raft technology. But what of Mahn? Would he be summarily put to death?

They came to the crest of the cutting and hurried down the other side. Ahead, the landscape was spectacular. The mountains fell away to a great silver ice plain, riven with fissures like lightning.

"And we must cross that?" she called out.

"First we must evade the Skelt and their wir."

"And the animal you claimed would aid our escape?"

"All in good time," Mahn said. "Now cover your nose."

"What?" Delia wondered if Imp had mistranslated.

"I said, cover your nose and do your best not to inhale when I tell you."

He left her and scrambled over boulders until he came to a stunted tree with swollen, arthritic branches bearing what looked like rotting, pear-shaped fruit. Mahn reached up and gathered an armload of the fruit, then hurried back to her side.

As she watched, he split the fruit one by one and removed a big, black seed pod from each. When he had a dozen of these, he looked at Delia and said, "Stand back."

She did as instructed, and Mahn cracked each seed pod on a boulder. Delia rocked back on her heels as an acrid stench hit her. She gagged, her eyes watering despite her face-mask.

Mahn, his big eyes streaming, lost no time in tossing the split seed pods like grenades back the way they had come.

"When the wir come upon the cacchia seeds, their sense of scent will be impaired for hours and they will be unable to track us. This way."

They moved down the mountainside and veered right, losing themselves in a tumble of giant boulders.

They ran on for thirty minutes, passing through a landscape of increasingly vast, moss-covered boulders, the ground icy underfoot. The boulders gave way to a forest of spiky trees rising like spires to three times her height, grey and uniform, as if wrought from steel.

"And the creature which will assist us?" she asked again.

"We are almost there."

They passed through the forest and emerged at the head of a valley, which widened and zigzagged to form one of the many fissures fracturing the vast ice plain.

Something moved within the deep gully at her feet, and Delia stared in wonder. The grey ribbed surface of the cutting undulated in a slow, steady pulse.

"What...?" she began, staring at the Fahran.

At the head of the valley, fifty metres further up from where they stood, she saw movement and stepped back in alarm. What she first thought was the surface of the gully resolved itself, like an optical illusion, into a tube as wide as her life-raft, its head rising and questing like that of an aroused snake. The leviathan appeared to be blind, with no features as such, other than a sphincter-like mouth. As she watched, the thrashing head found what it sought, like a suckling animal fastening upon its mother's teat: what appeared to be a pile of boulders. Its drooling mouthpiece fastened on one of the rocks and sucked, and it vanished into its maw with a loud, liquid sound.

"Follow me," Mahn said, setting off up the hillside.

She caught up with the Fahran and they paused on the edge of the pit above the creature's head. Its slavering, puckered mouth gave off an odour almost as bad as the cacchia seeds. The boulders turned out to be great dun seedpods longer than a human. The creature raised its head again, nuzzled blindly until it found more pods, then sucked. A pod vanished into the maw.

A forest of trees stood at the head of the valley; it was from them that the pods had fallen.

She looked down the length of the valley, attempting to locate where the creature ended, but it continued for as far as the eye could see.

She turned to Mahn. "What is it?"

"We call it a summer worm. It emerges from its lair deep underground as summer approaches, and swallows thousands of the gallia pods. They nourish it through the long winter."

Delia gazed at the fissure zigzagging away across the ice plain until it was lost to sight. "And how long is the summer worm?" she asked.

"It stretches from here to the territory of the Vo," he replied. "Some two hundred kilometres, in total."

Delia laughed in amazement. "And," she ventured, "this is the creature that will assist us, right?"

"The summer worms have helped the Fahran evade the Skelt for centuries," he said.

He looked up, staring back through the forest. He pointed. "Skelt," he said, "searching the land without their trusty wir."

She followed his outstretched arm and made out, in the distance, the tiny figures of the Skelt, appearing only when they stopped, becoming blurs again as they moved on down the mountainside.

Mahn hurried up the hillside and concealed himself behind the piled gallia pods. Delia followed him. "The Skelt won't take long to reach us..." she began. She glanced at the headpiece of the summer worm, apprehensively, then asked, "Just how – ?"

"We will be away from here in minutes," Mahn assured her, and fell to work.

He grasped a gallia pod and rolled it onto its side. "If you could hold it steady," he said.

Delia grasped the fibrous husk. Over two metres long, tapering at one end and rounded at the other, the pod resembled a huge, elongated coconut. She glanced over her shoulder, wondering when the summer worm would next reach for a pod. She had no desire to be close by when the slobbering mouth sought its next meal.

Mahn worked quickly. He found the seam of the pod and pulled it apart with his bare hands, splitting it along its length for a metre to reveal a sweet-smelling, mushy pink interior. As she watched, he reached into the pod and rapidly baled out the mush until the sickly sweet flesh was piled at their feet. Within minutes he had excavated a long cavity, and Delia's stomach turned at the sight of it.

"And now?" she asked, fearing the answer.

"Now we ease the pod to the edge of the pit, so that it will be the next one taken by the summer worm."

"Very well. And then?"

"And then we climb into the pod, draw the edges of the seam together, and wait until the summer worm obligingly saves us from the Skelt."

"I thought you might say that," she said. "But..."

"We will pass through the gut of the summer worm in a matter of two or three days," he said. "When we emerge, we will be in Vo territory."

"Wonderful," she said. "And we won't be digested and eaten away by its stomach acid?"

"The worm's digestive system will detect that the seed pod carries a foreign body, and will evacuate it whole in case it harbours poison."

"Ingenious."

Imp, this is insane. How will I breathe?

If the Fahran survive concealment and ingestion, then I surmise that it will be safe for humans. I will monitor your bodily functions, and if needs be ease you into a hibernative state.

She looked up. A platoon of Skelt blurred down the valley, heading ever closer. "It seems I have little alternative," she murmured.

Mahn was dragging the gallia pod towards the edge of the pit.

"How long might we have to wait?" she asked.

"The summer worm takes a pod every few minutes or so, and it took the last one more than five minutes ago."

They positioned the seed pod on the lip of the fissure, metres above the slavering maw of the summer worm.

Mahn glanced across the valley. "The Skelt approach. Do as I do, Delia, and do not be afraid."

The Fahran stepped over the side of the pod, as if casually boarding a canoe, and lay down, resembling an alien child in some bizarre biological coffin.

"Come."

She lifted a leg, eased herself into the sweet-smelling interior of the hollowed-out gallia pod, and lay down beside the Fahran. To her surprise, the flesh enclosed her like a comfortable, if moist, transition pod.

"And the Skelt do not know of this?"

"We are safe from the Skelt," he said, reaching up and drawing the seam of the pod shut; the edges came together over her head, sealing with an adhesive squelch, and she lay pressed against the alien in absolute darkness.

CHAPTER THIRTEEN

INVOLUNTARILY, DELIA FOUND herself reaching for Mahn's hand. She found it and squeezed.

"The gesture?" Mahn's question was muffled in the confines.

"One of friendship, affection," she said, "and trust."

His fingers squeezed hers in return.

"You say the Fahran use the pods to escape the Skelt...?" she said.

"And to travel long distances as summer approaches."

"And you? Have you used a pod before?"

"Never. This is the first time."

"And you're not... apprehensive?"

"Not in the slightest. My hive-sisters tell stories of their travels by gallia pod, and their dreams as they went."

"Dreams?"

"We will enter a deep sleep during the journey, and the atmosphere within the pod will affect our senses, and we will dream. My people believe that when in a gallia pod, we dream of the future, and our destiny."

"This should be... interesting," she said.

"Do not be afraid, Delia. Give yourself to the experience. In two or three days we will emerge."

"In the territory of the Vo?"

"As I said to you earlier, the Vo can be negotiated with. Not all their tribes are warlike. Many are peaceable, and consider themselves allies of the Fahran against the Skelt."

"And others?"

"It is true that some tribes are difficult to deal with."

"And where we will emerge? Is that territory held by friendly Vo, or not?"

"That is impossible to say. Ownership of the land changes hands all the time, as their tribes skirmish back and forth across the ice plains."

She was about to ask what they might do if they emerged in territory held by hostile Vo, when the seed pod tipped. She imagined the drooling mouthpiece of the summer worm sucking the seed into its maw.

The pod rolled; one moment she was on top of Mahn, and the next he was pressing down on her. She was wondering when the incessant tumbling might end when the pod suddenly settled. She eased herself into a more comfortable position beside the alien, arranged her arms and settled her head against a pad of flesh.

Would you like me to sedate you, Delia? Imp asked.

Not yet. Maybe later.

The movement of the pod now reminded her of the sedate progress of a punt floating downriver. She had once holidayed in Cambridge, and taken a punt along the Cam. In her mind's eye she recalled the dappled sunlight, the passing fronds of weeping willows.

"Mahn," she said a little later.

"Yes?"

"Why did you rescue me from the Skelt?"

"As I told you before, for many years I had dreamed of escape, but lacked the courage. That was one reason."

"And another was that you did not want my knowledge of the life-raft's technology falling into the hands of the Skelt?"

"That, too, yes," he admitted. "And also, I wanted to do something to spite the Skelt. For years they had kept me imprisoned, acting as a translator and a liaison between their leaders and other Fahran captives. For years they have enslaved and tortured my kind. I could do nothing to oppose the Skelt, until you arrived on Valinda."

He was silent for a time, then said, "Those were the reasons, but it is true that also I was sorry for you. You were a prisoner of the Skelt – I could empathise with that. You were far from home, amongst strange and cruel beings. I could empathise with that, too."

"Thank you, Mahn."

"You were helpless, defenceless, and at the mercy of the Skelt. I had no doubt that they would kill you when they had learned from you what they wished. As it happened, the military members of the Council voted to kill you before that, so it was imperative that I assisted your escape."

"And if the Skelt captured us, they would put you to death instantly."

After a silence, he said, "Yes."

"So, whatever the reasons for saving me, you acted selflessly. You could have done the safe thing and done nothing, and continued serving the Skelt."

"And how would I have looked upon my soul, then? I would have been... tarnished, corrupt. My life would have been diminished."

"You're a good person, Mahn."

"I simply did what a million other Fahran would have done in my position."

She allowed the silence to lengthen. She was light years from Earth, fleeing murderous locusts, encased in a seed pod in the alimentary system of a giant worm, heading towards the equator of the planet with a small furry alien on a religious pilgrimage...

A little later, Mahn said, "You are... a strange being, Delia."

"Strange?"

"You told the Skelt that you came from the stars, vast distances."

"That's right."

"Like our God; he too came from the stars."

"I'm no god, Mahn. Just a very lost human being."

"And yet," Mahn said, "you have many strange powers."

"I have?"

"Back there, you issued your soul for the Skelt to fire upon. You sacrificed your soul, to save us."

She tried not to laugh. "It was not my soul, Mahn. I sacrificed nothing."

"Then what was it, if not your soul?"

"As I demonstrated back in the pit, I have the ability to project pictures –"

"You are a magician!"

"No, it's technology, Mahn."

"And your ability to comprehend, and speak, my language. I do not understand: you speak in what I take is your own tongue, and then I hear your words in my language."

"As I mentioned earlier, I have a tiny machine in my head. An implant, the same which projected the image of both your world, and what you thought of as my 'soul.' I call it Imp. It's this that enables me to understand and speak your tongue. It translates for me. It's a tiny computer – a machine that thinks."

"A machine, in your head? What else is this machine, this Imp, able to do?"

She thought about that. "It speaks to me, advises me. It has access to vast reference libraries, great sums of knowledge. It's... I suppose it's also like a friend."

Mahn said softly, "I am glad you have a friend, Delia."

She squeezed his hand. "Thank you, Mahn."

*   *   *

SHE SLUMBERED, THEN awoke suddenly as the pod jolted. She wondered if she had slept for two days and arrived at journey's end.

"What was that? How long have I been – ?"

She felt Mahn's moist breath on her cheek as he said, "I think the pod might have collided with another. It is nothing to worry about. You have slept for perhaps two or three hours only."

"You've been awake all that time?"

"I have been considering my life, my fortune in meeting you, and the pilgrimage ahead."

"And when you have completed the pilgrimage? What then?"

"I will go back to teaching. I will find a quiet post well away from the Skelt, and teach hivelings for the rest of my days."

"That is a noble thing to do, Mahn."

"And I will tell my pupils of the time I rescued an alien from the hands of the Skelt, and how we fled across the face of Valinda with angry militia in pursuit."

"Do you think they'll believe you?"

"Perhaps not! Perhaps I should write of my adventures. And then other teachers will take my scroll and tell of my exploits to pupils all across Valinda." He paused. "And you? When the pilgrimage is over, what will you do?"

She thought for a time. "Do you know... I've looked no further ahead than the pilgrimage? I will accompany you, and take in the wonder of your planet, your people and their culture, their religion..."

"Delia, there will always be a place in my home for you."

She swallowed, emotion constricting her throat. She realised that she was still gripping the alien's hand, and squeezed. "Thank you. That means a lot to me, you know? It truly does."

"It must be so difficult, Delia... To be alone, on a strange world, without another of your kind."

"And with no prospect of ever returning to my planet," she murmured.

"No prospect at all? Perhaps, one day, if you could retrieve your life-raft and take off?"

She smiled to herself. "That would be impossible. Even if I could somehow retrieve the vessel, it would be useless. It was an escape craft only – it would be unable to achieve the power required to leave Valinda's gravity well. And even if it did..." She stopped, despair overcoming her. "Even if it did, it is so far from here to Earth that the life-raft would be unable to cover the distance."

"I am sorry."

"So... I must make the most of life on Valinda, and come to love my new home, and its people... or rather some of its people."

She stopped, choking back a sob.

I think I should sedate you, Delia.

No! No, it's all right... I'm okay. I'd rather remain awake, talking...

She recalled wondering something about Mahn earlier, and now she asked, "Mahn, do you mind if I ask how old you are?"

"Not at all, I am ten summers old."

One hundred Terran years old... She smiled to herself. She had thought of Mahn as being a young man, barely out of his teens.

"And is that old, by Fahran reckoning?"

"Not old, no, but not young. I am perhaps halfway through my life. On average, we Fahran live to an age of twenty summers."

Two hundred years... she thought.

"And you?" he asked. "How old are you, Delia?"

She told him that she was a little over three summers old, and felt him move as if in surprise beside her. "Three summers? But you are a child!"

She laughed. "Not by human reckoning, Mahn. We attain adulthood, on Earth, at the age of roughly one and a half summers. At that age, usually, we leave home and embark on careers."

"At that age," Mahn said, "we Fahran are still hivelings. We do not venture from the protection of our hive, and say goodbye to our hive-mother, until we are at least three summers old, sometimes four."

"I saw my first alien world, Delta Pavonis V, just half a summer ago, by your reckoning. Five Terran years. Since then I've seen five other colony worlds. "

"And what was it like, the first one?"

"It was very much like Earth, but much bigger. Vast. We had terraformed it, made it like Earth, green and rolling with great inland lakes. It was very beautiful. Perhaps all the more so as it was the first extra-solar planet I'd ever experienced."

"And the aliens of that world? What were they like?"

She shook her head, then realised the futility of the gesture. Even if Mahn had been able to see her, the movement would have conveyed nothing. She said, "There were no aliens on Delta Pavonis V – nor on any other world so far discovered by humankind. Oh, we've found plant life and animal life, but never sentient extraterrestrials. Until now."

She sensed his movement again. "Do you mean, Valinda is the first planet where you have found intelligent life?"

"That's right, and what's even more amazing is that on Valinda is not just one sentient species, but three. Until now, we wondered if we might be the only sentient species in the universe."

"Whereas we Fahran, who do not posses the means of travelling between the stars – who have not even left our planet – we knew that life existed elsewhere."

"Thanks to the Skelt..."

"When they came, with their stories of the conquest of other stars, other peoples, we knew we were not alone."

"So there are yet other intelligent races out there, suffering under the yolk of Skelt domination? That's an appalling thought."

"And then, long after the Skelt arrived, so our God, Chalto, came to Valinda. He gave us hope."

"In what way?"

"He told us that one day he would lead a revolt against the Skelt, and that we would defeat our oppressors."

She smiled to herself.

"That would be wonderful," she said.

"And..." Mahn said, "perhaps that is why you are here, on Valinda. Perhaps our God brought you here, especially, to bring about the end of Skelt dominion. Perhaps that, unbeknownst to you, is your destiny?"

"Well... if it is, then I don't know quite how I'll bring that about."

"Perhaps, Delia, you will be guided by our God. Perhaps in time he will show you the way."

She smiled. "Perhaps," she said. "Mmm..."

"Delia?"

"I'm feeling... feeling very peaceful, very sleepy. As if... as if I'm being anaesthetised, as if I'm about to... to undergo an operation..." She recalled having her tonsils removed when she was ten, and the wonderfully soporific sensation of drifting into unconsciousness.

"It is the pod," Mahn told her, as if from far away, "sending you to sleep. Good dreams, Delia."

"Good dreams, Mahn."

Then she slipped from one state of consciousness to another; she was not asleep, exactly, but neither was she conscious. She drifted in a state of gorgeous lassitude, without a care in the world, and presently she dreamed.

She was running towards her mother and father on a beach; she was five again, and they were on holiday in Mexico, and the sunlight limned her parents, made them glow like angels, like the supernal beings they were, and she knew a boundless love and trust for these people – and she had no awareness of her present self, but inhabited the body and consciousness of the five-year-old she had been.

Then, with the sudden, seamless transition of dreams, she was no longer five, but thirty-five, and she was dining in Paris with Timothy Greene, laughing at something he was saying... Then, later, she was in his arms, in bed in their hotel with the man she loved with all her heart... And yet, while she basked in the feeling, the recapitulation of the love she had known then, a small part of her consciousness was aware that all that was gone, taken away from her, and would never be regained.

And before she could cry out at her loss, she was no longer in the hotel bedroom in Paris, but on the surface of a strange new world, under a blisteringly hot sun, surrounded by swathes of multi-coloured blooms that sprang to life in a great wave of vibrancy and life.

And then she was jolted from this vision, from the dream-state to sudden consciousness, and she was back in the pod again, lying next to Mahn. Only a few hours could have elapsed.

"Delia."

"Mmm?" she responded drowsily.

"The journey is almost over."

"No... Surely not."

Imp, how long have I been out?

Almost three days, Delia.

She took a deep breath. The air on the pod was damp, fetid. Her limbs were stiff, her flesh sticky where it had come into contact with the walls of the pod.

She was aware of the pod's progress through the intestines of the summer worm, as smooth as a boat on a river.

Mahn asked, "Did you dream, Delia?"

"Yes. Yes, I did."

"Of the future?"

She recalled the plain of flowers suddenly erupting into life. "I don't know. Maybe. I was standing on a vast plain, watching a great carpet of blooms come to life. A million extraordinary colours, unfurling in fast-motion."

"That is the Blooming, Delia! If you dream of the Blooming, it means good luck."

"I hope so, Mahn. And you? Did you dream?"

"I had a curious vision. I was flying over Valinda, flying like a sqeer-bird over a swollen river and a great jungle."

"And what might that mean?"

"I don't know, Delia. I have heard no one speak of dreams of flying, or the import of such dreams."

"Were you happy in the dream?" she asked.

He thought about it in silence for a while. "I was exultant. I felt fulfilled."

"Then I think it was a good dream, Mahn. I think it means that your hopes and dreams will come to pass."

The pod bucked, jolting as if coming up against others. It was as if she were on some kind of precipitous fairground ride, in an enclosed vehicle she could not control. She was rattled this way and that and found herself clinging on to Mahn.

"I think the summer worm is evacuating our seed, Delia. Hold on. There is no telling how far we might drop."

She braced her head against the flesh of the pod, not wishing to crack her skull against Mahn's when they hit the ground.

The pod bumped and collided with others for a full minute, and so violent were the impacts that she feared her pod might split and send her and Mahn spilling out into the worm's lower intestine. Then the bumping ceased, and an odd calm prevailed as if they were sailing through the air.

They hit the ground with a bone-jarring impact. Delia cried out. The pod rolled, squashing them together face to face. She thought for a moment they were rolling down the side of a mountain and might never stop, but the motion slowed and then ceased. The pod rocked back and forth, settling, and soon all was still.

In the aftermath of their ejection, Delia held her breath. Now that the journey was over, all she wanted to do was leap from the confines of the pod, breathe fresh, cold air and stretch her limbs.

Mahn counselled caution. "We must wait a little while, and then split the pod very carefully. Scavengers gather around the lower reaches of the summer worm, picking through seed pods that have not been fully digested."

"Like ours," she said.

"Usually these scavengers are vegetarian," he said.

"But not exclusively?"

"Dangerous animals are rare hereabouts," he said. "But the Vo occasionally collect the spent seeds."

"The Vo are not carnivorous?"

"They are, but they collect semi-digested seed pods, fill them with melt water, and as the heat increases with the coming of summer, so the water reacts with the sugars in the pod and produces a fermented, alcoholic drink much valued by the Vo."

"That's all we need," she said. "Giant drunken spider-crabs!"

"The Vo festivities are some time off," he told her. "Only at the time of the Great Melt, with the plains flowing with a multitude rivers all tipping from the great equatorial escarpment, do the Vo feast and become riotously inebriated."

"I hope we're not around the witness the festivities," she said.

A silence stretched as they waited. At length Mahn said, "I hear nothing. I will open the pod. I would close your eyes, Delia."

She did so, and felt Mahn leaning across her and pulling at the seam. Bright red light pulsed through her eyelids as the seam split. She opened her eyes minimally, then covered them with her hand against the blinding dazzle. Cold air entered the pod and she took deep, grateful breaths.

She heard something, a high-pitched squealing.

"What's that?" she hissed.

Mahn leaned across her chest and peered through the seam, his fur sodden with pod juice.

He stiffened, then withdrew his head very slowly.

The squeals continued.

"What...?" she whispered.

"Very close by, perhaps ten metres away, is a Vo – but it is not the Vo we should fear. I recognise its markings and it is from a peaceable tribe. The Vo has been captured by a ghorn, and it is this creature we should fear."

"A ghorn..." Delia said.

"The ghorn are carnivorous creatures," Mahn informed her, "and will eat anything that moves."

CHAPTER FOURTEEN

DELIA CONTROLLED HER breathing and, cautiously, lifted her head to peer through the split in the pod.

They were sitting on a plain of grey rock and fractured, silver ice. The red sun bulged low over a flat horizon. Delia saw the Vo first; it was much smaller than those she had seen ridden by the Skelt, and she wondered if it were a child. It was no bigger than her life-raft, its bulbous headpiece and lobulated body marked with red and yellow chevrons – presumably adornments of some sort.

The Vo lay on its side, its multiple legs gathered and cinched by a rope. Its eyestalks waved this way and that, as if in distress. Beneath them, its mandibles opened and shut, issuing high-pitched squeals.

Its front left leg ended at the first joint, and ichor dripped to the ground and coloured the ice a sulphurous hue.

Only then did Delia see its tormentor, the ghorn.

It was a relatively small creature, a little taller than herself, and resembled a bipedal wolf – except in place of fur it had silver scales that ran with oily iridescence in the light of the sun.

The ghorn sat on its haunches before the Vo, sucking meat and juices from the spider-crab's severed foreleg.

Delia felt Mahn's mouth close to her ear as he whispered, "The Vo are a great delicacy for the ghorn. It will feast for days, eating the Vo little by little but ensuring it remains alive."

She shook her head in disgust at the predator.

"The Vo is from the Jeeri tribe, hence its distinctive markings. They formed an alliance with the Fahran many decades ago."

"We must do something," she whispered. "We can't let the Vo die such a death!"

"By saving the Vo we would gain kudos from the Jeeri tribe, and thus earn ourselves safe passage south through Vo territory. However..."

"Go on."

"The ghorn are fearsome... and we have no weapons."

She heard the squealing of the Vo, accompanied by the sucking and slobbering made by the ghorn as it feasted on the severed leg.

She whispered, "The Vo – is it merely crying out in pain, or speaking?"

Mahn listened, then told her, "It is chanting a prayer to its god, praying for death, claiming it has led a virtuous life and that such a fate, at the hands of mindless ghorn, is undeserved. It is a young Vo, barely one summer old, I would estimate – a child. This is perhaps the first time it has left its underground lair, come scavenging for summer worm seed for its tribe. It certainly did not deserve this fate."

"We can't just lie here for days, watching the ghorn feast and the Vo die slowly."

"As I said..."

"I know, the ghorn are fearsome."

She contemplated her options. "Mahn, we couldn't simply frighten the ghorn away, could we?"

"What, bare our teeth and run at it, screaming?"

"Well, something like that."

She detected scorn in his reply. "It would scythe us down with its claws, rip out our bellies and watch us die. And then, when it had had its fill of Vo meat, it would vary its diet by sampling our flesh."

"I get the picture."

Imp, she said, *we must do something.*

You have a plan?

A vague idea. The laser scalpel in the medi-pack...

It is hardly a suitable weapon.

It'll suffice, in lieu of a laser rifle. Its blade might be short, but it's lethal.

Tell me how you intend to go about besting the ghorn.

She thought about it. *As before, I want you to project a holo-image, to attract the animal's attention. One figure, beside the Vo and directly before the ghorn. While the ghorn's attention is on the projection, I will approach it from the rear and use the laser scalpel.*

And if I advise you not to risk your life in this way?

I will overrule your advice and go ahead anyway.

It would appear I have little choice in the matter.

None.

She looked at Mahn and whispered, "In the larger of the two packs on my back you will find a short, green device, as long as your finger. If you could get it out and pass it to me..."

She struggled onto her side so that her back was to Mahn.

"Delia?"

"A knife," she whispered, "but a special knife. Quickly."

She felt the alien's long fingers tugging at the fastenings of her pack, and then Mahn rooting through its contents. She rolled up the sleeves of her thermal suit to free her hands.

"Is this it?" Mahn asked, holding up the laser scalpel.

"Good work."

She took the scalpel and looked across to the Vo and the ghorn.

"Delia, I plead with you to be careful."

"I can't sit by and do nothing. You said yourself that we would earn kudos from its tribe if we saved its life. That's what I intend to do."

"But the danger to yourself..."

She stared at the little alien. "You must have considered the danger when deciding whether or not to save me, yes? You elected to go ahead, despite the risk. Well, there you are... And anyway," she finished, "I will have my Imp's assistance."

She eased herself into a sitting position and was about to swing a leg over the side of the pod when Mahn stopped her. He took her hand and looked into her eyes, then lowered his head and allowed her to proceed.

Imp, she said. *Wait until I'm standing, then project the image.*

Affirmative. But which image? Your own?

No... My father, okay?

Very well.

Taking shallow breaths, she lifted a leg over the seam and climbed from the pod. Her boots came down on the icy rock. She heard something crunch lightly beneath her weight and held her breath. Her legs felt shaky from enforced inactivity. For the first time since her arrival on Valinda, she felt the warmth of the sun through the material of her suit.

She activated the laser scalpel and pushed out the light blade to its ten centimetre extent.

Five metres separated her from the ghorn. If it were to turn now and see her, then she would be forced into a face-to-face fight. She had attended tae-kwon-do classes a few years ago, but had proved inept. She would have to rely solely on the scalpel. She only hoped that the creature didn't move as fast as the Skelt.

The ghorn hunkered down with its back to her, sucking at the severed leg.

Imp, I wonder if I should approach it now, without resorting to the projection. It seems intent on its meal.

I advise adhering to your original plan, Delia. It might appear absorbed in its meal, but it is an animal. It will be alert for predators, and jealous of its cache.

You're right. Very well. Project.

She looked across at the Vo; if it saw her, it gave no indication. Beside the bulbous body of the spider-crab, the image of her father suddenly appeared. He stood, tall and white-haired and a little stooped, smiling across at her. Something kicked in her heart and she smiled in response.

A split-second after the image appeared, the ghorn sprang to its feet, dropped the spider-crab's leg, and crouched as if ready to attack.

Her heart hammering, sweat gathering under her face-mask, Delia approached the ghorn step by careful step.

She readied the laser scalpel, tightening her grip around its shaft. She would bring the laser down into the creature's upper back and rip downwards, along the length of its spine. The blade was long enough to reach vital internal organs, split them apart...

She was two metres from the ghorn, and raising her weapon, when the animal moved. Draw by the image of her father, the ghorn took a step forward, then another. Delia found herself matching its steps, maintaining the distance between herself and her prey.

If it reached the projection and discovered it no more than a trick of light...

The ghorn slowed, wary. Delia took another step towards the creature. On her next step, she would plunge the scalpel into its back.

She raised the laser just as the ghorn, alerted by some hair-trigger animal intuition, growled and spun round to face her.

Instinctively she lashed out and slashed with the laser, back and forth so fast that she surprised even herself.

The ghorn stared at her with massive liquid eyes in its oddly vulpine face. Delia backed off, fear swelling within her. The creature appeared unharmed, and she wondered if the blade had merely scored impotently across the surface of its scales.

It took another step towards her. Delia backed off a step, too terrified to press the attack.

She saw a pink line appear just below the creature's jaw. It opened its muzzle in silence – as if to threaten her, or to protest at her actions – and something bubbled past the ugly, sickle arrangement of its fangs. It took another step forward and, as she watched, its long head made an odd movement on its neck, a sickening sideways slip.

Then the ghorn fell to its knees as if in supplication, its head sliding slowly from its shoulders and hitting the ground at her feet a second before its body thumped down beside it.

Delia stood and stared at the body, too shocked to move, as the ghorn's pink blood pulsed out across the ground and flash froze in a beautiful, spreading pattern of crystals.

Then Mahn was beside her, gripping her arm. "I was too terrified to watch, Delia! Only when I heard the ghorn hit the ground..."

She looked across at the image of her father; he was smiling tolerantly at her, as if in quiet approbation of her actions.

Imp, stop the projection.

Her father's image vanished.

She looked into the hideous face of the Vo. Its furred, jet-black mandibles clacked, and its eyestalks regarded her. She heard a high-pitched tweet issue from its slit mouthpiece, and Mahn translated.

"I cannot understand all it says," he said, "but it is asking what kind of creature are you."

She smiled. "And not a word of thanks!"

"No... it *is* thanking you. It... it is reciting a song... a poem... of debt, of thanks."

"Thank the Vo on my behalf," she said. "It isn't every day that someone composes a poem in my honour. Tell it that I am a human, from very far away, and that I couldn't just stand by and watch it die."

Mahn stepped towards the Vo, tiny beneath its clacking mandibles.

He looked up and spoke in an approximation of the spider-crab's language, gesturing with his long hands as he did so.

He turned to Delia and said, "She says that her name is Var."

She smiled. "Var the Vo..."

"And," Mahn went on, "she says also that we are in danger, here."

"Danger?" She looked around her. "More ghorn?"

"No," Mahn said. "Skelt. A party of Skelt militia."

"Not the same who followed us from Alkellion?"

"Unlikely. But perhaps another band of militia from Alkellion. They range far and wide in search of Vo and other creatures."

The Vo moved her slit mouthpiece, issuing a whistling sound painful to her ears.

Mahn reported, "Var says she saw the party riding harl – beasts of burden – a day ago, just north of here. She was near a tunnel to her underground lair, quickly concealed herself and so remained undetected."

"We'd better not hang around," Delia said. She lifted her laser scalpel. "Tell Var that I'll cut the rope binding her, and then we'll be on our way."

Delia slit the rope and pulled it free of the Vo's remaining legs. The severed foreleg was no longer dripping ichor; Delia stepped back from the frozen slick of fluid and watched the creature rise to her full height, twice as tall as her. The spider-crab moved up and down on her remaining nine legs as if testing their agility.

Delia asked Mahn, "She'll survive without...?" She pointed to the ugly stump.

"The Vo are not like you or me, Delia. They can lose two or three legs and still function."

Var scuttled towards Mahn, her mouthpiece working. "She asks where we are heading. I said that we are on a pilgrimage to Mahkanda. She says she will carry us as far as Million Falls, on the equator. This will greatly assist us."

"Tell Var that we will be grateful for the ride," Delia said.

The Vo lowered itself to the ground, and arranged the five legs on the right of its body so that they formed an ascending staircase. Mahn scrambled up first, settling himself on the creature's high domed back. Delia followed, finding her footing with difficulty on the polished chitin. At last she scaled the Vo's carapace and settled herself behind Mahn.

Var rose jerkily, and Delia was reminded of the one occasion she had ridden a camel while on holiday in Tunisia. She felt the same precarious, vertiginous sensation now as the Vo started up and moved off across the frozen plain. She pitched back and forth, soon accommodating herself to the creature's swaying motion.

"How far to Million Falls, Mahn?"

"Two hundred kilometres. However..."

"Yes?"

"Before we reach Million Falls, I would like to stop at my home village of Jhelam, so that I can tend to my mate's grave tree."

"Of course," she said.

"Jhelam is on the same escarpment as Million Falls, and we should reach the village by sunset."

Imp calculated that sunset would occur in sixteen Terran hours. She was in for a long ride. Var increased her pace, her nine remaining legs skittering across the iron-hard ground with mechanical precision.

Var spoke, and Mahn translated. "She says that we must remain vigilant for the Skelt hunting party."

As they rode, Delia looked back the way they had come, scanning for any sign of the Skelt. In the far distance was the mountain range beyond which was the city of Alkellion. The mountains were tiny, a jagged line drawn across the vast blue sky, above which rode the tiny disc of the white, second sun.

She made out a dozen zigzag fractures streaking from the horizon and down across the plain, and found it hard to accept that she had travelled this distance within a seed pod passing through the gut of a worm...

And now she was riding on the back of a sentient spider-crab.

She wondered what her friend Zeena, a xeno-zoologist, would have made of all this, and felt a stab of pain at the thought of Zeena's death and those of all her other colleagues aboard the *Amsterdam*. She pushed the thought to the back of her mind and concentrated on looking out for Skelt hunting parties.

Ahead, the land stretched away in a featureless, gun-metal grey plain, no longer scored by fissures and fractures. Occasionally she made out dark rents in the plain, which Mahn told her were entrances to the Vo's underground lairs.

Delia realised that she hadn't eaten for an age, and pulled an energy bar from her backpack. It was her last, and she asked Mahn if he would be able to scavenge food from this unlikely terrain.

"It is deceptive, Delia. It would appear devoid of life, but plants grow beneath the surface."

"Edible plants?"

"Delicious plants," he said. "Soon we will stop and eat."

She finished her bar and still felt hungry.

As they moved steadily south, Mahn and Var conversed. She said to Imp: *How long before you'll master the Vo's tongue?*

Very soon. It is not complex.

Excellent. I'd like to be able to speak to her.

From time to time Mahn reported his conversation with the Vo. "I was correct in thinking Var is a child. She is barely a summer old. This is only the second time she has ventured aboveground."

"Won't her family be concerned for her?" Delia asked.

She sensed chiding humour in Mahn's reply. "The Vo are not like you or me. They are born in great numbers from one queen, and go about their individual, independent lives after just a few days. Var was telling me that she will work as a trader when she attains the age of two summers. She desires to see much of the world, and meet its many peoples."

"A trader," Delia mused.

"Theirs is a complex society," Mahn said. "They have teachers and scholars and philosophers, poets and musicians..."

She wondered what Vo music might sound like. "And the Skelt use these intelligent creatures as beasts of burden?"

"And as a source of meat, also."

A little later Var slowed down and stopped, and Mahn announced that it was time to eat.

They climbed from the back of the Vo and Mahn moved off across the plain, proceeding slowly and peering down at the ground. Delia watched him drop on to all fours and brush his hand across the surface. He found a stone and scraped away at the soil, excavating a sizeable hole, and then pulled at something, tugging on what looked like a root. Hand over hand, he drew a long stem from the cold earth, then another and another. Each stem ended in a pale pink tuber the length of his arm.

"Neer root," he said. "A Fahran delicacy eaten raw or cooked in stew. Will you join us, Var?"

The spider-crab replied. Imp said in Delia's head, *She ate earlier. She said she will look out for Skelt while you eat.*

You've worked out their language? Can I converse with Var now?
Affirmative.

Mahn settled himself in Var's shadow, and Delia joined him. Mahn passed her a neer root. He snapped his own in two and bit into the flesh, and she did the same. The vegetable was sweet, but with an odd spicy aftertaste which tingled on her palate.

She turned to Var and looked into her great obsidian eyes at the end of their long stalks. "You ought to try some, Var. It's quite delicious."

Imp translated, turning her statement into a rapid whistling.

The trouble with conversing with aliens, she thought, was that their body language and facial expressions were impossible to decode. Var moved her eyestalks slightly towards Delia in what might have been a gesture of surprise that she had spoken in the Vo language.

Var whistled up and down the scale, and presently Imp translated: "You speak, red one! But you were silent for so long. Do you understand my words?"

"I understand, and... I was studying your language before I spoke, in case I made errors and you misunderstood me."

"I compliment you on your facility, red one."

"My name is Delia," she said.

"Delia... and Mahn claims that you come from the stars in a machine. He told me this, and I thought he jested. Tell me, is it true?"

Delia swallowed a mouthful of neer root. "It is true. I come from a world called Earth, a long, long way from here."

Mahn said, "Her vessel was captured by the Skelt, and Delia was imprisoned until I helped her to escape. She is all alone on our world. Her friends died in the accident that destroyed the vast ship which brought her all the way from her world."

"All alone..." Var said. Her great black eyes regarded Delia. "You are a strange creature indeed." She raised a claw, swung it around and, with a delicacy Delia found hard to credit, touched her midriff. "You are a strange colour, and so soft. How do you survive without armour, without claws?"

"Well, on my world there are few predators to threaten us, so we don't need armour, or claws." She indicated the Fahran, sitting beside her and chewing his root. "But look at Mahn, here. He is from Valinda and he has neither armour nor claws, and he and his kind survive. Each creature adapts to its own environment."

"For millennia," Mahn said, "we Fahran lived far underground, rarely venturing out even at summertime. There were no predators on the part of Valinda where we originated. Only recently, according to our scholars, have we made the surface our home for varying periods.

Though by 'recently,' I mean thousands of years."

Delia opened her backpack and took out a water canister, finding it almost empty.

"And we are in an area where water is difficult to obtain," Mahn said. "Perhaps we will have to wait until we reach Jhelam...?"

"I'll be dehydrated long before then," Delia said.

Var stood quickly, startling her. "But you are wrong, little Fahran," she said. "We can obtain water here. Or, at least, *I* can."

She scuttled off across the rocky plain, unfurling a long proboscis and probing the ground here and there, finding it unsuitable and moving on.

At last she stopped and applied her proboscis to the plain, working it little by little beneath the surface. A minute ensued, and Delia saw the thick, jet black hose throb with the uptake of fluid.

Var pulled free her proboscis, turned and scuttled back to join them. She stood over the pair, her proboscis dangling, and said, "You wanted water..."

From the hooked tip of her proboscis, clear fluid dripped as from a spigot, and Mahn bent his head and drank.

His thirst slaked, he gasped and wiped his wide lips with his fingers, then stepped back for Delia to take his place.

Do you think it'll be safe? she asked Imp.

Affirmative, but be cautious and take only a little.

She bent her head to the tip of Var's proboscis and sucked. The water was ice-cold and effervescent, with the tang of salty minerals. She took two mouthfuls and withdrew, thanked the Vo for her kindness, and then filled her canister.

They climbed onto Var's back and continued on their way. Delia accommodated herself on the shell, leaning back against a bulging hip joint in relative comfort.

Var increased her speed, so that shortly after resuming their journey they were travelling at what Delia estimated was thirty kilometres an hour. Certainly, she thought, she wouldn't like to lose her purchase of the shell and tumble to the ice-hard ground at this speed.

She scanned the terrain on every side for the first sight of the Skelt.

At one point Mahn, seated before her, indicated the sun in the sky high to their right. It swelled hugely, bigger than any celestial body Delia had ever seen; surely it was bigger now than when she had first arrived on Valinda.

"It grows by the day, Delia, and its heat increases. Soon it will fill half the sky, and we will be able to see great spouts of flame rising from its surface."

"And do you remain aboveground for the duration of the summer?" she asked. "Surely it must get too hot at some point."

"That is so. Four months into summer, the sun burns exposed fur, and dries up water in seconds, and we must retreat underground for another four months, until the time we call the Leaving, when Valinda begins to move away from the sun. It is still hot, but the Leaving means that the long winter is on the way, and our summer festivities take on a melancholy note."

"And we Vo," Var pronounced proudly, "remain aboveground all summer, for our shells can withstand the heat – just as we can withstand the intense cold of deepest winter."

"When we are well underground," Mahn said, "deepest winter is the time I like least, with little to commend it except that it is the time when my people tell the Aharah cycle of stories, about the time before the Skelt came to Valinda, when the Fahran built cities like Alkellion and Million Falls and went abroad without fear of being enslaved."

"And my people tell stories in high summer," Var put in, "stories of the great voyages of adventure made by Vo heroes. And our stories are accompanied by music, rousing songs from many centuries ago. I wish you could hear our songs, Delia."

"And so do I," she said, wondering what spider-crab music might sound like.

Mahn said, "And do you have music on Earth, Delia?"

"Indeed we do," she said. "In fact... would you like to hear some?"

Mahn stared at her, and Var exclaimed, "The music of another world? But how is this possible?"

Mahn said, "Delia has a tiny machine in her head. It is this – am I right? – which will play the music."

"That's right. But what to play?" she mused. "I know..."

Imp, how about a little Arvo Pärt?

Certainly. Which symphony, Delia?

I think perhaps his Third, yes?

Very well.

The speaker at her temple issued the opening notes of the symphony.

Var waved her claws in apparent delight. "But it is... beautiful," she declared.

Mahn stared at her. "Var is right," he said. "And to think, I am listening to music composed on a world far away..."

They proceeded across the alien plain accompanied by the ethereal strains of the Terran symphony.

CHAPTER FIFTEEN

ONE HOUR LATER Mahn touched her shoulder. "Delia, look! Look!"

She sat up and stared into the sky, where Mahn was pointing. She ordered her Imp to stop the music. Var had halted, and also directed her eyestalks to the heavens.

Delia blinked in the sudden silence, at first seeing only the red dazzle of sunlight.

"But what is it?" exclaimed Var.

Then Delia saw the laser-straight condensation trail high in the sky, streaking south, and her heart skipped.

Imp?

"I have seen nothing like it in all my time!" Var declared.

Mahn said, softly, "But I *have*..." He turned and stared at Delia. "My friend, when your vessel appeared in the skies above Valinda, we Fahran rushed to the windows and stared up in wonder. We beheld a strange white line, just like this one, pass high above the northern plain..."

Imp, can it be? Can it really be...?

I am attempting to assess the probability.

But what else can it be? she asked. *No other species on Valinda possess the technology of flight, and surely it can't be the Skelt, returning?*

But the alternative, she told herself, was just *too* much to hope for.

Surely it was beyond the realms of possibility that others had survived the starship blow-out, boarded a life-raft and managed to reach Valinda?

Imp? she cried.

The reply seemed an age in coming. *I have attempted contact with the vessel, but that proved unsuccessful. There might be any number of reasons for that. However...*

Yes? she said, frantic.

The craft's ion signature suggests the very high probability that it is a life-raft or a shuttle originating from the Pride of Amsterdam.

"Yes!" she cried aloud, unable to stop tears from streaming down her cheeks.

Mahn touched her hand. "Delia?"

She stared at him. She had the urge to drag him to her and plant a great kiss on his long, alien lips. "It's a life-raft from my ship, Mahn! It's another survivor from the *Amsterdam*. I'm no longer alone. There will soon be another human being on Valinda..."

I advise caution, Delia. It is not one hundred per cent certain.

Ignoring her Imp's words, she looked up at the condensation trail, trying to make out the miniscule shape of the craft. Perhaps there would be more than one survivor, she thought – perhaps the raft was full of humans.

And that thought was followed by another, a thought so dangerous she knew that she should not even entertain the idea, for fear of being crushed by disappointment.

But Imp... what if one of the survivors is Timothy...?

Delia, Timothy was in the stern of the Amsterdam *when the explosion occurred. That section of the ship, in all likelihood, would not have made the transition through the wormhole.*

I know, I know... but – but what if he did manage to reach a life-raft, and the life-raft just set off and... and inadvertently shunted...?

But even as she said the words, she knew she was fantasising.

Delia, I am sorry. That is impossible.

She nodded. *I know, Imp. I know...*

And, as I say, I counsel caution. There is a high probability that it is a human life-raft. But it is not a certainty.

She watched the con-trail fluff out, the tiny speck of the vessel disappearing from sight, and felt a great swelling of joy in her chest.

Imp said, *Analysing the vessel's trajectory, Delia, I estimate that it will come down two hundred kilometres below the equator, directly south of our present position. Ask Mahn if there are any Fahran cities in that vicinity.*

She relayed the question, and after some thought Mahn replied, "The city of Alarah lies that way, Delia."

Imp said, *We should make for Alarah, then.*

Deli repeated this, and Mahn said, "We can do so, yes. Alarah lies some way off our intended route, but we can make a detour."

"And how long will it be before we reach Alarah?" she asked, hardly able to contain her excitement.

"We will reach Jhelam in one day, and the Falls a day after that," he said. "Then we will take a boat south to Alarah, which we should reach in perhaps half a day." He squeezed her hand. "And then, my friend, you will be reunited with your kind."

She looked ahead – despite her Imp's reservations – to the meeting with her fellow survivors, and wondered at their reaction when she hove into sight on the back of a giant spider-crab.

CHAPTER SIXTEEN

DELIA WAS ASLEEP when the Skelt appeared.

Mahn shook her shoulder and she came awake, smiling.

Var was no longer moving, but had settled herself on the ground, very still. "Mahn?" Delia asked.

Var whistled. Imp translated: "On the horizon, to the left. Look."

Delia scanned the horizon but saw nothing. "What is it?"

The Fahran said, "Var thought she saw a party of Skelt."

Something turned to ice in her stomach. "I don't see anything."

"The Vo are famed for their acute eyesight," Mahn said.

"I saw Skelt," Var said. "Another hunting party. A dozen, maybe more, far to the north."

Delia looked around in desperation. The plain was flat and still, with not a sign of movement.

She let out a breath. "Perhaps they've moved on."

"It would be safer if we concealed ourselves," Var said.

Delia looked around. "That's a great idea, in theory. There's one slight problem – a distinct lack of hiding places."

"One hundred paces ahead and to the right," Var said, "is a fissure in the ground. It will lead to a Vo underground lair."

Delia made out a discoloration in the cracked, grey stone ahead. "How can you be sure?"

"Pheromones," Var explained. "Vo have come this way many times before. It is a narrow cleft, so I suggest you dismount and follow me."

Var arranged her legs to form a staircase and Delia followed Mahn down, her stomach tight with apprehension. Var scuttled over the iron-hard ground towards the cleft, and Delia and Mahn hurried to keep pace.

Perhaps Var had been mistaken, Delia thought; perhaps she'd seen a flash of sunlight on a rock or a sliver of ice, and ascribed it to a Skelt's lightning movement? They seemed to be alone on the vast face of the featureless plain. Nevertheless, she was cheered by the thought that soon they would be safely underground in the lair of the Vo.

She wondered if they would proceed to Jhelam underground; another extraordinary experience. She wondered if the Vo had cities down there, and if so, what they might be like.

They had almost reached the rent in the ground when Var whistled in alarm. Almost before Imp had time to translate, "Attention! Skelt!" the locust creatures appeared en masse.

"Run!" Mahn yelled, reaching for her hand.

She saw a blur of silver motion to her right, and another straight ahead. Var was scuttling at speed towards the cleft, a dark slash ten metres away. The spider-crab collided with a silver streak, and the Skelt went rattling off across the ground. For a second it lay on its back, then vanished from sight as it picked itself up and ran.

Var reached the cleft, slipped through the gap and disappeared.

Mahn gripped Delia's hand and dragged her along – and then he was suddenly no longer at her side. Something hit him and he went flying across the ground and lay very still. Delia started towards

Mahn, but something restrained her. She turned, crying out, and stared into the elongated face of the locust creature gripping her arm.

In an instant a dozen Skelt materialised around her, armed with sickle swords, spears rising from quivers on their backs.

Delia struggled, attempting to free herself from the Skelt, but its grip was like iron. She had the laser scalpel in the pocket of her thermal suit, and her left hand was free... But with so many Skelt around her she would be a fool to play the hero.

Do not resist, Imp counselled. *Do not give them an excuse to harm you.*

She looked desperately across to where Mahn lay, unmoving.

One of the Skelt thrust its face at her and worked its mandibles. Imp translated: "What are you?"

They're not the Skelt we evaded earlier, she said.

I am not sure that this is to our advantage.

What should I tell them? She was shaking in fear and it was all she could do to hold on to the contents of her stomach.

We don't want to be returned to the Skelt at Alkellion, Imp said, *in light of the militia's decision to put you to death.*

"What are you?" the Skelt asked again.

I think the best course might be to plead ignorance. Do not respond to its questions. This might buy us time.

Very well... But time for what?

Time to allow me to consider the situation.

She stared at the Skelt before her, then looked away. The party seemed uninterested in Mahn, who lay unmoving ten metres away. He had hit the ground with force... but perhaps he was merely unconscious, not dead. His tiny form, loose-limbed and pathetic, brought tears to her eyes.

The Skelt were joined by the others, who crowded around and stared at her with obvious curiosity.

The first Skelt brought its face close to hers and spoke again. Imp translated: "You do not comprehend? You are ignorant? An animal? Perhaps the Vo planned to eat you, yes? Perhaps you are good meat?"

Another Skelt spoke, and Imp said, *This one says that it thinks you are intelligent, and not an animal. It calls you an enigma, which ought to be investigated.*

This brought a clacking cacophony of response from the rest of the party.

What are they saying, Imp?

They are debating what to do with you.

And? What are the suggestions? And don't spare my feelings.

Very well, they range from eating you themselves, feeding you to the harl, or taking you back for their leaders to question.

'Back'? she asked. *To Alkellion?*

They did not specify.

A Skelt stepped forward, drawing its curved sword and gesturing towards her. The creature rattled its jaws.

Imp?

It said that you are meatier than a Fahran. It has volunteered to be the first to sample your flesh.

Wonderful. I think I'd better say something.

I agree.

She stared at the Skelt with the drawn sword and said, "I understand you."

The translation brought a clatter of comment from the surrounding party. Their leader bent close. "You speak our tongue even better than the Fahran."

"I am a scientist, from another star. I came here in a flying ship. I have knowledge which I will share."

This brought another round of clattering comment. *They speak of the light in the sky they saw many days ago,* Imp said, *evidently your life-raft. They say they must take you back to their city. They will be well rewarded, they say.*

The leader spoke. "We will not eat you, yet. First, you will speak to our chiefs, and then we might feast upon your flesh."

"My flesh is poisonous to the Skelt," she said. "But your leaders will reward you well for the knowledge I will share."

The leader gestured, and Delia saw a blur of movement as two Skelt moved towards her. Then she was tipped on to her side and carried through the air, a dizzying rush all the more vertiginous for being unexpected. Sharp claws bit into her arms and legs and it was all she could do to stop herself from crying out in pain.

She tried to look back, to see whether they had gathered up Mahn too, but was unable to bend her head far enough.

The disorienting rush lasted for a few minutes; eventually she came to a stop and was unceremoniously placed upright. She staggered, gaining her balance, and looked around her.

She saw a hundred Skelt gathered on the plain, and a procession of a dozen strange creatures. They resembled turtles without shells, but turtles twice the size of bull elephants, with iridescent scales and multi-horned heads. Each creature – the harl Var had spoken of? – bore a cargo of dead animals with jet black pelts, and other, smaller animals, slung like trophies across their domed backs. Behind the caravan of harl she made out a dozen spider-crabs, their legs shackled, each one ridden by a Skelt.

She was tipped up again and carried off at speed. When she stopped again, she was being lashed to the back of the leading harl. A Skelt – she guessed it was the leader who had questioned her earlier – crouched beside her and called out a command to a colleague hunkered behind the head of the beast.

The harl started up and plodded ponderously forward, its breath coming in great stertorous wheezes. Behind them, Delia heard the rest of the caravan trudge in wheezing pursuit. She closed her eyes and wondered what fate awaited her at journey's end.

CHAPTER SEVENTEEN

HOURS ELAPSED. DELIA dozed and woke. She ached from being tied in an unnatural position to the back of the beast. The sun was directly overhead, a bloodshot eye staring down on her dispassionately. They were still on the great plain, but she could not make out the northern mountains. With the sun at its zenith, it was impossible to say in which direction they were heading.

Do you know where they're taking us? she asked Imp.

No, in that I have no knowledge of our destination. However, as for our direction...

Go on, she said, fearing the worst.

Imp confirmed her fears. *North.*

That's bad, isn't it?

It does not necessarily mean that we are heading for Alkellion.

She grunted. *Pull the other one. And even if we're making for another city, word will soon reach the Skelt at Alkellion that they have me, and what then? The militia there want me dead, or have you forgotten that?*

If we are heading towards another city, that will be to our advantage. It will give us the opportunity, perhaps, to play one set of Skelt off against the other. I can promise scientific knowledge, perhaps offer knowledge for privilege, until such time as I can effect your escape.

She was of a mind to say that she never realised that machine intelligences were prone to fantasize, but kept the thought to herself.

We're unlikely to come upon another Fahran as good... she began, and could not continue.

Imp, what of Mahn? Do you think...?

It is impossible to say with any degree of certainty, Delia. I attempted to assess his status after the ambush, but without success.

At least Var managed to get away, she thought. Perhaps she had returned, searching for her friends, found Mahn and taken him to safety.

In the blink of an eye, a Skelt appeared beside her. She still couldn't tell them apart, but suspected it was the leader of the scavenging party again.

The Skelt regarded her, its mandibles clacking. Imp translated: "You claim to come from the stars."

"That's correct. I do."

"And the name of your planet?"

"Earth."

How did you translate that, Imp? she asked.

Simply as the Skelt word for soil.

"And how far away is this Earth?" the Skelt wanted to know.

"Thousands of light years," she said.

The Skelt listened, its head cocked. "And why did you come to my world?"

"I came to explore, in peace."

"You were alone?"

She had a thought. "I was alone in my vessel, yes. But my colleagues followed in another craft. By now they will have landed on Valinda.

They will come looking for me – in their ship, which has powerful weapons."

Ingenious, Imp said.

"How powerful?"

Recalling that the Skelt had damaged her life-raft with their own ground-to-air weapon, she said, "Much more powerful than anything possessed by the Skelt."

The alien regarded her without speaking for a while. "You are a fearsome warrior race, you people of Earth?" it asked at last.

"We can defend ourselves, if we need to."

The Skelt turned its long, equine head and looked into the sky. "We, too, came from the stars, many summers ago. My people are a powerful warrior race. We have conquered more than a hundred planets on our travels through space."

Unable to stop herself, she said, "That is hard to believe, given that now you fight with swords."

"The Skelt on Valinda occupy an outpost, and quell the world with a level of technological sophistication deemed requisite for the task at hand. The Fahran and the Vo are feeble foes. My ancestors, when they left my people here, equipped us appropriately and moved on. But our history books say that my people have weapons capable of destroying worlds. I have read of the world of Kalash, defended by a suicidally proud race. They would not cede their planet to us, and so suffered the consequences."

"And... are you in contact with your people amongst the stars?"

The Skelt just stared at her in silence, unwilling or unable to give her the information.

Imp, is there any way this Skelt might know in which direction its race moved around the spiral arm?

I very much doubt it. But I can ask.

Imp spoke to the Skelt, who replied. Imp said to Delia, *I asked the creature whether its people moved along the arm towards the core, or contrariwise. As I suspected, it does not know. It is my opinion that the concept of star travel, and the distances involved, are things of magic to this creature.*

Delia said to the Skelt, "It must make you proud, to hold sway over a foe as peaceful as the Fahran?"

Either her sarcasm was lost in translation, or the Skelt chose to ignore it. It said, "We are proud to rule Valinda as decreed by our ancestors."

"And use races like the Fahran and the Vo as your slaves?"

The leader turned its inscrutable eyes upon her. "But that is their destiny, as an inferior race. Is it not written in nature, that the weak succumb to the strong?"

"And when my people come to rescue me?" she asked, her heart thumping.

The Skelt regarded her for long seconds. At last it said, "Then we will prove, when we have vanquished your compatriots, that we Skelt are the true masters of Valinda."

Delia stared at the grey, unchanging landscape.

After a minute she looked back at the Skelt. "And where are you taking me now?"

"To our city, Alkellion," said the Skelt, "where I will hand you over to our Council. They, in their wisdom, will decide what should be done with you."

As rapidly as the leader appeared, it vanished from her side, leaving her staring into space.

Alkellion... she said. *Imp, I must get away before then!*

That will be difficult.

I have my laser scalpel, remember?

It is not an efficient weapon. We are surrounded by almost one hundred Skelt. They are trained warriors, I might remind you, and move at speed. You would do well to bide your time.

The harl caravan trudged on. The wheezing of the creature became metronomic, lulling her. The Skelt leader did not return to quiz her, for which she was thankful. She considered the possibility that, somewhere upon the face of the planet, other humans breathed the same air as her.

Imp.

Go on.

Perhaps Mahn survived and made his way to Alarah to get word to the other survivors... Or perhaps Var might have the wherewithal to do that?

It is a possibility, but of course you assume that the survivors are armed, or capable of coming after you and defeating such a well-drilled foe as the Skelt... And, indeed, that there are survivors.

But if there are survivors...?

I calculate that the chances of a successful outcome, should there be survivors, and should they elect to come after you, are remote.

Then... you're saying that I'm as good as dead?

I am saying nothing of the sort.

You imply as much, she accused.

I simply stated that a successful outcome to the scenario you posited is unlikely. That does not mean, therefore, that I think your chances of remaining alive are limited.

But once I'm back at Alkellion, with the military members of the council wanting me dead...

Many days have elapsed since then – time enough for the parties involved to have reconsidered the situation. By now, the scientists of the council might have won over bellicose factions. And once it is known that another human vessel is upon Valinda – that, in my opinion, will concentrate Skelt minds and make them reconsider your destiny.

Some hope of that, she said.

In a flash the leader was beside her again, leaning forward to issue commands to the harl-driver. The great beast lumbered to a halt, and Delia watched as a dozen Skelt, blurring on either side of the harl, moved off into the distance.

Look, Imp said.

A party of Skelt came into sight a hundred metres ahead of the column. They stopped as one, then vanished as they moved, appearing again before her harl and staring up at her. A newcomer spoke to the Skelt leader at her side.

What are they saying, Imp? she asked.

It seems that these Skelt have come directly from Alkellion.

She stared down at the newcomers, aware that they were discussing her.

The leader turned to her. "It would appear, little one, that you have been far from truthful with me."

"Meaning?"

"You did not tell me that you escaped from Alkellion, evading our guards with the aid of a Fahran."

She replied, holding the Skelt's implacable gaze, "You didn't ask."

The Skelt said, "A decree was issued for your death. No-one defies the Council and survives."

One of the Alkellion Skelt, down below, called up to the leader.

Delia said, *Imp? What did he say?*

The guards from Alkellion demand that the leader hand you over so that they can carry out your immediate execution.

Thank you for that, Imp.

You did ask.

I'm not complaining. And what does the leader say?

He is equivocating. He thinks it wise to deliver you to the Council, citing that the situation has changed with the arrival of more beings from Earth.

The Alkellion Skelt gazed up, its mandibles working.

It says that the presence of other humans makes no difference. He will kill you, and then the other humans. He also points out that he outranks the leader of this party.

Wonderful. But I've got my scalpel, Imp, and if they decide to kill me I'll go down fighting.

The leader turned to Delia and said, "I have orders to hand you over to my colleagues from the city."

"Tell him about the other ship," she said in desperation. "Tell him that my colleagues will avenge my death. They'll kill every one of you complicit in my death – tell him that!"

"I have my orders."

He moved swiftly, slashing through the ropes binding her to the harl. She felt claws pinch her arms and legs as she was lifted from the creature and deposited, staggering, on the ground before the party of Alkellion Skelt.

She raised her head and stared at the leader of the new arrivals. Her heart pounded. She wondered whether to reach for her scalpel and lash out at the Skelt now, at least do the bastard some damage before she died.

The Skelt drew its sword and pushed up Delia's chin with its ice-cold blade. She tried not to flinch.

"Your blood will freeze on the ground of Valinda, and wild animals will feast on your carcass."

She pressed her right hand against the pouch of her one-piece, felt the outline of the laser scalpel beneath the material, and slowly moved her hand to reach for the weapon.

She was stopped by a deafening cacophony as the gathered Skelt clicked and chattered in consternation. At first she thought they were objecting to her execution, unlikely though that was. Then the Skelt turned, staring around them, and instantly dropped into crouches, alert and poised.

The leader of the Alkellion Skelt, before her, lowered its sword from her chin and whirled around.

Behind her, the harl raised its massive head and gave a startled snort.

What's happening?

Look, Imp said.

The combined forces of the Skelt – both the scavenging party and the new arrivals from Alkellion – formed a great protective circle around the caravan, swords and crossbows at the ready.

As Delia stared across the plain of ice, she saw a Vo emerge from a hole in the ground a hundred metres away, then another and another. She counted a dozen of the giant creatures, and then more – twenty, thirty – and still they came. She whirled around, aware that on every side, in a great encompassing circle, the Vo were popping up from the icy ground and moving carefully towards the beleaguered Skelt.

And they're armed, Imp said.

The spider-crabs carried staffs topped with great scythe-like blades, and many Vo bore more than one weapon. Some hefted clubs of bone, while others were unarmed but for the natural defence of their huge, swinging pincers. Perhaps two hundred Vo advanced, step by step, towards the Skelt.

Delia, back off and take cover beside the harl.

She glanced over her shoulder. As if in fear, the harl had collapsed to the ground. She took a step backwards, then another, away from the Skelt, then crouched down beside the flank of the creature and watched as battle was joined.

The Vo advanced in fits and starts, scuttling forwards and then stopping, a phalanx of bristling legs and waving claws. The Skelt moved to meet them, crouched and wary – but it was clear that the bipeds were massively outnumbered.

Imp said, *I suspect that the Skelt capture Vo only when the numbers are in their favour. Now they face a fight.*

I can't see them overcoming the Vo, she said, *but I hope the spider-crabs don't take me as just another Skelt.*

The Skelt had remained visible as they advanced slowly, but now they moved in a blurred wave and were among the spider-crabs in an instant. Delia heard the ringing clatter of steel on chitin, the frenzied knocking of a hundred pairs of mandibles and the high, whistling battle cries from the Vo. She saw a few spider-crabs fall, their legs hacked from under them – but she witnessed even more Skelt succumb to the onslaught. One second the Skelt were silver-grey blurs, and then they materialised on the ground as corpses, often nipped in half at the midriff, or missing arms, legs and heads.

She watched the Vo dart forward relentlessly, hacking and slashing, and Skelt bodies flew through the air and rained down on all sides. The sound of their bony bodies hitting the frozen ground was deafening; Delia cowered beside the great bulk of the harl, covering her ears and fearing that a Skelt, in an act of petty barbarism, might decide to despatch her before its own inevitable end.

She found herself clutching her laser scalpel, with no memory of pulling it from her pouch. Beside the sickle swords of the Skelt, and the Vo's bladed staffs and murderous claws, her weapon was pathetic. She held it before her like a talisman, daring any Skelt to come within striking distance.

I wish the thermal suit was grey, she said. *I'm more than a little obvious in this crimson suit.*

I think the combatants have more to occupy their minds at the moment.

Yes, but when the battle is over...

I would advise you to put the scalpel away, Imp said. *Whatever happens next, you should not be seen as a threat.*

Very well. She retracted the blade and slipped the device into her pouch.

I've noticed something, she said seconds later.

Go on.

The markings on the shells of the Vo, she pointed out. *They're not all the same. I've counted a dozen different sigils.*

This suggests a coming together of tribes, Imp said.

She looked across to the Vo imprisoned by the Skelt, who were watching the battle but were unable to join in due to the shackles around their limbs. The markings on the prisoners' shells were, likewise, varied.

An uprising to rescue their fellow Vo? she said. *I just hope they don't associate me with the Skelt.*

We will explain the situation, given the chance. But look, it appears that the battle is approaching its finale.

The blurs that were the Skelt became less numerous, and here and there the huge Vo halted amid the carnage and looked about them as if seeking their next opponent. The sound of battle diminished, and soon the conflict was reduced to scattered skirmishes as the Vo mopped up the remaining Skelt.

Delia hunkered down in the lee of the harl's bulging gut, trembling; it was only a matter of time before one of the victorious Vo noticed her.

She counted five dead or badly injured spider-crabs, while not one Skelt remained standing. Vo passed amongst the carnage, beheading those Skelt still living with economical snips of their great pincers. Others crossed to where their brethren were imprisoned and, amid whistled greetings and celebrations, cut through their shackles. Still more Vo pulled the animal carcasses from the backs of the harl and feasted: Delia averted her eyes from the macabre sight of mandibles chewing dead flesh.

A towering Vo, scuttling by, stopped suddenly and turned its great dark eyes upon her.

She pushed herself back against the harl, then forced herself upright so that she was facing the spider-crab. Her hand crept, instinctively, to her pouch – then stopped. What possible protection might the pathetic laser scalpel afford her against the Vo?

A great claw moved towards her, plucked her up with a delicacy she found incredible, and swung her through the air.

She was set down away from the harl so that she was in full view of all the Vo, silent now and staring at her. A strange calm descended on the gathering, the spiders dispensing with the feast and turning to her in silence.

A hundred pairs of compound eyes turned on their stalks to regard her, and the silence was broken by a sudden high-pitched whistle from the creature that had found her. Then others joined in, taking up the cry, and soon the entire spider-crab army was whistling and chirruping and waving legs and pincers.

Imp?

I don't know, Imp admitted.

The phalanx of Vo before her parted, and a lone Vo, much smaller than all the others, advanced towards her – its right foreleg severed at the first joint.

And riding on the spider-crab's back, his right arm in a makeshift sling, was the small, blue-furred Fahran Delia knew as Mahn.

CHAPTER EIGHTEEN

THE SELF-APPOINTED LEADER of the massed Vo clans – a huge brute the size of an earth-mover – declared a famous victory over the accursed Skelt and suggested the combatants, joined by Delia, Mahn and Var, return to the nearest underground lair to celebrate. The Vo had vast quantities of gallia pod wine with which to lubricate tired throats, and a hundred night worms were being roasted in preparation for the feast.

Mahn thanked the leader but said that time was pressing – the three friends were on a pilgrimage to the valley of Mahkanda, and must make haste. The leader accepted this but insisted that she and a dozen other Vo escort Delia, Mahn and Var south to the escarpment and the Fahran's home village of Jhelam.

Var scuttled along proudly at the head of the procession, while Delia and Mahn sat on her back and shared a meal of neer root and water.

They passed along the bank of a river now melting in the rising heat. Huge floes of ice loosened and floated off, and meltwater sparkled silver in the midday light. The riverbank was turning green, thick with a mat of fast-growing vegetation, interspersed with pink blooms which snapped open in an instant.

Delia reached out and touched Mahn's shoulder, then tapped Var's shell. "You don't know how good it is to see you both. I thought you were dead, Mahn, and I never thought I'd see you again, Var."

"When the Skelt retreated," Var said, "I came out of hiding and found Mahn. His arm was sprained, and he told me how he'd seen you carried off. I took him belowground to my people, who attended to his arm while I explained that you, Delia, had saved me from the ghorn but had been taken by the Skelt."

"And they readily agreed to help me?"

"My people admired your bravery, Delia, and could not leave you to the depredations of the Skelt. My elders petitioned other tribes, raised a small army, and set off across the plain in search of the cowardly Skelt."

"And there I was, thinking that a Vo might do for me when the battle was over."

"My people rescued not only yourself, but a dozen enslaved Vo, with the loss of only three brave warriors. When the remains of the Skelt are discovered by their fellows, they will realise that we can resist their dominion; we can fight against their injustice and assert our rights."

"I wouldn't mind being a fly on the wall at the Vo celebrations," Delia laughed.

Mahn looked at her. "A fly on the wall?"

Delia explained.

"I too would have enjoyed seeing the Vo celebrate," Mahn said. "But time is pressing. I will spend only a brief time in Jhelam, and then we will be on our way again. We should be there in half a day, by sunset."

Delia chewed on a neer root for a time, then asked, "Your mate, who passed away in the Skelt raid... How long had you been with her?"

"We were together for three summers, Delia, and were anticipating many more summers together. Like me, she was a teacher, though far more skilled and knowledgeable than me. She was a bright spirit, and illuminated everyone she met."

"I'm sorry..." The response was inadequate. Delia stared across at the Fahran, who sat cross-legged, with a half-eaten neer root in his lap. "Your time in Alkellion must have been appalling."

He turned his hand. "The odd thing is, Delia, that looking back on the last long year, I do not know how I managed to survive. I was in despair, and grieving the loss of my mate. You see, I saw her cut down by a Skelt sword during the raid..." He was silent for a time, staring down at the nibbled root. "The terrible thing was that her death was so needless. We were on the steps outside the village – gardens that we have fashioned on the side of the escarpment. It was the end of a long day in early summer, and we were walking and enjoying the setting of the sun. I look back and think that I had never been happier than at that time. Then I heard a scream from along the steps, and looked up to see a Skelt raiding party. They were making their way along the step, attacking the light huts the farmers erect at springtime, and putting the inhabitants to the sword. Mareen, my mate... she saw the Skelt attack the hut of a family she knew – she taught their daughter... I told her to run. There was a sinkhole leading to an underground passage just a few metres away. We could easily have escaped... But Mareen was more concerned about the safety of her pupil. She ran towards the hut just as a Skelt emerged."

He fell silent and stared across the flat landscape, then closed his eyes and murmured, "It is a blessing that she died with one stroke of the sword, so suffered no pain... I collapsed in a faint, and that probably saved my life. The next thing I knew, I was corralled with a dozen other males while the Skelt leader moved from one to the other of us, demanding to know our professions. I was bound and taken away, and then tied to the back of a harl along with five other of my people. Six days later I found myself in Alkellion, being taught the language of our oppressors so that I might act as their interpreter."

Var waved a claw. "Sad times, my little friend. But they are over."

But the Fahran's eyes were still far away. "I endured. My loss burned like a fire in my chest. Many was the time I almost threw myself from the ramparts of the city – but always something stopped me. My death would have gained nothing – in fact, it would have been an acknowledgement that the Skelt had won. And they would only have gone on another raid to find a Fahran to replace me... and that was a fate I wished on no one. So I lived one day at a time and dreamed that at some point in the future I might escape."

Delia reached out and touched his hand.

Mahn looked up and said, "But you know how I feel, Delia, for you too have suffered your own loss, and more recently."

She smiled. "More recently, yes, but we had only been together for a matter of months. I loved him, though. What is so painful... what really hurts... is that Timothy's death has robbed me of a possible future. I'm an incurable romantic, you know. I looked ahead and saw myself with Timothy in a year, two years... five. Hell, I even dreamed of having children with him... and I've never admitted that to anyone before." She shook her head. "Perhaps I was foolish to do that, invest so much after just months with him. But he was a good man, a gentle, loving man... And maybe it wouldn't have lasted, like all the others... but now I'll never, ever know."

She fell silent and stared out from her vantage point high on the spider-crab's back on a world more than ten thousand light years from Earth. She saw Timothy's smile again, across the table in the Paris restaurant. She heard his avowal of love, just minutes before the starship blow-out: *Delia... I love you.*

And just seconds before the explosion, she had opened the channel to Timothy and said, *Love you, too...*

So at least he would have died knowing her feelings for him.

And his death would have been instantaneous, she told herself. Like Mahn's mate, Mareen, he would not have suffered.

It was a small consolation.

From down below, Var lightened the mood, piping up, "I feel very young, you know?"

Delia smiled. "You do? Why?"

"Because I have just ventured from my hive, and I have never mated, and I have not experienced anything like the things you two have experienced."

Mahn laid a long hand on Var's striated shell. "But look at what you *have* experienced, Var. How many Vo just one summer old have trekked this far across the world, met an alien from Earth and helped rescue her, and been part of an army that defeated the Skelt? For a young Var, you have accomplished much."

"And," Delia added, "you will accomplish much more."

They fell silent. Delia finished her neer root and drank more water. Their Vo escort bulked on either side of them, great bristling monsters that scuttled along, legs pumping like great black pistons. From time to time their high-pitched whistles passed back and forth: Imp informed her that they were trading reminiscences of the battle just gone, feats of bravery and derring-do, and jubilation at the sight of the slaughtered Skelt. At one point they fell into concerted song, like a dozen faulty electrical appliances competing to be the loudest.

Delia dozed, only to be awoken an hour later when Var stopped and exclaimed with a high-frequency whistle. She sat up, groggily, and Imp said, *Var called out in wonder, a word that is hard to translate. It sounds like:* siiiik! *An appreciation of beauty, and awe, and at the same time gratitude that she has come upon a sight she has heard so much about.*

Mahn, beside her, was staring south.

Imp said, *The great escarpment that very nearly cuts the world in two.*

They stood, it seemed, on the side of a mountain. At their feet was a sheer drop that fell forever – though her Imp informed her that it measured two kilometres. The world expanded below them, extending to the long southern horizon, a jagged line of snow-capped mountains. The land between was flat, but already turning green with the approach of summer. Delia made out vast forests – swathes of jade green growth as large as cities – and huge contorted trees ten times the size of a Terran oak.

The huge Vo leader approached Var and whistled. Imp translated. "The Great Escarpment! We leave you here, to continue your journey. But you must promise to return, to celebrate – and bring the Fahran and the strange red creature."

Var spoke, thanking the leader and wishing her a safe return journey to her underground lair.

Delia watched the dozen Vo turn and march off across the flat plain, a powerful troop the sight of which, just days ago, would have struck fear into her heart.

The sun was moving little by little towards the far horizon, a huge bloated red sphere without clear definition.

Mahn said, "My village is nestles on a ledge a hundred metres below the lip of the escarpment, and there is the track leading down to it."

He fell silent. Delia could only guess at what Mahn must have been experiencing, as Var set off along the track down the wall of the escarpment.

THE GREAT WALL curved away into the distance. A dozen terraces stepped down the escarpment, reminding Delia of farmers' fields in the Himalayas. In each long strip a skinny, pink animal drew a plough, tended by a Fahran. Towards the centre of the crescent hillside, a hundred or so beehive-shaped mud huts huddled on the tiered ledge. This, evidently, was Jhelam. Below the village, the escarpment fell away steeply to the plain far below.

Mahn said, "Var, would you pause for a short while, please?"

Var duly came to a halt and all three gazed upon the peaceful rural scene.

"My home village," Mahn said at last. "Nothing has changed. It is just as I left it, one summer ago. Continue, Var."

They proceeded down the track, and as they passed along the curving terraces, the farmers ceased their work and stared at the arrival of the spider-crab, bearing one of their own and another strange, bipedal creature.

Silently the farmers left their animals and approached the track, then stood in silence and watched as Var scuttled by. One or two Fahran called out to Mahn, and he replied. They summoned their fellows from the village, and more and more of the small, blue creatures emerged to witness Mahn's return.

What are they saying? Delia asked her Imp.

Greetings, for the most part. The first Fahran asked, 'Who are you?' and Mahn gave his name, and then another said, 'Mahn? Can it be? But you were taken by the Skelt!' Mahn assures them that it was indeed he, returning home after a long winter...

By the time they reached the mass of mud huts that climbed the tiered terraces, perhaps a hundred Fahran stood in the light of the dying sun, staring with their huge dark eyes in silence.

Var came to a wide terrace of packed earth, which clearly acted as a kind of village square; the crowd gathered there, blocking the way, and Var halted.

A Fahran emerged from one of the beehive dwellings, a tiny, white-furred figure clutching a staff and bent almost double. He looked up at Mahn with rheumy eyes and uttered a few words.

Imp translated, *Ahntan an Mahn, mate of Mareen, son of Naran and Lheer, you have returned.*

"I escaped the Skelt," Mahn said, "fled their far northern city. I have returned, but cannot stay. I am on pilgrimage, and head south to the valley of Mahkanda. I can stay but a short time, to tend the tree of my Mareen."

"And the fate of Gahan and Vaal, and Hovar and her sisters who were taken with you?"

"Gahan and Vaal are as well as can be expected. They toil for the Skelt. Hovar and her sisters died soon after arriving at Alkellion, Hovar at the hands of a Skelt, Ramar and Fawl succumbing to disease."

"It grieves me to hear this news. I will communicate the tidings to their families."

Mahn turned to Delia. "The grave garden occupies the uppermost terrace, where the line of pharl trees grow. You and Var may accompany me."

"I will be honoured," Delia said.

Var moved forward little by little, and the crowd parted to allow her through, past the mud dwellings and up another track to the grave garden. Delia looked behind her; the entire village followed in silence.

They came to the first of the trees and Mahn asked Var to halt and let him down.

An air of restfulness filled the grove; the pharl trees were short, thick-boled, with spreading canopies of purple leaves. Mahn climbed down from Var's back, and passed along the avenue of trees. Delia climbed down also, but did not follow. Var folded her legs and settled herself on the ground, and Delia stood by her great head, happy to watch at a respectful distance.

Three Fahran hurried past them and approached Mahn, who turned at their greetings. They came together and Mahn touched his cheek to the forehead of each Fahran in turn, his hands on their shoulders. They spoke for a minute, and Delia wondered if they were old friends. Then the trio turned and hurried back along the grove, passed Var with a twittered aside, and rejoined the crowd.

Imp said, *They uttered a short greeting, wishing a safe journey to Ahntan an Mahn's travelling companions.*

Delia watched as Mahn approached a small, sturdy tree. Each tree stood beside a carved post – presumably a grave marker beneath which the body of a Fahran lay. Mahn was very still for perhaps a minute, staring at the tree. Then he knelt, and prostrated himself before the gnarled root system, his arms outstretched before him.

Delia felt uneasy, and looked away. There was something humbling about Mahn's obeisance, as if the ceremony should be undertaken away from prying eyes. Mahn was grieving, and vulnerable, and it seemed a sacrilege to look upon him.

Not that her uncertainty was shared by his fellow villagers. They massed behind Var and looked on in reverential silence, and Delia found something ineffably moving in their sharing of this moment with their grieving fellow.

She found herself weeping, her tears hot beneath the face-mask, and she could not say if she were weeping for Mahn and his old loss, or for herself. She lifted her mask and rubbed at her cheeks with the cuff of her sleeve.

Mahn stood and stepped towards the tree. For the next minute he picked dead leaves from the branches, then pulled weeds from around the base of the trunk; then he backed away from the tree, and turned and rejoined Delia and Var.

"I feel much better, my friends. I felt Mareen's spirit, wishing us well on our journey south. Shall we continue?"

"You don't wish to stay a while, meet with friends...?" Delia began.

"We must arrive in time to witness Chalto rise," Mahn said, "and before then we must find your people at Alarah. There will be time enough in future to return and meet old friends."

Delia was about to remount Var when a small Fahran, a child half Mahn's height, darted from the watching crowed and passed Mahn a woven satchel. Mahn peered into the bag and spoke to the child.

He climbed up on to Var's back, and Delia followed him.

As Var rose and proceeded along the track that climbed from the village to rejoin the plain above, Mahn said, "Food, donated by the village, so that we will not go hungry on the journey south."

She turned and watched as they left the village, and the silent crowd of Fahran, in their wake. She found herself lifting a hand in a gesture the aliens would have no hope of comprehending.

They reached the plain, and proceeded along the lip of the escarpment, heading east to Million Falls. Ahead the sun sank, a huge bloated hemisphere straddling half the far horizon.

Mahn recounted the many wonders of the city of Million Falls, and dipped into the satchel and pulled out sweet cake and strange fruit. He passed fruit down to Var, who took it delicately in her great right claw and slipped it into her maw, masticating noisily.

Delia sat back and ate a sour-sweet fruit shaped like a pear as night time came.

CHAPTER NINETEEN

MILLION FALLS WAS every bit as beautiful, and spectacular, as Mahn had promised.

The city was strung out along the lip of the escarpment. Low, curving domiciles like sand dunes, and rearing towers curved like scimitar blades, rose against the red sun, which had swollen to five times its former size since Delia's arrival on Valinda. The hemisphere straddled the horizon, huge and crimson, spouting a constant fire-show of looping and spurting ejecta. In its dying light the town was busy with Fahran going about their business, most on foot but some riding ugly, skinny beasts like hairless alpacas.

But most beautiful and breathtaking of all, even more striking than the bloated sun, were the waterfalls that tipped like rainbows from the escarpment and dropped in perfect parabolas to the plains a kilometre below.

Var had come to a halt in a plaza beside a waterfall. The meltwater surged with the momentum of the river behind it, launching itself out over the edge of the cliff, the spume catching the sunlight and creating a million dancing, effervescent rainbows. Delia stared at the waterfall, and the others spaced along the drop, as they cut arcs through the air to the plain below, a vast green expanse shot through with a thousand silver rivers.

"Beautiful..." she breathed. She stared at the town. "And the Skelt never venture this far south?"

"The plain between where you were captured and the Falls is vast, with scant pickings for their raiding parties. Once they came this far south, many summers ago, but not in living memory."

Mahn offered Delia fruit and water, and something that resembled bread. She ate as she took in the view, and luxuriated in the warmth of the sun.

Imp said, *Delia, it is safe now to remove your face-mask. I have deactivated your thermal suit.*

It'll be strange to feel the sun on my face, she said.

Aware that Mahn was watching her, she reached up and peeled off the mask; the sensation was a welcome relief, akin to removing an old plaster. She blinked and rubbed her face, smiling at Mahn.

"The strange thing is," he said, "I always thought you would have hair beneath the covering."

"Well, I do." She lowered her hood and shook out her long black hair. "But not on my face and body."

The Fahran stared at her. "You are a curious colour, like sand in the sun. Your eyes are tiny, and your nose large. And your mouth..."

"Yes?"

"So thin, and yet so narrow."

"You think me ugly?" she laughed.

"I... No, not ugly, exactly. Just strange." He turned a hand. "You're very different from we Fahran, and yet curiously similar."

Var said, "Like the Vo and the Fahran, I think."

"With the proviso, Var, that I do think you're ugly," Mahn said.

"And I must admit that I have always thought the Fahran peculiar,"

Var said, "so thin and spindly, like a child's doll."

"So much for inter-species amity," Delia said, "and I thought we were getting on so well."

She recalled something Var had told her, days ago. "You said you were accompanying us only as far as the Falls, Var. I think I speak for Mahn when I say that I hope you'll reconsider, and come with us to Alarah, and maybe even beyond."

Var whistled in response. "I have given it much thought over the past two days," she said. "So much has happened, so much might yet happen which I would be loath to miss. Your people have come from the skies, Delia, and it would be a blessing to witness the reunion with your kind. And the thought of accompanying you on a pilgrimage to your holy valley, Mahn, is attractive."

Mahn said, "Then come with us. You said that your ambition is to travel, to see the world and gain experience."

Delia knocked on Var's hard shell. "It's settled, Var. You're coming with us."

"I would be honoured," Var said.

Delia regarded Mahn. "Now, I'm intrigued. How do you get from the escarpment to the plains below?" Here the drop was sheer, with no sloping roads leading to the plain below.

Mahn pointed, and Delia saw what looked like a great jellyfish floating up from the plain. Its domed skirt billowed and pulsed, propelling its ascent; below the dome, a gondola carried a dozen Fahran, waving to crowds lined up at a receiving station.

"But what is it?"

"A yarm," Mahn told her. "It's a very simple animal. They rise and fall up the wall of the escarpment at this time of year, and hibernate through the long cold winter. Many summers ago my people had the excellent idea of harnessing the creatures and attaching carriages to their skirts. We will descend to the plain by way of a yarm," he finished.

Var rose and scuttled along a boulevard that ran parallel with the escarpment. Crowds of Fahran, until then intent on the view, turned to watch their passage.

"They have never before seen anything like you, Delia," Mahn said, waving to the crowds like royalty.

The yarm Delia had seen was not the only one ferrying citizens up and down the Falls. She counted the pink, membranous skirts of a dozen more of the creatures, fading into the distance. The first station they approached had a long queue of waiting travellers; Mahn suggested they continue on to the next.

"Have you ever ridden a yarm?" Delia asked.

"Never," Mahn said. "This will be the first time."

The yarm seemed insubstantial, and the flat-bottomed gondolas attached by ropes to the cartilage below their skirts appeared almost as flimsy.

They lined up at the next station, climbed down from Var's back, and presently stepped aboard the gondola. Delia felt it rock beneath her feet and hurried across to the rail; it was ridiculously low – made for the convenience of Fahran citizens – and she was compelled to sit down to forestall a queasy tide of vertigo.

Var settled in the centre of the gondola, and Mahn joined Delia. He stood beside the rail and pointed across to another Fahran. "The ferry-master," he said. "Watch."

The tiny Fahran approached a long rope depending from the skirt of the yarm high overhead and swarmed up it, coming to a halt five metres above the gondola. He twisted his right leg around the rope, cupped his hands around his long lips, and began whistling what sounded like a mournful, heartfelt lament.

"What is he doing?" she asked Mahn.

"The yarm are amenable to music," he explained. "They are attracted to the love songs of the Fahran. This was discovered many summers ago, when Fahran choristers, practising one dawn, attracted an audience of a dozen floating yarm. The ferry-masters have perfected the art of calling, and controlling, the creatures."

High above, the circumference of the yarm's skirt pulsed and eddied, and the gondola floated dreamily down the sheer face of the escarpment. Delia peered over the rail and watched the land below resolve itself.

Verdant farmland stretched for as far as the eye could see, shot through with silver rivers. Farmers worked the plantations with their fleeceless-alpaca beasts, piling bales of produce onto wheeled carts.

Mahn explained that it was the first harvest of summer, and that from now until high summer the farmers would make three more harvests, all across Fahran territory, and the crops would last well into the next winter.

"And when fresh produce runs out?" she asked.

"Then we will eat fungus grown underground, and animals reared for winter slaughter. Some children, born in mid-winter, won't enjoy the delicacy of fresh fruit and vegetables until they're all but grown. They're often the weakest, and hive mothers attempt to conceive so that their hatchlings will be born towards the end of winter."

"And you?"

"I was spring born," Mahn said, "and as such was destined to be a teacher."

She stared at him. "The time of year you were born denotes your profession?"

He blinked at her. "Why, of course. Is it not the same on Earth?"

She explained that the time of one's birth had nothing to do with the choice of one's vocation, a concept both Mahn and Var found bizarre.

"On Valinda," Var said, "we do not have a *choice* when it comes to our profession. It must be very confusing not to know one's destiny as you grow to adulthood."

Delia laughed and marvelled at the differences between their worlds.

In due course the yarm floated to the ground; the ferry-master wound a hawser around a tree and the passengers filed off one by one.

Delia and Mahn climbed on to Var's back and she set off along the riverbank towards a moored ferry, again drawing stares and comments from the strolling crowds.

Delia looked along the length of the escarpment. Million Falls could be seen stretching east and west, the silver arcs of individual waterfalls connecting the highland to the plain like so many curving cantilevers of steel. Below, the spume of spray was spangled by a myriad dancing rainbows; and long-billed birds, with wingspans far greater than any Terran albatross, cut arabesques through the mist.

They boarded a riverboat and accommodated themselves on bales of cloth in the prow of the vessel. The captain cast off and the broad, shallow barge drifted along the sedately flowing river.

As the trip progressed, and the boat moved through farmland to a flat, grassy plain interspersed with tall, corkscrew trees, Delia moved to the rail and stared out across the twilight land.

Soon they would dock in Alarah, and in time Delia would learn if other survivors from the *Amsterdam* had made landfall on Valinda.

Imp?

Yes?

What if the con-trail we saw was not from a human life-raft? What if it was a Skelt vessel, returning to check on their old colony?

The coincidence of a Skelt vessel appearing so soon after your arrival here is vanishingly small.

She nodded. *I know, but...*

She felt silent, then asked, *Still no contact with...?*

Negative. I will keep trying.

I wonder why the silence, if it is a life-raft from the Amsterdam?

If it is a human vessel, then the survivors have either switched off their implants, or – more likely – evacuated the Amsterdam *without their chargers.*

Delia contemplated the years ahead. It was impossible to envisage how she might cope, alone, without human company – despite the companionship of Mahn and Var – but the thought of fellow human beings to share her grief, her nostalgia, when considering all she had lost... Well, it made the idea of life on Valinda almost bearable.

If the vessel was from the *Amsterdam*, then she would have people with whom to share memories, compare experiences, people whose frames of reference and cultural values were the same as hers; she would be able to tell them things that only another human being could comprehend, share intimacies and confidences...

She thought of Timothy, and then her parents who she would never see again, and fought back her tears.

Delia ... rina about the years that it would be impossible to operate how she in the conversation, without light in conditions — before the consummation of Alexandra Vanda and the thought of labour in each house as about her mind, her force pair when comparing it. If she had held... With a standard edition similar in Valenti shadow in guide.

The vessel was born the Attra when seen she would have elastic with a sun to show at time example's expressed people, whose frames of esteem and culture of value, once the author was first, she would see the ... of them things that only care for human being could complete with, if it compared a...

the thought of Timothy and that is a parcel, who she shall never see again and Papa Will little remind...

CHAPTER TWENTY

IT WAS LATE into the night when the riverboat approached the city of
Alarah. Delia joined Mahn and Var at the rail.

The architecture was familiar from Million Falls, with flowing,
sweeping dwellings that seemed almost to have been formed by the
wind, but Alarah was far more sprawling than the Falls and built
upon one bank of the river only. A glowing mass of stars rose behind
the city, so that the buildings appeared silhouetted on the horizon like
a line of alien script.

"Are all cities on Valinda so beautiful?" she asked Mahn as the boat
approached a stone jetty.

"We Fahran pride ourselves on our architecture. The cities of the
north, like Alkellion, are ancient and more severe in style; those of the
equator were built to celebrate summer."

"And the Vo?" she asked Var. "Do your people build cities?"

"Great underground lairs ten times the size of Alarah," she said,
"though I admit they are not as beautiful."

The boat nudged the jetty and several gangways were lowered.

Delia felt a pressure in her chest at the thought of what lay ahead.

Crowds of Fahran had gathered at the harbour, hawking food and drink and trinkets, or come to meet friends and family. Fat, glowing insects floating on long cords lit the streets, and above the hubbub of conversation Delia made out soft melodies played by musicians on stringed instruments like wheeled harps. Here and there, conspicuous above the crowd, stood half a dozen bulky Vo.

Mahn led the way from the boat, but as soon as her feet were on dry land, Delia was the centre of attention. A hushed crowd had gathered, staring at her and her companions; one or two children reached out, tentatively touching her crimson suit. A murmur passed through the ranks, a susurration of comment and curiosity.

"I think it might be best if you climb upon my back and I'll ease my way through the crowd," Var suggested.

"One moment," Mahn said. He stepped forward, approaching a bent, white-furred Fahran. They spoke, each extending a hand to the other's shoulder as they did so, and at last Mahn returned and said to Delia, "Good news!"

Her heart skipped.

Mahn reported, "The people are excited by an amazing event – the arrival of a starship that fell from the sky a day ago."

She picked up on the verb. "Fell? You don't mean...?"

"It landed safely, and the entire city gathered at a distance, and watched as a hatch opened and two strange beings appeared."

"Strange beings? Do you mean, like me?"

Mahn turned to the oldster and questioned him. The old Fahran spoke at length, and Mahn reported: "He did not witness the beings himself, just heard reports. He said the beings were tall, much taller than we Fahran."

"But not Skelt?"

"No – certainly not Skelt."

Delia's heart pounded. She climbed unsteadily on to Var's back, joined by Mahn, and the Vo edged forward through the crowd.

"The ship came down on the bank of the river, a kilometre west of the city," Mahn said. "We will head there now. This way, Var."

They left the harbour and proceeded along a wide, lighted street thronged with strolling Fahran.

Imp?

Delia?

The chances are that the ship is from the Amsterdam, *isn't it?*

That looks increasingly likely, yes.

She told herself that she wouldn't really believe it until she saw the other humans, and embraced them in order to establish their reality.

"Look," Mahn said a while later, pointing ahead.

In the distance, against the night sky, reared the silhouette of a large spacecraft on ramrod stanchions. Delia's heart leapt again. She recognised the vessel. It was not a simple life-raft, but a Terran survey shuttle – a ship-to-ground craft.

She let out a small gasp and almost wept with relief.

The ship had come down on a rise of land in a loop of the river. At the foot of the hill a crowd had gathered, staring up at the ship as if in expectation.

Delia gazed at the lighted lozenge of the forward viewing screen, but saw no evidence of anyone inside. The hatch was open and the ramp extended, and a warm orange glow spilled out into the night.

They approached the crowd and Var eased her way through; the Fahran parted, turning to see who demanded access, and twittered with surprise when they saw Delia.

Var emerged from the crowd and stopped at the foot of the hill. "Go on," Delia said, her voice catching in her throat.

She rode up the hillside, her heart pounding.

A small figure appeared at the top of the ramp, dark against the interior glow. Delia felt something tighten within her.

The figure took one step forward, and another – then stopped, turned and called something to whoever was inside.

Var came to a halt at the foot of the ramp and lowered herself to the ground.

Now that the time had come to climb down and approach her fellow humans, Delia was gripped by a strange paralysis. The sight of the small woman at the top of the ramp – joined then by a tall, thin man – reminded her of all the people she had lost, all the people she would never see again: Timothy and Zeena, and her family and friends, and all the lost crew of the *Amsterdam*.

The man and woman staring down at her were still wearing their face-masks, so she was unable to see their expressions as, at last, she climbed down from Var's back and jumped from the last foreleg.

She raised a hand in greeting, then climbed the ramp to meet them.

The woman came forward slowly. She wore the blue flight suit of a pilot, and was shorter than Delia by a head. Her face-mask concealed her identity.

Delia reached out, touched the woman's hand, and then, in a rush, they embraced, and her tears came in a great torrent of unrestrained emotion.

"I thought I was alone!" she gasped. "I thought... I never thought I'd see..."

"How the hell, girl...?" The woman's voice was rich; South African-English, Delia guessed.

"A life-raft. I managed to get aboard a life-raft..."

"I thought I was seeing things," the woman said. "I looked out and I saw this giant spider thing, and riding on top of it... I said to Javinder, 'We have company'..."

Javinder, in the orange suit of an engineer, stepped forward and embraced Delia.

Delia cuffed the tears from her eyes and laughed, "And you can remove the face-masks, both of you. The air's perfectly safe."

"You sure?" the woman asked. "Our implants ran out of charge before we landed."

"My Imp gave the all clear," Delia said, "and I haven't come down with any nasty alien bugs yet."

The woman pulled off her mask to reveal a round, smiling face. "Oma Massinga, pilot first grade, at your service."

"Dr Delia Kemp, damned glad to see you."

Javinder peeled off his mask, uncovering a long Indian face. "Javinder Lal, shuttle engineer."

"My Imp tried to establish contact when I saw the ship come down..." Delia said.

"We were in the shuttle," Oma said, "running a few repairs on the drive, when the *Amsterdam* blew. We didn't have time to go and fetch our chargers. We've been six days, limping through space to get here, and the mind-silence came down after four." She shook her head. "It's driving me mad, Delia. I don't know how I'll cope."

Smiling, Delia reached out and touched the woman's hand. "It's okay. There was a charger among the supplies in the life-raft." She regarded the shuttle. "It was damaged in the blow-out?"

"We nearly didn't make it," Javinder said. "The drive's compromised. But if we could scavenge parts from your life-raft..."

Delia was about to ask him why, because even if they could escape Valinda they would still be stranded many light years from Earth. But Oma made a moue with her lips and shook her head minimally – let the man have his dreams.

Delia smiled in brief acknowledgment.

"I don't suppose there were other survivors?" she asked.

Javinder shook his head. "It was the first thing I did when we jettisoned – scanned for other ships. We were the only one."

Oma looked down the ramp to where Mahn and Var waited, staring up at them. "And who the hell are those two?"

Delia turned to the aliens, seeing them through new eyes now, seeing first their strangeness but then, she thought, apprehending their... *humanity*, for want of a better word.

"They just happen to be the first sentient extraterrestrials discovered by humankind. They are also my friends, who have saved my life. Without them... well, I wouldn't be here to tell the tale."

She called down for Mahn and Var to climb the ramp, and then one by one the humans and aliens entered the ship.

DELIA WAS A little drunk.

Javinder had produced a bottle of genuine Indian whisky and toasted their meeting. Delia gave Javinder and Oma her charger, then instructed Imp to squirt its translation cache to their implants. Minutes later all five beings, alien and human, were conversing like old friends.

Delia recounted her adventures across the face of Valinda, stories added to and embellished by Mahn and Var. Oma and Javinder listened with a mixture of disbelief and astonishment, and even Delia, considering the events of the past few days, found many of her exploits hard to credit.

At one point Javinder explained the extent of the shuttle's engine problems. He would be able to work on the drives for a while before having to cannibalise parts from her life-raft. Seeing the warning flash in Oma's eyes, Delia kept quiet. The Indian was in deep denial.

He knocked back his fifth shot of whisky. "And I'm pleased the only other survivor is a doctor. I mean..." He waved drunkenly across the deck to a sloping console. "The ship's surgical smartware is all very well, but..."

Oma laughed. "As you'll find out, Delia, Jav is a hypochondriac."

The Indian shrugged. "It's just that... I'd rather place my trust in a human doctor than a machine. With you around the place from now on –"

Delia interrupted. "Tomorrow I'm setting off with Mahn and Var. We're heading south. Mahn is on a pilgrimage, to witness the Rising of his god, Chalto."

"But..." Javinder said, glaring at her, "we need you here."

"You'll get by for a week or two. When Mahn rescued me from the Skelt, I gave him my promise that I would accompany him south, as a small token of my thanks."

Javinder leaned forward, glancing at Oma as if for back-up. "But your duty, Doctor, is to your own kind."

She lowered her glass and stared at the Indian. "My personal duty is to my friend, Ahntan an Mahn. I gave him my promise."

Javinder pointed to the sigil on his upper arm. "Might I remind you, Doctor, that I outrank you...?"

Delia stared at him, then burst out laughing. She waved. "I'm sorry – it's just... We're more than ten thousand light years from Earth, with no hope of ever getting back, and you try to pull rank? Get real! Whatever authority you had, major, ended when the front end of the *Amsterdam* shunted itself through the wormhole."

Javinder winced, suddenly vulnerable, and Delia almost regretted her outburst.

"But we need you," he said pathetically. "We need to stick together..."

Delia swore, pushed herself to her feet, and hurried from the ship.

She paced down the ramp and crossed to the riverbank. Many of the Fahran sightseers had left the area, and only a small knot of curious locals remained. They kept their distance, for which Delia was grateful.

She stared across the rippling river to the massed bank of stars rising high above her, and worked to control her breathing. Somewhere out there, orbiting an anonymous star in the glowing firmament, was Earth. She tried to imagine all the people she had known, going about their daily business; she tried to imagine her mother and father, attempting to cope with life in the aftermath of losing their only daughter.

She had to face the fact that, however unpalatable it might be, she would never return to Earth; Valinda was her home now, for better or for worse. Tomorrow she would set out on the pilgrimage with Mahn and Var. She would throw herself into the trek south – despite Javinder's objections – and relish the many wonders she would no doubt encounter on the way.

She had a thought.

Imp.

Delia?

The Skelt weapon that brought us down...

Go on.

You said, days ago, that it was somewhere south of the equator, right?

That is correct.

Do you know where?

Approximately, Imp said.

Project a schematic of Valinda.

A split second later a three-dimensional image of the planet hung in the air before her.

Where are we? she asked.

A flashing red dot appeared just south of the equator.

And do you know where the valley of Mahkanda is situated?

Going by the distances mentioned by Mahn, I estimate that it is in this approximate region...

Another, larger dot, flashing blue this time, appeared south of the red dot that represented Alarah.

And the position of the Skelt weapon? she asked.

Here, Imp said.

A pulsing green light appeared midway between Alarah and the valley of Mahkanda, though approximately one hundred kilometres to the east of both.

So... she said tentatively, *with a slight detour, we might be able to locate the weapon?*

Affirmative.

She nodded to herself, satisfied.

Imp, open a direct com-channel to Oma.

Accomplished, Imp said.

Delia: *Oma, I need to see you...*

Oma: *Hokay... I'm on my way.*

Delia kept the projection of Valinda in situ, hanging before her like an oversized yuletide bauble.

Oma appeared at the top of the ramp, looked around until she saw Delia and the illuminated projection, then hurried across to her. She sat down cross-legged, sighing. "Sorry about Jav back there. Male hormones. Just ignore him."

"I fully intend to." Delia indicated the projection.

"Pretty," Oma said, squinting at the globe.

She told the South African about the strike that had brought down her life-raft. "And the weapon could only have belonged to the Skelt."

"But earlier" – Oma waved towards the shuttle – "you said the Skelt were technologically backward."

Delia nodded. "They are."

"So..." Oma indicated the projection. "I'm intrigued how a race as technologically undeveloped as the Skelt have such an advanced weapon?"

"It occurred to me," Delia said, "that it might be a leftover from when the Skelt invaded Valinda. They were once a star-faring race."

"And how long ago was the Skelt invasion?"

"One thousand Valindan summers ago," Delia said. "Around ten thousand Terran years."

Oma shook her head. "Could a weapons system last that long without degrading? Sounds doubtful to me."

Delia shrugged. "It makes me all the more curious to get down there and see what gives." She hesitated, then said, "Is the shuttle equipped with weapons?"

"A cache of laser rifles, nothing else."

"That'll do."

Oma stared at her. "For what?"

"I want to find the Skelt weapons system," Delia said, "and make sure the damned thing is put out of commission. I've rather taken against the Fahrans' oppressors, and I want to do something to nullify their threat."

"And if the Skelt object to this, and have militia guarding the weapon?"

Delia thought about it. "The Skelt can't tolerate the heat," she said. "They migrate underground during summer. My guess is that a weapon capable of winging a vehicle in low orbit is pretty sizeable, too big to take with them underground."

"And you're doing all this alone?"

"With Mahn and Var, if they want to come along." She regarded Oma. "And you, if you're up to it?"

The South Africa screwed her lips to one side. "I don't know... Let's talk this over in the morning, when I've sobered up, okay?" She sighed and pushed herself to her feet. "I'm going back to the party. You coming?"

"I'll be along in a second."

She watched Oma cross to the ship and climb the ramp.

She wondered if her scheme to put the Skelt weapon out of commission was anything more than a hare-brained reaction to Javinder's rank-pulling. In the morning, when she too had sobered up, would she still be as enthusiastic?

Yes, she decided at last; it needed to be done. The Skelt were a threat to peace on Valinda, and there could be no peace if they possessed a weapon with the firepower capable of bringing down a life-raft.

She stared at the massed incandescence of stars in the heavens; the sight was breathtaking, a pulsing effulgence like nothing she had ever seen before. And the planet itself was beautiful, too, and it seemed all the more tragic that such a world should be blighted by a race as vile as the Skelt.

She had to face the fact: she would be spending the rest of her life on Valinda. A member of the Fahran race had saved her from certain death at the hands of the Skelt, and his people had proved peaceable and accepting of her. There were worse places she could be stranded, she decided, and helping the Fahran would give her life some purpose. She would work to bring some form of détente to the planet – by peaceful, conciliatory means if possible; but if that proved impossible, then by force.

A tiny figure appeared at the top of the ramp. Mahn called down to her, "Delia, what are you doing out there, all alone? Come and join us."

She stared up at the alien, his figure blurring in her vision.

Wiping her eyes, Delia stood and made her way back to the shuttle.

CHAPTER TWENTY-ONE

DELIA LEFT THE shuttle and sat on the end of the ramp, admiring the hilltop view.

She was on an alien world thousands of light years from Earth – a world inhabited by the first sentient extraterrestrials discovered by humankind – and still she found it hard to believe.

The sun was rising above the flat horizon, a great molten ball with geysers of flame writhing across its bloody surface. The planet was heading into a period of intense summer, which would last just one Terran year before the onset of a long, cold, nine year winter.

Imp, she said.

Her Implant responded. *Morning, Delia.*

How long have I been on Valinda?

Eight days, five hours and three minutes, Terran reckoning.

Just over a week! It seemed much longer than that since she had crash-landed on the then ice-bound world and been captured by the locust-like Skelt.

She turned to see Mahn coming down the ramp.

"Are you feeling better for a night's sleep?" he asked.

"That, and refreshed after the first shower I've had in a long time."

Mahn sat cross-legged before her. "I have been speaking to Oma," he said, "about my pilgrimage to witness the Rising of Chalto. She said she is coming with us."

"She did?" Delia smiled. "That's great."

Mahn said, "I was surprised, Delia, when I finally met your fellow humans."

"In what way?"

"You are all different colours. Oma is dark, Javinder a little lighter, and you lightest of all."

"And are all Fahran the same shade of blue as yourself?"

"Yes, other than our elders who are white with age."

"My friends and I are different colours," she told him, "because our species adapted to different geographical areas. Oma's ancestors are dark-skinned Africans, while my pale-skinned ancestors were from the cooler north of our world."

She looked up. Oma Massinga emerged from the shuttle and sat on the grass. She passed Delia a bulb of juice. "Thought you might be thirsty."

Delia read the label. "Mango," she said. "Oma, I could weep." She felt herself welling up. "I'm sorry. It's silly, the way some things affect..."

Oma gave her an odd look. "You okay, girl?"

"I'm fine." Delia wiped her eyes on the cuff of her one-piece. "Other than Javinder's whisky last night, all I've had for the past eight days is water. I remember drinking mango juice for the first time on holiday at my aunt and uncle's in Vancouver." She flipped the lid and took a long drink. "Hell, that's good. It brings back memories."

Mahn said, "I wonder, Delia, if I might take a sip?"

She asked Imp about the advisability of giving the alien a drink; so far she had refrained from sharing her Terran provisions with Mahn, for fear of poisoning him. *A small sip should do him no harm,* Imp replied.

She passed Mahn the bulb and he raised it to his long, thin lips experimentally. He took a sip. His eyes widened and he jerked forward, spitting the fluid across the grass. "Aghh! But it is *terrible!* So sweet and unpleasant."

Oma tapped the Fahran's thin, furry arm. "If you think mango juice is sweet..." she said, "we have some lemonade aboard the shuttle."

Delia said to Oma, "Mahn said you're coming with us. You thought about what I said about the Skelt laser last night, and you agree we need to destroy it?"

"That's what I came to see you about," the South African said.

Oma sub-vocced a command to her Imp, and it projected an image into the air. A schematic of Valinda hung before them, showing the city of Alkellion where Delia had been imprisoned, and the city of Million Falls on the equator. Further south was the valley of Mahkanda.

"Your Imp patched this up and squirted it across," Oma said. "I want to get a sense of where we're going."

Delia stared at the slowly turning projection in the air before them.

"This is the orbital route the shuttle took," Oma said. She pointed a bitten fingernail at a dotted line arcing over the globe from the south pole to the equator. "A thousand kilometres south of here, we avoided hostile ground-to-air fire. You said you were brought down by the same – and yet the Skelt, from what you've seen of their technology, aren't capable of manufacturing such a weapon."

Delia nodded. "That's right."

Mahn leaned forward and peered at the projection. "Where exactly did the hostile fire come from?"

Oma commanded her Imp to increase the magnification. She indicated a position south of the equator. "There."

Mahn tipped his head. "That is the ancient city of Khalamb," he said. "Many summers ago it was an important stopping off place for pilgrims *en route* from the equator to the valley of Mahkanda. But then the Skelt overran the city, killing many citizens, Fahran and Vo alike, and since then we have avoided the place as we trek south."

Delia said, "Mahn, I would like us to make a detour to the city."

"It is certainly possible, yes."

"And the Skelt?" Oma asked.

"By the time we get to Khalamb," Delia said, "the increasing heat will have driven them underground." She turned to Mahn. "How do we reach the city?"

"We will take a riverboat and alight at a town called Lerah," he said. "From there it is a short distance, perhaps thirty kilometres, to Khalamb. We will proceed on foot, or rather on the back of Var."

"I hope she's amenable to that," Delia said.

"She will be delighted to be of service."

Oma was staring at the projection. "What kind of terrain are we talking about here?"

"The Blooming will be well underway by then," Mahn told her. "So the land will be riotous with growth. However, Var will have no difficulty traversing such terrain."

"And the heat?"

"It will be very hot," Mahn said. "We Fahran, and the Vo, will easily withstand the heat. But you and Delia..."

"We have thermal suits," Delia said. "They can be programmed to cool us down as well as to provide warmth." She reached out and took the South African's hand. "I'm glad you're coming along."

Oma frowned. "But what if the Skelt's weapon is movable, and they've taken it with them underground?"

Delia shrugged. "As they say back on Earth, we'll cross that bridge..." She took a long drink of mango juice.

Mahn looked from Oma to Delia. "And how will you destroy the Skelt's weapon?"

"We have weapons of our own aboard the shuttle," Delia said, "hand-held lasers which should prove effective."

Javinder stepped from the shuttle, chewing an energy bar, and sat beside Oma. Behind him, Var squeezed herself from the exit. The great spider-crab scuttled down the ramp and settled herself on the ground beside the engineer, her jet black shell coruscating in the morning sun.

A small crowd of blue-furred Fahran had resumed their silent vigil at the foot of the hill; Delia was becoming quite accustomed to the attention by now. It would wear off, she thought, in the years to come.

"Work on the auxiliary drive is going well," Javinder reported. "I might have it running again in a few days. Var here has been assisting me."

"Well," the spider-crab said, "I have been passing Javinder various tools."

There was a sudden, uneasy tension in the air. Javinder had broached something unspoken between the two women – the state of his mind – and he knew it.

"There's always hope," he said defiantly, "until you give in. Those who don't even try, fail. Look –" He turned his dark gaze from Oma to Delia, "I know what you're thinking. 'Let Jav, well into the infra red of the autistic spectrum, tinker about with the drive if it will occupy him.'"

Delia said, "That's a pretty astute thing for an autistic to think, Jav. We never thought that."

"Well, you played along with each other and didn't mention what you were thinking – that even if I did get the shuttle up and running, so what? Without a wormhole lattice, we're stranded here."

Oma shifted uncomfortably. "You said it yourself. There's always hope."

He nodded, looking from Delia to Oma. "We don't know exactly where we are, do we?"

"Right..." Delia said tentatively.

"Well, what if I get this thing up and flying, try to work out where the hell we are?"

Oma opened her mouth, but Delia shook her head, minimally, to deter her.

Javinder looked at them, then smiled. "I see you're not convinced." He shook his head. "I'll see you later. I have work to do."

He pushed himself to his feet and paced up the ramp.

Oma moved a little way from the shuttle. She gestured to Delia to join her, then murmured, "I'm worried about him."

"He's delusional," Delia said. "He must know we're stranded here." She stopped. "How long have you known him?"

The South African shrugged. "A couple of years."

"And he's been okay in that time? I mean, mentally stable?"

Oma nodded. "As far as I know. A little literal minded, sometimes withdrawn. A typical engineer. The thing is, he left someone back on Earth."

"Serious?"

"Very. She was a tech on the *Valladolid* and Jav was head over heels. He's taking it hard."

"Poor man."

Oma hesitated, then said, "I feel guilty, Delia."

"Guilty?"

"Don't get me wrong, I like the guy. But at the same time I want to get away from him. You don't know what it was like, cooped up in the shuttle with him for days."

"Don't feel guilty," Delia said. "He'll be fine on his own, working on the shuttle. Have your Imp set up a private link and call him every couple of hours. Progress reports, updates to tell him how we're doing."

"That makes sense. I'll do that."

Delia sighed. "After a week of non-stop, life-threatening action, it's strange to be among human beings and their psychological problems again. All I thought about was how I was going to survive for the next few hours."

Oma glanced at her. "And now? I mean, how are you?"

Delia smiled. "Don't worry about me, Oma. I'm fine."

Var rose to her feet and approached them with Mahn; she told them that a riverboat was due to leave in just under an hour.

They moved into the shuttle, said goodbye to Javinder, then loaded up with provisions. Javinder was back on his slide-bed, working away, by the time they exited the craft.

Delia and Oma climbed onto Var's back beside Mahn, and they made their way down the hillside and along the road beside the river, followed by a small crowd of locals like a posse of blue chimpanzees.

Beside Delia, Oma was counting on her fingers. "Eight," she announced at last.

Delia glanced at her. "Eight what?"

"Modes of transport. Horse. Elephant. Donkey. Camel. Zebra. Giraffe. Even an antelope, when I was a kid. I've ridden them all, back home in Africa. And now a Vo!"

CHAPTER TWENTY-TWO

DELIA LEANED AGAINST the rail and enjoyed the view.

The sun sank behind ribbons of bloody cloud far to the east, and the riverboat floated down a river so wide that, at some points, she was unable to make out the banks. She had spent the morning playing chess with Oma – her Imp projecting a board and pieces in the air before them – and that afternoon she'd rested on a padded divan in one of the berths that lined the decks. Privacy was not a concept very highly regarded by the Fahran, whose tribes encouraged communal living. Delia didn't mind sleeping in full view of her fellow passengers, but she was acutely embarrassed when having to perform her toilet before a host of staring Fahran.

As the massed stars rose above the horizon, an incandescent glow unlike anything Delia had seen from any other world, Oma sought her company and murmured, "It's beautiful."

"It reminds me of the lights of a city seen from orbit," Delia said. "I recall the first time I saw Rio de Janeiro from the *Amsterdam*, coming in slow over the terminator." She shook her head. "It took my breath away. I... I recall how good it felt to be back on Earth again."

"Delia, how are you? How are you taking...?"

"How am I taking the fact that I'll never see Earth and loved ones again?" She shook her head. "It's going to take a long time to come to terms with the idea." She smiled at the South African. "It's a bit like grief. A bitter pain, at first so severe you wonder how you'll cope. But you do. It gets a little less painful as time goes by, but never in a way that makes sense. I mean, you think the worst is over, and then you'll be pole-axed a week later by the realisation..."

"You sound as if you've lost someone close."

"My brother. I was twenty, Daniel just sixteen. A stupid, stupid traffic accident. My parents were devastated."

Oma reached out and took her hand.

"The strange thing is," Delia went on, "I had someone on the *Amsterdam*. Timothy Greene. We'd only been... I'd only known him a few months. I suppose I should be grieving – but the odd thing is I can only really think of the pain my parents must be going through." She smiled, brightly. "But anyway, what about you?"

Oma shrugged. "I have no family, and few friends on Earth. My parents are dead and I'm an only child. I split up with someone a couple of years ago and there's been no one since." She shrugged. "So I can't say I'm grieving for lost loved ones. Of course I'm missing a few people, most of them on colony worlds. But what's more painful is just the small, inconsequential things. The thought of never tasting real coffee again, or a good Thai meal – or any Thai meal! – and never seeing the Kaizer Chiefs playing in the cup final." She glanced at Delia from under her eye-lashes. "Does that make me a shallow, self-centred egotist?"

Delia laughed and squeezed the young woman's hand. "Of course not. I know exactly what you mean. Oh, the things I miss... Maple syrup on waffles, *On the River* – a holo-drama serial set in Toronto – Iced Leaf tea, Belgian chocolate." She frowned. "And it's not really these things we miss, is it? They're just symbols, denoting our incredible isolation out here... denoting lost opportunity."

Oma laughed. "Hey, before we both get tearful, I've just remembered I have something for you."

"Don't tell me, a bar of Maeterlinck's milk chocolate?"

"Afraid not." Oma opened her backpack and withdrew two laser pistols. She passed one to Delia. "Pulsers. Activate there, push that button there and you get a one second laser burst. As easy to fire as water pistols."

"I hope we don't need to use them to defend ourselves."

"Me too. But we'll be entering the city of Khalamb. I know you said the Skelt might have skedaddled, but if there's one or two of the critters hanging around..."

Delia slipped the pistol under her waist-band. "And they're powerful enough to destroy the Skelt weapon?"

"A ten second blast on maximum power would turn an armoured tank to slag," Oma said.

They played another game of chess – Delia lost for the third time – and then she slept *al fresco* beneath the massed stars.

She was woken early next morning by dazzling sunlight and Mahn offering her a tray laden with an array of strange foodstuffs.

They ate together on the prow of the boat, Delia and Oma, Mahn and Var sitting on the deck and chatting. Delia had awoken frequently during the long night as the boat docked at small towns along the river, disgorging passengers and picking up new, noisy travellers. They were Fahran for the most part, with one or two Vo in amongst.

The land on either side was flat, though the coming of summer was bringing the plains to life. Overnight, what looked like a phantasmagorical jungle had appeared. Tall, graceful trees, more like curving reeds than trees proper, arced into the air and overhung the river. Purple vines, sprouting great crimson blooms, wound up the tree trunks and gave off vulgar blares of sickly sweet scent.

As she ate, she watched the land change before her eyes like time-lapse photography. A dense carpet of small flowers sprouted between the trees, covering the land in a sudden sweep of crimson which faded to cerise as she watched. Small, darting birds, or bat-like creatures, swooped amid the blooms, and she made out the occasional, distant yarm floating high above like giant jellyfish.

They stopped at another small port, this one servicing a village of timber villas almost consumed by the rampant vegetation. A dozen Fahran bearing crates of fruit and vegetables climbed aboard, and as many travellers alighted. They set off again, drifting in silence beneath the boat's three full-bellied sails.

Oma gestured to the passengers on the deck behind them. "How many of them do you think are pilgrims, Mahn?"

He studied his fellows. "My guess is not many. Most of them are traders and farmers selling produce further downriver. Not many pilgrims come from the north – most are in the south, where the religion of Chalto is more established."

"Are you from the south?" Oma asked.

"I was born in the north, but my tribe originated in the south. In fact, it was members of my hive who first encountered Chalto on his arrival many years ago."

"Tell me about your religion," Oma said. "What do you believe in? Who was – is – Chalto?"

"Chalto is a great being who arrived in a boat from the heavens thirty summers ago. He came with his disciples, who died defending a Fahran city from the Skelt. Chalto then decreed that he would do all within his powers to help the Fahran, both in our everyday lives, and in our struggle against the Skelt."

Oma said, "And did he?"

"He gave us tools, or showed us how to make them, and instructed us on the manufacture of weapons with which to fight the Skelt."

"What kind of weapons?" Delia asked. She had seen no weapons of any kind carried by the Fahran.

"Devices which fire bolts and stones, crossbows and catapults."

"Pretty rudimentary stuff," Oma murmured. "What happened to Chalto?"

"He slept – and every summer rises to address his followers."

"Slept? For thirty summers – three hundred Terran years?"

"He is truly a god," Mahn said.

Oma looked dubious. "And what does he say when he addresses his followers?"

Mahn stared into the sky, where a dreamy yarm floated by. "I have never witnessed a Rising. Those that have report that Chalto exhorts the Fahran to be patient, to await for the time when he will assist in the overthrowing of the Skelt."

Delia asked, "And what kind of being is Chalto? What does he look like?"

Mahn regarded her with his huge brown eyes. "Many have looked upon Chalto, and know what he is; but they are not allowed to create images of him."

"But why not?"

"It is simply forbidden by our elders," Mahn said.

"And has Chalto said how he might help you overthrow the Skelt, other than instructing you in the manufacture of weapons?"

"That is Chalto's secret," Mahn said.

The boat was passing down an avenue of overhanging trees. The richly scented blooms bobbed an arm's-reach overhead, attended by swarms of humming insects. Var lifted a great pincer, snipped off the pistil of a bloom, and proceeded to eat it.

"A delicacy of my kind," she reported, "available only during the Blooming."

"Presumably the Skelt know of your God," Oma said. "But have they done anything to combat the threat he poses?"

"Chalto's boat, in which he came to Valinda, is fortified and impregnable. Though the Skelt have mounted raiding parties and attempted to breach its walls, they have failed. And then winter comes and covers the boat with layers of ice, and Chalto sleeps again."

"And the boat? What does it look like?"

"It is hard to describe. We Fahran have an analogy – we say it resembles a kuhrl nut."

"What do they look like?" Delia asked.

"Long and brown, tapered to a point at one end and flat at the other. Its surface is seamless, though it bears script along its length."

"Script? What does it say?"

"That is a mystery," Mahn said. "No one but Chalto knows that."

Imp spoke to Delia: *I'm opening a private channel between Oma and yourself, at Oma's instigation.*

Oma: *Delia, that sounds like an alien starship to me, don't you think?*

Delia: *I agree. I think we have a form of cargo cult here. An advanced being comes from the stars, bearing gifts, and promises to overthrow the oppressive Skelt.*

Oma: *And this reawakening every ten years?*

Delia: *Intriguing. Some kind of holo-projection?*

Oma: *Maybe. But why? I mean, why would an alien landing – or crash-landing? – on Valinda set up this primitive belief system? What's in it for the alien?*

Delia: *Perhaps we'll find out when we get to Mahkanda.*

Mahn was saying, "Beyond Khalamb is an important town on the pilgrims' route. This town is called Larahama, and there is situated the shrine of Chalto's boat."

"And why is there a shrine at Larahama, especially?" Delia asked.

"Because it is a special place in our religion," Mahn told her.

"Larahama is where Chalto's disciples fought the Skelt, and fell. They sacrificed themselves in order to save the Fahran of Larahama. The great Fahran artist, Yarly, built the shrine and a model of Chalto's boat as a reminder to the Fahran of the fallen disciples."

Oma asked, "When will we reach Larahama?"

"It is a few days' trek beyond Khalamb," he said, "deep in the jungle and accessible only on foot."

"And how far away are we from Khalamb now?" Delia asked.

"At sunset we will dock at Lerah. We disembark there and take the path through the Blooming to Khalamb, perhaps a day away on foot."

Delia sat back, having finished her breakfast of a heavy fruit mash and a liquid not unlike thick apple juice. The heat of the day was pleasant but not oppressive: a warm Mediterranean Spring morning, she thought. Into her mind, unbidden, came the memory of a holiday in Crete, with Greek yoghurt and honey for breakfast.

The sun rose above the riotous jungle, and Delia and Oma sought the shade of the latter's berth, leaving the aliens to bask in the sunlight.

Oma got through to Javinder, projecting his image into the air and setting up a reciprocal arrangement so that Javinder could view them.

"How's it going, Jav?" Oma asked.

The Indian mopped sweat from his brow. "The locals are becoming even more curious, and brave with it. They're at the foot of the ramp, now. They'll be sneaking aboard in another day. I've struck up quite a friendship with a little guy who says he'd like to visit the stars. You?"

"We're enjoying a leisurely voyage downriver, and sampling the local fruits. How are the repairs going?"

"Very well. Another day and I think I'll have the auxiliary running." He stared from Oma to Delia. "You said that your life-raft, back at Alkellion, was guarded by the Skelt? The thing is, sooner or later I'll be needing to scavenge parts."

"The Skelt have the life-raft," Delia said, "but they abandon the city in summer. As to whether they'll take the raft with them, or leave it where it is..." She shrugged.

"I'll have the shuttle ready to make a short hop in a day or so. By short hop I mean a planetary jump from here to Alkellion, not into space. We won't be able to do *that* until I've finished work on the main drive. So when you get back we could fly to Alkellion and see what the situation is, right?"

Delia glanced at Oma, then nodded tentatively. "That sounds fine, Javinder. I don't see why not. I just hope the Skelt haven't taken the raft with them underground."

They chatted about other things for a while, Oma describing the jungle and listening – with assumed interest – while Javinder went into minute detail about the drive's inertial failures.

Later that day, as the sun set and the stars came out in a great glowing proscenium above the jungle, the riverboat docked at a long jetty running parallel with the riverbank. A small settlement of ancient timber buildings – warped by the sun in summer and torqued by the winter ice – nestled in the riotous jungle beyond.

Mahn announced that this was Lerah, and they disembarked.

CHAPTER TWENTY-THREE

RATHER THAN ATTEMPT to navigate the track through the jungle to Khalamb by starlight alone, Mahn suggested they spend the night in the settlement and set off at first light. He found an old Fahran willing to rent a couple of rooms in his riverside dwelling, and an hour later, after a communal meal of what Mahn called vegetable stew – though it was oddly sweet – Delia found herself lying on a very short palliasse in a room beside the murmuring river. She told Oma about her childhood in Toronto, then listened as Oma told her about being brought up by a strict Methodist pastor in Johannesburg.

In the morning, after a quick breakfast of what she suspected was the vegetable stew – reheated and with added sugar – they left the villa and Var lowered herself to the ground and arranged her legs so that the others could mount her back.

Mahn was about to climb up when the grizzled oldster emerged from the shack and spoke hurriedly with him, gesturing at the jungle.

Mahn heard him out, then climbed up beside Delia. Var set off along the track, and Delia said to Mahn, "Bad news?"

He turned a long-fingered hand. "A Skelt hunting party was seen south of here, a little north of the town of Khalamb."

"I thought you said the Skelt vanished underground during summer," Oma said.

"They do, but some remain until the conditions become unbearable. With the coming of summer, certain beasts they consider delicacies proliferate and the hunting is good."

Delia smiled. "That's a relief. For a second there I feared they might have been searching for us."

"I very much doubt it," Mahn said. "We lost them far north of here. It is simply a hunting party, making the most of the start of summer."

They fell silent as Var perambulated along the overgrown track. They sat high on her back, vines and tendrils whipping at them as they passed. Mahn called down to Var, who obliged by lifting a huge claw that acted as a protective fender against the jungle's attack.

At one point Delia called down to her, "Are you sure you're okay with all of us on your back, Var?"

"I am hardly aware of your presence. You are as light as flies."

"And a day's walk through sultry heat?" Oma said.

"At home I would walk for days and think nothing of it, and I relish the heat after all the years of cold."

"We appreciate your effort," Delia said.

At least they were spared the direct glare of the huge sun. The jungle canopy provided a dappled filter, so that, looking up through the leaf cover, Delia made out only slices and slivers of the molten primary. She had experienced the jungles of South America and Asia, but nothing compared to this. Motion was constant. Trunks and stalks, leaves and vines and flowers, writhed and sprouted in a heady tapestry of movement. Almost as exhilarating as watching the jungle growing before her eyes were the overwhelming surges of scent. Some had analogues with earthly aromas: she caught tantalising whiffs of cinnamon and lemon; but others, as sharp as smelling salts, had her gagging or covering her face. From time to time she made out flashes of iridescent plumage as bird-like creatures racketed through the foliage, and at others she glimpsed small red bipeds brachiating through the treetops.

At one point, midway through the journey, Mahn suggested they stop to eat. Var found the shade of a vast, veined leaf, which seemed to have reached the limit of its growth and stopped moving. They climbed from Var's back and ate a meal of coarse bread and fruit that Mahn had bought at the last stop.

He asked Delia to project a map of Valinda into the air before them, showing their present position. They were a little below the equator, two hundred kilometres south of Million Falls and around fifteen from Khalamb.

"It will be sunset by the time we arrive at Khalamb," Mahn said.

Delia looked at Oma. "How do you think we should go about this, on the off chance that there are still Skelt in the area?"

"We'll approach slowly, play it by ear," Oma said.

Delia asked Mahn, "Have you ever heard of a Skelt weapon that can bring things down from the sky?"

"Nothing. The Skelt have swords, and crossbows which they developed after capturing Fahran hunters. It is worrying that they might have such a weapon."

"Of course," Delia said, "they might have taken it with them underground. At first I assumed it was some kind of artillery piece embedded in an emplacement. But we're talking about alien technology here. The Skelt invaders might have left something mobile, but still capable of incredible firepower."

Oma indicated the projection. "And after Khalamb?"

"We rejoin the river further south." Mahn pointed a long finger at the erratic squiggle of the river. "We take a track south west through the jungle to the township of Xelem. There we will pick up a riverboat to Phara, then disembark there and trek through the hills. In two days we will arrive at the holy city of Larahama."

Delia finished her water, and they climbed up onto Var's broad back and resumed the journey. She stretched full length along the hot striated chitin, her head resting on the bulge of the Vo's upper leg. Oma sat cross-legged beside her.

"How about some music?" Delia asked. "Ever heard of Arvo Pärt?"

"Can't say I have," Oma said.

Delia commanded her Imp to play Pärt's third symphony, and soon the soothing melody issued from the speaker at her temple. "Soulful," she said. "It works here, somehow."

"I wonder if the composer thought his music would be listened to under the light of a distant star?" Oma mused.

"I'm sure it never crossed his mind," Delia said.

Var said, "Your music is very strange to Vo ears. We prefer our music to be faster, more insistent. I am sorry, I cannot describe it any better than that."

Mahn said, "Vo music is like stones falling down a mountainside. It is a clatter that assaults the senses and makes no sense... to the Fahran, at least. Forgive me, Var."

Delia asked the Fahran, "And you? What do you think of human music?"

Mahn tilted his head and listened. "It is beautiful. It seems to reach into my soul and soothe it."

"I think that that's just what the composer would have wanted," Delia said, "an alien touched by his music composed four hundred years ago and many, many light years distant."

They fell silent and listened to the music as they moved through the jungle, Delia overcome by a sudden, intense sadness.

She reached out, found Oma's hand, and gripped it as if she were the survivor of some calamitous shipwreck.

"Hey, hey there... Don't cry, Delia. It's all right. You'll be fine."

She rolled into the South African's soft embrace and wept herself to sleep.

CHAPTER TWENTY-FOUR

SHE AWOKE TO silence – or, rather, not to silence, as jungle sounds swelled around her – but to an absence of music.

"I'm sorry," she sniffed, wiping her face on the cuff of her one-piece.

Oma stroked her hair as they lay side by side. "No need to apologise. I know what you're feeling."

"You do?"

"The music brought it all back. The loss. The fact that what we've got here doesn't compare to what we've left behind."

Delia nodded.

Oma shook her head. "But that's defeatist thinking, girl. It's futile, allowing yourself to give in like that. Futile and self-pitying. We're all in this together, and we'll get depressed from time to time, but we'll pull each other through, right, and we'll make the very best of what we've got here or die trying, okay?"

Delia smiled through her tears – not tears of despair, now, but of delight at finding herself marooned with Oma, whose fortitude was infectious.

"Right?" Oma insisted.

Delia squeezed the woman's hand. "Right."

"How about you tell your Imp to play a little more music?" Oma said.

"I'll do that."

A single, melancholy note rose through the jungle, filling Delia's heart with gratitude. A rift had opened in the foliage and high up in the silver-white sky she saw something that matched exactly the serene mood of the music: drifting high up and far away were a dozen floating yarm, heading south west.

She touched Oma's arm and pointed. "Look."

"They're beautiful," Oma said. "I wonder what they are."

"They're called yarm," Delia said, and described the gondola ride back at Million Falls.

Mahn gestured towards the floating life-forms. "The yarm originate in this region," he said. "They spend all the summer months airborne, riding the thermals above the equator."

"And the winter?" Oma asked. "What do they do then? Do they perish, like Terran butterflies?"

Mahn said, "Then they undergo a miraculous transformation. They lose their tendrils – those floating ribbons dangling beneath their hoods – fasten themselves to a certain type of rock near the equator, and await the coming of winter. Soon the ice comes, and freezes them. The yarm hibernate, go into a dormant state, taking salts and other nutrients from the rock, and so see out the long winter. Then summer comes again, and they revive, then mate, and celebrate the return of the sun with their great aerial dance."

Oma looked at him. "Are they sentient?"

"Well, not as we think of sentient," Mahn said. "They have no spoken language, or writing, and they create nothing. But Fahran elders claim that the yarm communicate telepathically, and are philosophers, who do nothing with their time but ponder the ways of the universe."

"I like that," Delia said. "Floating philosophers."

"Look," Mahn said, pointing.

Delia started up through the gap in the canopy. The dozen yarm had ceased their south-west drifting and pulsed high overhead. As she watched, first one, then another and another, lowered itself towards the treetops so that soon their domed, diaphanous hoods muted the silver-white light of the sky, the frilled edges of their hoods coming together and touching in long, sensuous ripples. Their pendant tendrils – though tentacles was a better description of the half-dozen appendages that hung from each hood – fell through the gap in the foliage and swayed a metre or so above Delia and her friends.

She reached up and touched the sphincter-like end of a tentacle, and was reminded of the slimy, questing trunk of an elephant.

Oma laughed. "Look at them! Just look! Delia, look at the way they're moving! The tentacles are swaying in time to the music!"

Oma was right. The music rose and fell, and in absolute accordance the tentacles rippled along their length like so many vertical sine waves.

"The yarm respond to music," Mahn said. "The ferry-masters on the gondolas at Million Falls sing to them."

"I'll perform an experiment," Delia said. "I'll cut the music and see what happens. Here goes."

She sub-vocced her Imp to silence the Pärt. The symphony died and was replaced by the cacophony of the jungle's animal inhabitants.

"Look!" Var called out, waving a pincer.

One by one the yarm rose, their tentacles trailing away now that the musical attraction had ceased.

"Okay, and now we'll see what happens if..." Delia said, and ordered her Imp to resume the music.

A violin solo trembled through the air, and the Yarm, attracted to the otherworldly harmony, descended and trailed their tendrils in appreciation.

"That's seriously weird," Oma said. "If only Pärt were around to witness this."

They continued on their way, the music playing. For the next hour, the yarm kept pace, their pendent tentacles trailing just above the treetops in appreciation of the symphony composed thousands of light years away.

When the music concluded and Delia allowed the silence to continue, the airborne aliens gained altitude and were soon lost to sight in the silver-white heavens.

Delia was dozing, an hour later, when Var stopped suddenly and jerked her awake. Mahn said, "What is wrong?"

The Vo was silent for a time, then said, "Alert! I smell Skelt."

Instinctively, Delia reached for her laser. Oma had already drawn hers and was standing up on Var's back, scanning the jungle.

Mahn moved forward and knelt on Var's great domed head "A recent scent?" he asked.

Var replied, "Very recent."

"Within the hour?"

"Even fresher," Var said. "Half that, or less. They came this way and crossed the track, heading south towards Khalamb. There were..." she paused, then went on, "I detect the passage of at least twenty Skelt."

"It is strange indeed that so many should be abroad in the summer heat," Mahn said. "Hunting parties usually consist of no more than six Skelt."

Oma frowned, her full lips screwed to one side. To Mahn she said, "Is it more than just coincidence that they should be around now, just as we're in the area?"

"I do not know," the Fahran replied. "They *might* just be hunting."

"Yeah," Oma said. "Hunting us."

"But how would they have known?" Delia began. "Surely they couldn't have tracked us all the way south, Mahn?"

"I think that very unlikely," he said.

"So, okay – they saw the shuttle come down," Oma said, "and decided to investigate. You said they're hot for Terran technology, Delia."

"Any technology," Delia whispered, staring into the suddenly hostile jungle.

Oma asked Mahn, "Could they have spies amongst the Fahran?"

"Impossible!" he said. "My people detest the Skelt! We have been oppressed by the insects, hunted and killed by them, ever since they set foot on our planet. No one of my kind would commit such treachery!"

"Then they saw where we came down," Oma said, "kept to the jungle and waited for us to move."

Var asked, "Should I continue towards Khalamb?"

"I don't know about anyone else," Delia said, "but I want to see that weaponry. If anyone objects, I'll understand."

Mahn said, "We should proceed with extreme caution. Var, you will be able to scent Skelt if they approach, yes?"

"Yes."

"And as Delia and Oma are armed with their superior weapons – and the Skelt have only crossbows..."

"As you say," Oma said, "we should proceed with caution."

Var started up again, and Delia and Oma peered into the jungle, weapons at the ready.

A little later Oma said, "It occurred to me: if the Skelt did see the shuttle come down..."

"Go on."

"Then they'll know where it is." She turned to were Mahn was squatting atop Var's head, peering into the jungle. "Mahn, have the Skelt ever been known to raid Fahran cities?"

"Frequently, but usually in winter."

"I'd better call Javinder," Oma said.

Heart thumping, Delia watched Oma sub-voc a command to her Imp. Seconds later the Indian appeared floating in the air before them. His face was covered in beads of sweat and he looked far from happy at having his work interrupted. "Yes?"

"Look," Oma said, "we think the Skelt might know where the shuttle came down."

Javinder glanced off-screen, and Delia imagined him reading a diagnostic softscreen and finding its readings far more interesting than what Oma was saying. "Those locust things Delia went on about?" he said off-handedly.

"That's right. Thing is, this might be something or nothing, but in case they do know where the shuttle is, and decide to come and have a look-see, I'd up the security, Jav, okay?"

He nodded, his attention still off-screen. "I'll keep the hatch locked and the ramp up."

"And set up surveillance cameras and program the smartcore to alert you if anything bigger than a Fahran approaches the ship within a hundred metres, okay?"

"Will do."

"Are you armed?"

"Ah, no. Not at the moment."

"You'll find a laser in one of the units. Arm yourself and for God's sake think about something other than your precious drive, okay? The Skelt want our knowledge, and if they think they can get it from you, you're in danger. Got that?"

"Loud and clear."

"Good. I don't want to come back and find you whisked away to an underground Skelt lair, Jav."

"I'll batten the hatches now, set up a security cordon and arm myself."

"Good. And I'll be in contact every hour, on the hour, okay?"

"Affirmative. Over and out."

He cut the connection and his image disappeared.

"Damn him!" Oma said. "He's too obsessed with the repairs to consider anything as personal as his own safety."

"Chances are..." Delia began.

"That's not the point. He's a pro, a trained spacer. He should know the ropes by now. He's not a little boy, mired in some tunnel-visioned obsession with his hi-tech toys."

"Except, Oma, that's exactly what he is."

The South African relented. "Perhaps you're right, and we don't have anything to worry about. It's just... I got close to the idiot and I don't want to see him end up as insect food."

They fell silent and turned their attention to the jungle, Delia reassured by Var's insistence that she would smell any Skelt from way off.

"How far are we from Khalamb?" Oma asked Mahn.

"Perhaps three hours, a little more. We should be there well before sunset."

"Var," Delia asked, "no more signs of the Skelt?"

"Nothing," Var reported. "I detect the same hunting party, heading south. They will reach Khalamb a little before us."

Delia asked Mahn, "Do you know if the Skelt have passageways to their subterranean lairs at Khalamb?"

"They have them all over Valinda," he said, "though those close to Fahran cities we have endeavoured to close up or set with traps. There will be entrances at Khalamb, yes."

"So they might be heading there in order to retreat underground, their hunting over. Or is that wishful thinking?"

Oma grunted. "I hope we don't find out," she murmured.

Delia gripped her laser, her hand slick with sweat.

The next hour seemed to go on for ever. Delia expected a Skelt ambush at any second. She jumped at every odd noise that issued from the jungle. Once, when Var lost her footing and stumbled slightly, she feared that the Vo had been hit by a Skelt crossbow bolt.

Var apologised and they continued on their way.

CHAPTER TWENTY-FIVE

THEY PAUSED ON the crest of a hill and stared down in silence at the faded magnificence of the city.

Khalamb was a series of sand-coloured blocks and stepped ziggurats, rounded with the depredations of time and decorated with the jungle's fecund embroidery: the smaller buildings wore bright green mantles of vegetation, sporting occasional multi-coloured blooms. The occasional tower rose from the floral morass like the beseeching arms of victims claimed by quicksand. The streets between the buildings were hardly visible, being mere conduits now for the passage of vines and ferns.

"Any sign of the Skelt?" Delia murmured to Var.

"They passed this way more than thirty minutes ago and presumably entered the city."

"Do you know if there are any other Skelt in the city itself?" Oma asked.

"At this distance," Var replied, "it is impossible to tell."

Delia cast an eye over the buildings, looking for a ground-to-air missile battery or gun emplacement.

Oma was evidently doing the same, as she said, "Trying to find the Skelt weapon in there will be like trying to find the proverbial needle in a haystack."

Mahn looked at her. "What does that mean?"

While Oma explained, Delia eyed the approach roads. "Just how do we go about this?"

"I suggest that you and me, Delia, slip into the city and search for the weapon. Mahn and Var, remain here. We're armed, after all, and present less of a target."

Var protested. "You might be armed, but you cannot detect the Skelt as I can. It would be foolish to leave me here when I can forewarn you of the approach of the Skelt."

"And I am not staying here on my own," Mahn put in.

Oma looked at Delia. "What do you think?"

"Var has a point. I think it'd be unwise to go in there alone. Let's go in together. I wonder if there's a Skelt track through the vegetation?"

"If there is," Mahn said, "then perhaps it would be best to avoid it and make our own way into the city."

Var said, "When we reach the margin of the city, I'll lead the way, creating a tunnel through the vines. You three can follow."

Oma nodded. "Take the track down the hillside, and we'll dismount at the bottom."

Var set off, picking her way carefully down the incline. Oma said, "Delia, keep an eye out to our right and I'll cover our left flank. Mahn, watch our backs. Var, yell if you detect the faintest whiff of Skelt."

"Understood."

Delia gripped her laser and looked to her right, up the precipitous slope. Above its serrated canopy, the swollen sun was setting with a spectacular show of molten geysers.

A flotilla of yarm drifted peacefully by, high overhead, moving over the city and the jungle beyond.

She turned her attention to the nearby jungle, chastising herself for being so easily distracted by the beauty of this alien world.

They reached the foot of the hillside without mishaps and Var halted. Ahead they faced a wall of vegetation and, beyond, the first of the honey-hued buildings rising from the tangle.

"The Skelt, Var?" Oma asked.

"Nothing. They took a pathway that skirted the city."

They dismounted and Var led the way. Delia high-stepped over springy, recalcitrant vines, keeping her eyes right while Oma scanned their left flank and Mahn watched their rear.

Var made good progress. She snipped away blockading vines and lianas where necessary, but for the most part employed brute force to barrel her way through the overgrowth. The further they penetrated into the city, the safer Delia felt: they were breaking new ground, after all, with no evidence of recent Skelt passage. Sunlight fell over their shoulders, ruddy and full of floating dust motes. Disturbed insects buzzed in protest and, now and again, small animals, the Valindan equivalent of rodents, scampered away to safety.

They were heading down a wide, jungle-choked boulevard, when Delia made out patches of stonework through the foliage to her right.

Var stopped suddenly and turned to them. "Alert! Skelt!"

Delia dropped into a crouch, her pulse thudding. "Where?"

"Ahead of us, thirty seconds – a hundred metres."

"Coming this way?" Oma whispered.

"Stationary, for now."

"Sit tight," Oma said. "Wait it out."

Delia moved closer to Var's bulk, as if for protection. Mahn was at her side, staring apprehensively into the jungle. She raised her laser, alert for the first signs of movement.

"Var?" Delia whispered.

"Still there," the Vo said. "Unmoving."

"Do you think they know we're here?"

"Impossible to say."

Oma murmured, "Can you tell how many Skelt there might be?"

Var hesitated, then said, "Perhaps ten, certainly no more."

"I wonder what the hell they're doing here?" Delia said, more to herself.

Oma shook her head. "Can't be a coincidence that they're so close."

Var said, "They're moving – this way! What do we do?"

"We split up," Oma said. "Delia, take Mahn and disappear. I'll take Var. Head right, we'll go left."

Her stomach churning, Delia grabbed Mahn's hand and yanked him into the undergrowth. She hauled him through the clinging vines, came to a high wall and turned left, pushing through the Valindan equivalent of ivy. It was a relief to be moving; she only hoped that Oma, encumbered with the bulky Var, might be making as much progress.

She said to Imp, *Open a channel to Oma.*

Done.

Delia: *Oma, ask Var where the Skelt are now.*

Oma: *Will do.* And seconds later: *Moving away from Var and me.*

Delia: *So... moving towards me and Mahn?*

Oma: *Affirmative.*

Great, she thought.

Delia: *Do they know we're here?*

Oma: *Hard to tell.*

Gripping her laser in one hand and Mahn's paw in the other, she pushed her way through the obstructing vines, trying not to cough at the clouds of desiccated dust that filled the air.

Oma: *We're sitting tight. They're moving further away from us.*

Delia came to the corner of the building, facing a tangle of jungle.

Delia: *Can you tell if they're still moving towards us?*

Oma: *Judging from my Imp's positioning of you, and Var's sense of scent, they're almost on top of...*

The first Skelt came from nowhere in a terrifying explosion of vines directly ahead of her. The second came from behind, grabbing Mahn in its pincers, while a third emerged through the undergrowth to her left. She swung her laser and fired, but the crimson pulse missed the Skelt in front of her and the third Skelt grabbed her wrist and pulled the weapon from her grip.

Oma: *Delia?*

Delia: *They've got us.*

Oma: *Right, I'm tracking you. Keep calm. I'll be in touch.*

Oma cut the connection.

Delia felt suddenly bereft, wanting nothing more than to hear the comforting tones of Oma's voice in her head.

She cried out as she was tipped and carried by more than one Skelt. She tried to struggle, but the Skelts' grip prevented movement. She was forced through the jungle, vines and foliage tearing at her exposed face. She felt Skelt claws on her legs and torso and recalled being carried from her life-raft what seemed like a lifetime ago now. She inhaled the Skelt body odour – that peculiar combination of hot engine oil and spice – and tried not to gag.

She heard Mahn's fluting, plaintive voice, somewhere behind her. "Delia, be brave."

"I'll do my best, Mahn. And you too. Don't worry – Oma and Var are still free."

She felt a ringing blow on the side of her head, her Skelt abductor demanding silence.

Her headlong flight continued. She cursed herself for not being quicker with the laser, and for allowing the Skelt to disarm her so easily. But she was being hard on herself. She'd reacted as rapidly as she was able: she was up against a foe who moved with frightening alacrity.

She wondered where they were being taken, and hoped it wasn't to the underground lair of the Skelt. How might Oma effect her rescue, then?

She opened her eyes. Greenery passed in a blur, interspersed with dazzling flashes of dying sunlight. She glimpsed the locust face of her captor, then closed her eyes and wished for journey's end.

It came sooner than expected. She felt a cessation of sunlight on her face as she passed into cool shadow, heard the clatter of Skelt feet on a hard surface. The temperature plummeted. She opened her eyes, seeing only darkness.

One second she was horizontal, pincered painfully by locust claws; then she was on her feet. She was pushed forward savagely, staggered and fell to her hands and knees. Mahn tumbled down beside her with a grunt.

She heard the Skelt's footfalls, retreating, then a door slam shut behind them.

CHAPTER TWENTY-SIX

DELIA CLIMBED TO her feet, then assisted Mahn upright. "You okay?"

"I am unhurt," he said, massaging his thin wrist. "You?"

"I'm fine."

She looked around. They were in a chamber, ten metres by ten, but low: the slabbed ceiling was just centimetres above her head, constructed for Fahran dimensions. In the far wall was a timber door, and at intervals of a couple of metres along the four walls were barred windows. She crossed to one, clutched the bars and peered out. The chamber was largely below ground; the openings were at street level. She made out a wide boulevard – cleared by the Skelt? – with a ziggurat beyond, and then the jungle.

She crossed to the small door and tried the handle, then rejoined Mahn.

"Don't worry. Oma and Var are still free. We'll be fine."

She got through to Oma.

Delia: *Where are you?*

Oma: *Still in the jungle, about a hundred metres from where you're being held. My Imp's plotting your position. Sit tight and we'll have you out of there in no time. Do you still have your laser?*

Delia: *The Skelt took it.*

Oma: *Hokay. Sit tight and don't worry. I'll be in touch.*

"I'm in contact with Oma," she told Mahn. "She's working to get us out of here."

"But how will she do that?"

"She's armed, and she has Var."

Mahn moved to the barred window, having to stand on tip-toe to peer out. Delia joined him. The sun had set, haemorrhaging across the sky beyond the ziggurats.

The door at the far end of the chamber opened. A Skelt ducked and entered in a silver blur of motion, followed by a second and a third. They halted before her and Mahn, having to bend low in order to accommodate themselves.

The trio wore bandoliers and carried sickle swords. Their skeletal appearance, their stick-like arms and legs, and scooped pelvic bowls, filled her with nausea.

They turned their long heads, with protuberant compound eyes, first to Mahn and then to Delia.

The jaw of the central Skelt snapped open and shut, clicking an interrogation.

Imp translated. "Where is your ship?"

So they don't know where the shuttle landed! she said to Imp. *I wonder if they're in contact with the Skelt in the north, and know of my escape – or if they saw Oma's shuttle overhead and assumed I was on board?*

I suspect the latter.

Contact Oma, she said, *and tell her that the Skelt are not aware of the location of her shuttle.*

I am doing it now, Imp replied.

The Skelt rattled its jaws and again and Imp said: *The same question, where is the ship?*

She faced the alien defiantly. "It crashed on landing, and we ejected. The shuttle is destroyed."

Imp relayed her words.

The Skelt turned to each other and conferred.

One of the aliens drew its sword and placed it under her chin. She lifted her head away from the cold blade, but the Skelt applied pressure and she felt the razor-sharp edge nick her skin.

Its jaws worked, and a second later the translation came: "You lie. We saw your ship pass overhead. Where is it?"

What should I tell it, Imp?

Say that it is beyond the equator, but you don't know its precise location.

She did as instructed and Imp relayed her words.

"You lie!" The Skelt pressed the knife into her throat and she felt hot blood trickle down her neck.

The Skelt to her right reached out, touching the bony arm of its companion and forcing the alien to lower its weapon. Her saviour's jaw clicked. Imp said: *It says that you are more valuable alive, undamaged. It also said that if anyone should die, it is the Fahran.*

One of the Skelt moved, holding Mahn to its concave belly and looping its sickle blade around his neck. It pulled on the weapon, forcing Mahn's head back.

Mahn regarded her, seemingly impassive to his fate. He blinked at her. "Do not tell it where the shuttle is, Delia."

The Skelt threatening Mahn said, "You will take us to your ship, or the Fahran will die."

"Do not give in," Mahn said.

"But..."

The Skelt said, "Tell me – or the animal dies!"

She had no choice. "Very well," she said. "I'll take you to the ship, but only if you release my friend. And also we need time to rest. We have travelled a long way without sleep. At sunrise, we will set out."

The Skelt conferred. The alien threatening Mahn with the blade pushed the Fahran to the floor. "We will return at sunrise," it said. The trio of Skelt crossed the chamber in a quicksilver streak and the door slammed shut.

Delia knelt beside Mahn and helped him to his feet. "Are you...?"

"I am fine," he said, "but you are bleeding."

She touched her neck, her fingers coming away sticky with blood. "It's nothing."

Oma opened a link between their implants.

Oma: *Your Imp relayed all that. Well done. You okay?*

Delia: *A flesh wound. I'm fine. We have until sunrise.*

Oma: *That gives me plenty of time.*

Delia: *Where are you?*

Oma: *Close by. We have the ziggurat in sight. Give me a little while to work something out, okay?*

Oma cut the connection.

Delia told Mahn what Oma had said, then pulled the medi-pack from her backpack and attended to her cut, applying stinging antiseptic.

She sat down against the wall, and Mahn dropped into a cross-legged position before her. "I'm dog-tired, Mahn, but I'm too damned nervous to sleep. And anyway, Oma might come up with a plan at any minute."

"How will she get us out of here?"

"Good question." She looked around the chamber and up at the thick embrasures of the barred openings. "You Fahran certainly built things to last. This is rock solid and the walls are a metre thick, at least."

"This was a temple, as were all the other ziggurats."

Delia regarded the Fahran. "How old are they?"

Mahn turned a palm, "They were built many millennia ago."

"So they pre-date the coming of Chalto?"

"By many thousands of summers," he said.

"They're temples – religious buildings, right? But to which gods?"

"Gods which came before Chalto, but which have been lost in the mists of time."

She stretched her legs out before her. "And the Skelt? Do they know that Chalto is one of your gods?"

"It is difficult to tell what the Skelt know. They do know that a great ship came down, thirty summers ago, because they battled with Chalto's disciples and slew them, and attempted to open Chalto's ship in order to learn its secrets."

"It must be a strange situation for these Skelt to find themselves in," she mused aloud. "They know they're descended from a great star-faring race, which crossed space in vast ships and conquered worlds, and moved on. And they have devolved, lost so much knowledge, and desperately want to regain it, to restore themselves to their former glory."

"But can you imagine the Skelt amongst the stars," Mahn said, "terrorising innocent races? The thought is appalling."

"The cousins of the Valindan Skelt *must* still be out there, marauding from star to star. Unless, of course, down the millennia they've evolved morals, ethics, and become civilised."

The Fahran was regarding her with his head cocked to one side. "Do you really think that, Delia?"

"I'd *like* to think it," she said. "I like to believe in amelioration and redemption on a racial scale. But no, going by what I've seen of the Skelt here, I think that's a forlorn hope."

She was silent for a time, and then said, "I just hope that the human race, in its expansion across the galaxy, never comes across the Skelt."

Impatient, she jumped to her feet and crossed to the nearest opening; each one was secured with two thick bars. She gripped a bar and twisted, grunting.

"Delia, what are you doing?"

She moved to the next opening and grasped a bar. "Attempting," she said, "to work one of these things loose. Even if the resulting opening wouldn't be big enough for us to squeeze through, then at least I'd have a weapon. It'd give me great delight to cosh the Skelt when they return."

She hurried to the next opening. So far, all the bars had been set solidly into the embrasures, immovable. She gripped bar after bar with both hands and exerted all her strength. She wondered if she was doing this to keep her mind off the inevitable return of the Skelt, or if she really thought she might be able to prise a bar loose.

And then, after two dozen attempts, she felt a bar give slightly in her grip. "Yes!"

"Delia?"

"It's moving." She felt the stone crunch as the bar turned. She twisted it back and forth, working the bar like a pestle in a mortar. The bar gave at both top and bottom. She rocked it back and forth, pulling it towards her, and after three minutes of strenuous effort she managed to work the bar free. It came away suddenly, sending her sprawling across the floor.

"Delia!"

"I'm fine," she laughed, sitting on her backside and holding the bar up like a trophy.

She returned to the opening. The gap in the window was still not wide enough to admit her, or even Mahn. She gripped the second bar and twisted, then gave up after two minutes. She was succeeding only in giving herself blisters.

"At least we've got this," she said, hoisting the bar. "I don't feel quite so defenceless now."

"You must be careful," Mahn said. "You know how fast the Skelt move."

"Don't worry. I won't do anything stupid."

She moved to the timber door and pressed her face to a gap between the planks. She made out a cleared boulevard, and a pair of Skelt guards stationed a metre from the door. The second alien had her laser tucked into its bandolier.

If she attacked the Skelt when they returned, and managed to grab her laser...

She rejoined Mahn. "There are two Skelt out there, and one of them has my laser."

"What do you plan to do?"

Before she could answer, her Imp said, *I have Oma here.*

Oma: *They've caught us...*

Delia: *What? Oma...? Oma!*

Silence.

Imp, what's happening?

I am liaising with Oma's Implant, Imp said. And two seconds later: *Oma and Var have been caught. They are moving this way, under armed escort.*

"That's all we need," Delia said to herself.

Mahn was staring at her. "Delia?"

She told him that Oma and Var had been apprehended, and the little Fahran leaned against the wall and slid down onto his haunches.

The double door at the far end of the chamber opened and Oma was bundled inside, followed by Var. The door was unceremoniously slammed shut behind them.

Delia rushed over to Oma. "Are you –?"

"I'm fine. I'm sorry. There was nothing I could do – there were so may of the damned things. They had us surrounded."

Var said, "I tried to fight them off, Delia, but they caught Oma and threatened to kill her."

Oma sat down against the wall and mopped her brown with the sleeve of her jumpsuit.

"They're coming for us at dawn," Delia said. "I said I'd lead them to the shuttle. It's bought us a little time, at least."

Oma looked at her, bleakly. "Time for what?"

With the iron bar, Delia pointed to the opening from which she'd extracted it. "I had intended to use it as a weapon, but I have an idea."

Oma peered at the gap. "But it's hardly large enough..."

"I know, but like I said, I have an idea. I've tried to move the second bar in the opening, but it's set solid. However..." She turned to Var. "Do you think...?" she began.

The spider-crab danced across the stone slabs, piping, "I'm sure I can dislodge it, Delia."

Oma jumped to her feet. "Be careful. We don't want to alert the guards."

They joined Var as she raised a giant claw to the opening. Rather than attempt to grip the remaining bar and work it loose, she inserted her claw into the gap and used it as a lever, exerting ever more pressure.

Var whistled, adjusting her stance and leaning towards the wall. The bar shifted suddenly; the stone surround cracked with a sound that Delia was sure would alert the guards.

Var stopped and all three stood, frozen, and listened.

The Skelt made no move to open the door and investigate.

Delia nodded. "Okay... easy does it, Var."

The Vo leaned towards the wall again, levering her claw. Delia approached the opening and gripped the bar so that, if it did come free, it wouldn't clatter off across the floor.

She felt the bar shift, grinding the stone, and a second later it came loose and sent her sprawling for a second time. She lay still, her heart thudding as she listened for the Skelt guards. After five seconds she picked herself up and joined the others at the opening.

Oma said, "Good work, but we can't all squeeze through. Maybe you and Mahn, Delia. But there's no way Var or I would make it."

Delia stared at the opening. "I'll go. One of the guards has my laser. I'll make my way around the zig and jump them."

Oma stared at her, concern etched on her face. "That's risky."

"What else do you suggest?"

Oma bit her lip, thinking it over. "Hokay... and then what?"

Her heart thudded. "Once I have my laser I'll attend to the door. I don't know how it's secured, but it'll be no match for a quick laser pulse. Agreed?"

She looked around at her friends.

Mahn said, "Be very careful."

"Jesus..." Oma said. "I almost think that we should wait, take out chances when the bastards come for us."

"What chances? Knowing the Skelt, they'd kill Mahn and Var once we get anywhere near the shuttle – and maybe despatch you and me as well."

"I was thinking we might overcome them before that," Oma said uncertainly.

Delia shook her head. "No. This is the best option. There are only two of them out there. And even if I fail, they want me alive for the time being."

Mahn said, "I want to come with you, Delia."

"You could do nothing to help her, little one," Var said.

"I'd be better off working alone," Delia said. "Okay, Oma?"

Reluctantly, the South African nodded. "Okay."

"Right," Delia said, looking up at the opening. "Var, if you'd give me a leg up."

She stood on Var's great claw and was lifted towards the opening.

Tucking the irons bars into her waist-band, she inserted her head and shoulders through the gap and squirmed out.

CHAPTER TWENTY-SEVEN

SHE STOOD IN the star-speckled night, taking deep breaths.

A channel had been cleared along the side of the ziggurat, but the jungle was encroaching. She reckoned the best way to approach the Skelt guards would be to climb on to the first tier and move stealthy towards the entrance. This would give her the advantage of coming upon the Skelt from above. Using the ledge of the opening as a step, she hauled herself up. She climbed to her feet, gratified to find that the stone beneath her boots was covered with a fine coating of moss which would cushion her footsteps.

Stealthily she made her way along the first tier of the ziggurat towards the entrance.

Her Imp said, *I have Oma here.*

Oma: *You okay, girl?*

Delia: *Fine. Approaching the guards.*

Oma: *Anything I can do?*

Delia: *Just be ready to run out when I overcome the guards. I'll grab my laser and disable whatever locking mechanism is on the door.*

Put like that, it seemed a tall order.

Oma: *Will do.*

Delia cut the connection and instructed her Imp to maintain silence until further notice.

She came to the corner of the ziggurat, crouched down and listened.

The boulevard before the edifice had been cleared, and thankfully she could see no Skelt along its length. From this angle she was unable to make out the guards. She controlled her breathing and pulled the bars from her waist-band. They would make formidable weapons – but how she might attack and disarm the Skelt, lightning fast as they were, was not something she could pre-plan. Play it by ear, she thought.

She crept along the tier. The ledge was broad, perhaps two metres deep, and this had the advantage of allowing her to hug the wall of the second tier so that she could not be seen by the guards.

Halfway along the ledge, where she judged the entrance to be, she paused and listened again.

She was unable to see the pair, but she could hear them, their clacking conversation loud in the sultry night air.

Hunkering down, she crept forward little by little and peered over the edge.

The two guards stood close together, engaged in conversation. They seemed to be discussing something that one of them was holding. Delia smiled as she realised that it was a second laser – the one the Skelt had evidently taken from Oma. Her own laser, she saw, was tucked into the bandolier of the first guard.

But how to do this, she wondered...?

She looked left and right along the boulevard, paranoid at the thought of Skelt reinforcements.

She was staring up at a rearing ziggurat three along the boulevard when she saw it.

She gasped, hardly daring to believe her eyes, and instructed her Imp to open a channel to Oma.

Delia: *Oma?*

Oma: *Here, girl. What gives?*

Delia: *I've found the Skelt weapon.*

Atop the ziggurat, silhouetted against the stars, was the erect barrel of the artillery piece aiming into the skies.

Oma: *Well done. Where is it?*

Delia told her.

Oma: *And the guards?*

Delia: *Just below me. And they have your laser.*

Oma: *Great, but be careful. Hell, I wish I was out there with you.*

Delia: *With luck, you soon will be.*

She cut the connection and peered down at the guards.

They were still fascinated by their new toy.

She adjusted her grip on the bars, holding each one at the very end to give her maximum heft when it came to swing them in anger.

The way to go about this was to launch herself down between the guards, clubbing their long, equine skulls as she dropped. She would have the element of surprise on her side, even if they could move far faster than her. With luck, they would be dead or concussed within seconds.

She hunkered down and crept closer to the edge of the tier.

The guard to her left was fingering the laser, as if attempting to work out how to operate the weapon. The second guard stood perhaps half a metre away, peering at its colleague.

She took one last look up and down the boulevard and, seeing no other Skelt, stood up and took a deep breath.

She jumped.

She brought the bar in her left hand down with crushing force, and the Skelt's skull split with the impact, spraying brain fluid over her hand. The alien crumpled without a sound, dropping the laser.

The alien on her right, perhaps glimpsing her descent, moved fractionally as she brought the bar down, and instead of catching it true on the skull, the bar deflected onto its shoulder. She heard bone crack and the Skelt cry out as it dropped to its knees.

Delia crouched, facing the alien as it staggered to its feet and faced her. It moved lightning fast for its sickle sword, and Delia lunged in fear and desperation.

She clubbed the creature across its head and watched it drop to its knees. She hit it again, mercilessly, and the alien pitched forward at her feet.

Breathing hard, she pulled the laser from the Skelt's bandolier and retrieved the second weapon from the floor beside its colleague, then turned to the door.

She had expected to find some crude locking mechanism, perhaps a padlock, and was gratified to see that the door was secured by an even more primitive device. A length of timber like a beam barred the double door.

Delia: *Oma, I've done it.*

She hefted the beam, from its brackets and dropped it to the ground, kicking open the door. Oma and Mahn rushed out, followed by Var. Oma stared at the dead Skelt.

"Good going, girl."

Delia wanted to take the South African in a big bear hug, but instead passed her the second laser. "This way."

"Where to?"

Delia indicated the ziggurat, three along. "To do what we came here for," she said.

She sprinted across the boulevard and ducked into the shadow of the opposite ziggurat. The four crouched together and Delia said, "It can't be long before the Skelt realise what's happened. I suggest you three vanish into the undergrowth and I'll scale the zig and destroy the weapon –"

"I don't like the idea of splitting up..." Oma began.

"Nor do I," Mahn said.

"It makes sense," Delia hissed.

"Too late!" Var cried out. "Look…"

Delia turned, her stomach heaving.

Fifty yards along the boulevard, a platoon of a dozen Skelt seethed around the entrance to the erstwhile prison, taking in the open door and the dead guards. Seconds later, spotting the four cowering escapees, they fired a barrage of crossbow bolts. Delia ducked and laid down a tracery of laser fire, accounting for three of the Skelt. More appeared beyond the first platoon, at least twenty aliens who fanned out across the boulevard and advanced. Oma crouched and picked off the Skelt one by one.

"This way!" Delia said, grabbing Mahn's hand and pulling him along the boulevard towards the ziggurat on which the weapon was situated.

CHAPTER TWENTY-EIGHT

SHE SPRINTED, TURNING from time to time to fire at the Skelt. Ahead, she made out a tumble of stones that had once been the corner of the base of the ziggurat. "Over you go – take cover!"

Mahn and Var scuttled over the tumble and vanished. Delia turned and picked off the approaching Skelt.

"There's even more of the bastards!" the South African cried.

Twenty or so Skelt emerged from the jungle fifty yards along the boulevard. Crossbow bolts whickered through the air, striking the ziggurat behind Delia and Oma.

"Over the stones," Delia said, taking Oma's arm and scaling the tumbled masonry.

They jumped over the crest and ducked for cover. Delia raised her head above the stone, and wished she hadn't. Along the boulevard, more Skelt emerged from the jungle, a smear of movement flowing towards them in a solid, quicksilver river.

Oma fired, and Delia picked off the aliens one by one.

Mahn cowered beside her, shaking in fear. She glanced behind her, to where Var was attempting to hide her giveaway bulk behind the stones.

Then, beyond Var, she made out a shimmering phalanx of advancing Skelt. She swung and fired her laser five times in quick succession, skittling the aliens.

"They're coming from behind," she warned Oma.

Crossbow bolts lanced through the air. Delia laid down a barrage of fire to the rear, scattering the Skelt and gaining a temporary reprieve.

She looked around in desperation while firing strategic shots to slow down the advance of the Skelt. She and her friends were trapped. She looked up at the stepped side of the ziggurat rising against the glowing starscape.

"I don't want to sound defeatist," Oma called, "but I don't see a way out."

"How many of the damned things are there?"

"Is that a rhetorical question? We must have killed a hundred, but they keep on coming."

"From their underground lair?"

"Maybe. Hell, don't they fear death?"

"Insect hive mentality," Delia said. "The collective mind. Perhaps they don't see themselves as individuals."

"Interesting. Let's get into a philosophical debate with them when they capture us."

"I don't think they'll be in any mood to trade xenological theory, Oma. They might not be so lenient with us now we've put up a fight."

"As I said earlier, I don't see any way out."

Delia looked up at the summit of the ziggurat.

"But I do."

"Do what?"

"See a way out," Delia said. "Look."

She pointed.

Oma said, "So, how do we do this?"

"We lay down a barrage of non-stop fire and run like hell up the zig."

"Hokay. You brief the troops while I keep the hordes at bay."

Delia turned to Mahn and Var. "When I give the word, make your way up the ziggurat, okay? I'll cover you."

"But they will surround us and have us trapped!" Mahn objected.

"Trust me. It's the only way. Okay, after three. One, two, three – move it!"

Showing surprising agility for a creature her size, Var leapt and scuttled up the stepped side of the ziggurat. Mahn followed, scrambling like a child.

Delia fired left and right, hosing blinding laser fire at the advancing Skelt. She called out to Oma, "You next. Run!"

Oma leapt from the crest of the rubble, gained the first tier, and climbed at speed.

Delia followed, falling into a rhythm of ascent. Each stepped tier was waist high and she leapt, landed, turned and fired. Crossbow bolts rattled against the stonework all around her. She looked over her shoulder. Five metres below, a Skelt had reached the ziggurat and jumped onto the lowest tier, pausing to take aim. Before it fired, Delia loosed a laser bolt that burned through its sternum and sent the alien tumbling into its fellows. She took off up the tiered flank of the edifice.

Something hit her back, a dull thud that could only be one thing. Don't dwell on it, she told herself, just run. She'd heard accounts of being hit by projectiles – how the pain was not immediate; first came the realisation of the impact, a dull thump... *Don't think about it!*

Above her, Var had reached the summit beside the hulking weapon and turned to peer down. Mahn followed quickly, ducking into the protective custody of the Vo's many legs. Oma was on the tier three above Delia, firing right and left with manic energy.

Oma gained the summit and hauled Delia up after her. On all four sides of the ziggurat, Skelt militia climbed towards them.

"We're surrounded!" Mahn cried.

Delia stared at the weapon, its great barrel thrusting into the night sky. Its working end was a bubble enclosing a bucket seat and a control array.

"They coming!" Oma yelled.

Delia thrust her weapon at Mahn. "Join Oma. She'll tell you what to do."

Mahn ran to Oma's side, gripping the laser, and Delia hauled herself up into the great weapon's bubble cover.

It was as if the bucket seat had been expressly fashioned for her. A good omen, she thought. She gripped two handholds before her, with firing studs set into their housings. The seat tipped on gimbals and the barrel of the weapon dipped suddenly towards the jungle.

"Whoa!" Delia cried.

Surely, she thought, as she thumbed the firing studs, it couldn't be so easy...

She almost wept with delight as a great pulse of white energy lanced from the muzzle of the weapon and screamed off into the jungle.

She cried over her shoulder, "Get behind the gun!" and didn't have time to ensure that her friends obeyed before leaning forward and bringing the barrel of the weapon to bear on a phalanx of Skelt swarming up the flank of the ziggurat. She was blinded by the resulting laser discharge, and when her vision recovered from the after-blur she made out a falling line of charcoaled aliens. She leaned right, the barrel swinging with her. She depressed the firing studs and blitzed the advancing Skelt.

Behind her, Oma said, "Move clockwise, okay? We're dealing with the bastards on this side."

Delia did as instructed.

She blazed away at the Skelt swarming up the flanks, mowing them down in their dozens – but as she made one circuit of the ziggurat and came back to the flank fronting the boulevard, it seemed that the alien attack was relentless. The Skelt came and came again, as if their numbers were being renewed from a limitless source.

On her third circuit, however, she noted that not as many aliens seemed as willing to make the sacrifice.

"They're retreating," Oma called out.

She ceased firing. A sudden silence replaced the deafening sound of laser fire.

Oma was at her side, her round face sweating in the starlight. "So far, so good, but you do realise that they have us trapped. And look," she went on, pointing down at the boulevard, "they're massing for another attack."

Delia looked up, into the heavens. "I think we're going to be fine, Oma."

"How do you work that out?"

She smiled to herself and issued a command to her Imp. Instantly, the silence was replaced by the soothing strains of Arvo Pärt's third symphony.

"Delia," Oma said, staring at her, "now is hardly the time for a musical accompaniment."

"Oh, I don't know about that..."

Beside her, Mahn and Var looked up in unison.

Three diaphanous yarm, their pulsing domes phosphorescent in the starlight, drifted towards the summit of the ziggurat.

Oma grinned. "Hokay... but will we make it in time?"

Delia followed her pointing finger, and her heart sank. The Skelt had begun their counter-offensive up all four sides of the edifice.

Delia brought the super-weapon to bear yet again and fired at the Skelt swarming up the ziggurat; not all them, she saw with relief, were armed with crossbows. Most of them wielded swords, useless in anything but close combat. She swept the laser around, while behind her Oma laid down a constant barrage.

Delia glanced up at the yarm. Their trailing tentacles were perhaps ten metres away and descending. She felt something swell in her chest, a response to the music and a reaction to the realisation that her scheme to evade the Skelt might just work.

She waited for the pain in her back to kick in, but felt nothing. Adrenalin, she thought; I'm running on adrenalin.

A crossbow bolt seared past her head, missing her by centimetres, and thwacked into Var's upper left foreleg. The spider-crab grabbed the bolt with a great pincer and pulled, removing it along with a spurt of green ichor.

Delia looked up. The first yarm was hovering over the summit, its tentacles dangling, and she yelled, "Mahn, Var, grab a tentacle each and hold on for dear life!"

Mahn tossed Delia her laser, then reached out, embraced a swinging tentacle and hung on. Var, dancing in what she thought might be fear, took hold of two trailing tentacles in her forelegs and swung. The yarm moved off with its cargo, losing altitude due to the sudden burden, then regained its equilibrium and rose.

Oma hauled Delia from the control seat. "What?" Delia yelled.

"We came here to destroy this thing, didn't we?" Oma said.

Two yarm hung over the summit of the ziggurat, tentacles trailing.

"Do it and get out of here," Delia said.

As she watched, Oma stared at the control panel, wide-eyed.

"What?" Delia shouted.

"Nothing..." Oma said. "Just... just trying to work out the best way..."

Oma raised her laser, aimed at the control array before her, and fired. The array smouldered, then sparked, and she jumped clear of the resulting explosion.

A yarm tentacle swung towards them and Delia steadied it for her friend.

"Take it!" she yelled. "I'll cover you."

Oma grabbed the tentacle, swarming up its length like a trained gymnast. She hung on and leaned out, firing down at the advancing aliens. A dozen Skelt had reached the tier below the summit. Delia aimed at those armed with crossbows and picked them off, glancing desperately around her. She was unable to see a handy tentacle. For a second she wondered if this was her fate, to be overwhelmed by alien hordes while her friends drifted to safety.

"Behind you!" Oma yelled at her – and thinking that a Skelt was approaching on her blindside, she pirouetted to see a tentacle swinging through the air towards her. She reached out, took hold, hoisted herself and swung. As she lifted with an exhilarating buoyancy, and the Terran symphony swelled in the alien night air, she wound her leg around the tentacle, easing the strain on her arms, and peered down.

The nested squares of the ziggurat fell away. A dozen Skelt gained the summit and looked up. One was armed with a crossbow, and before Delia could bring her laser to bear, the alien fired. The bolt missed her by centimetres and tore through the yarm's pulsing cowl. She expected the creature to react by descending, but the yarm merely increased the rate of its pulsing flight and rose swiftly. Delia took aim on the crossbow bearer and fired, delighting in its loose-limbed tumble down the side of the ziggurat.

Ahead, silhouetted against the stars, she made out Mahn and Var hanging onto their yarm. Oma swung on her own yarm, ten metres ahead. Delia looked down. The stepped shape of the ziggurat was diminishing rapidly, individual Skelt now lost to sight.

She was unable to feel the crossbow bolt in her back. She wondered if she were still anaesthetised by adrenalin. Soon, when the rush abated, the pain would kick in.

Oma called across to her. "Delia, you've been hit."

"I know, but I can't feel a thing, at the moment."

Oma laughed.

Indignant, Delia asked, "What's so funny?"

"Of course you can't feel a thing, Dr Kemp. The bolt's embedded in your backpack."

"What?" She reached an arm up behind her, contorting herself, and found the bolt. She pulled it out, felt nothing, and inspected its point for blood in the starlight.

"And I thought I'd earned my first battle scar," she called out.

Serenaded by Arvo Pärt, the yarm and their cargo drifted serenely through the sultry alien night.

CHAPTER TWENTY-NINE

DELIA OPENED HER eyes, startled.

She'd resisted dozing off during the night for fear of losing her grip and falling to her death, but exhaustion must have got the better of her. She looked around, wondering how she'd managed to hold on while asleep, and saw that a second thick tentacle had wound itself around her torso, securing her.

The night had passed and the huge, bloody face of the rising sun spanned a quarter of the far horizon.

She looked around for the others.

The yarm carrying Oma was a hundred metres ahead; Mahn and Var swung on their yarm just ten metres away. Similarly, they were secured by multiple tentacles, as if their saviours had somehow guessed at their passengers' need for sleep.

She called across to Mahn, "But I thought you said the yarm weren't sentient."

"They're not, Delia."

"And yet while we slept, they moved other tentacles around us to keep us safe."

"A mystery. But by all reckoning, the yarm are not intelligent."

"But empathetic, perhaps?" She looked up at the beating skirt of the alien creature. "Thank you, yarm."

She looked down. They were drifting five hundred metres above the jungle, a multi-coloured tapestry of visible growth. Vines writhed like a pit of serpents, flowers opening and turning towards the hemisphere of the sun. A flotilla of multi-winged butterflies – or rather the Valindan equivalent – drifted *en masse* through the air, the perfect visual accompaniment to the symphony still issuing from her implant.

She instructed her Imp to stop the music, then got through to her friend.

Delia: *Oma, you awake?*

Oma: *I've just woken up. I must've slept. Hey! How come I didn't fall?*

Ahead, Delia saw Oma's tiny figure start and stare about her.

Delia: *The kindness of the yarm. Mahn insists they're not intelligent, but I don't know.*

Oma: *Well, we got away from the Skelt. But where are we now?*

Delia asked her Imp to plot their position, and a second later it responded: *Currently three hundred kilometres north west of Larahama, and heading due west.*

She communicated this to Oma.

Oma: *We've made progress to Larahama, but we need to be thinking of saying goodbye to the yarm.*

Delia: *Good idea. But just how on earth do we communicate that to them?*

She called across to Mahn and explained the situation.

"Don't worry," he called back. "We're descending."

"We are?" She looked down, and sure enough the treetops were closer now than they had been just minutes ago.

Mahn clung to the tentacle with one arm and pointed. "Look, the river."

Delia looked down and saw the winding, serpentine length of the river looping its way through the jungle. "But how do the yarm know we...?"

Mahn interrupted. "They don't. But they do need to drink from time to time."

"They're not the only ones. I could kill for a beer."

"And look," Mahn said, "further along the riverbank, a settlement. Riverboats ply the river every day. So we won't have long to wait for a boat to take us the rest of the way."

"And Larahama?"

"A day south of here by boat," Mahn called out, "followed by a trek of half a day inland to the city."

The yarm came in low over the treetops and descended towards the river. The tentacles unwound from around her – further convincing Delia of the yarm's empathy, if not sentience. She caressed the smooth skin of the last tentacle, murmuring her thanks.

She peered down at the river, then let go and dropped three metres and hit the warm water with a deafening splash. She surfaced, spluttering, and swam to the bank.

She watched Oma fall feet first, resurface spouting water, and helped her out. Mahn and Var dropped a little further downstream, the Vo hitting the water with a smack, disappearing for a second, before resurfacing and paddling towards the bank with Mahn on her back.

They stood together and watched as the three yarm hovered above the river, a sight at once awe-inspiring and moving. The tentacles dropped to the water and the yarm hung, taking in sustenance. Then, having drank their fill, as stately and silent as ever, one by one they rose high into the air and drifted off across the treetops.

Delia and her friends watched them disappear from sight, then made their way along the riverbank towards the settlement.

CHAPTER THIRTY

THEY CAUGHT A riverboat at midday, this time sharing the deck with a group of Fahran making the pilgrimage for the first time. Mahn joined their group and Delia watched him chat to his fellows; she wondered if he were recounting his adventures so far. He was certainly animated, gesticulating with his long arms as his audience sat spellbound.

The jungle grew high on either side of the river. In the distance, to the south west, a hazy range of mountains created a saw-toothed horizon. In the foothills of this range, according to Mahn, was the valley of Mahkanda, where Chalto's ship had come to rest. Halfway to the valley, buried deep in the jungle, was the shrine at Larahama.

She inspected the shattered chitin of Var's left foreleg; but there was little she could do to heal the wound, and Var assured her that she was not in pain. "It will heal in time," she told Delia. "In the meantime, I have plenty of other legs to serve me well."

"That's the trouble with being bipedal," Delia said. "Lose one leg and we're disabled, two and we're in dire straits."

Var reached out a great pincer and touched Delia's hand with surprising delicacy. "And your flesh is so soft. The slightest knock must pain you."

"Well, we're careful," she said. "But I admit there are times when I wish I had a shell."

Var raised an eye-stalk to take in the passing jungle. "The stories I will have to tell when I return home: a Skelt attack, imprisonment, yarm flight, and a long journey to the Fahran god of Chalto. My hive siblings will not believe me."

Delia moved into the shade of a great sail. The sun was growing hotter by the hour; already the temperature was in the high thirties, and Imp had said that at the height of summer the mean temperature would be in the mid-fifties. And added to the heat was the humidity, making every breath a labour.

She thought of her parents, no doubt grieving her death, and her friends on Earth and the colony worlds. She would never see them again, and even the possibility of being able to reassure them that she was alive and well was denied her.

She considered Timothy; this was the first time in days that he'd entered her thoughts. She'd had much to occupy her, but still felt guilty that events had pushed him to the back of her mind.

She looked across the deck to where Oma sat alone, cross-legged, staring down at the passing river. The South African had been quiet since boarding the boat, withdrawn and abstracted – not at all her usual, buoyant self. Delia crossed the deck and sat down beside her.

"Admiring the view?"

Oma looked up and smiled. "Miles away."

"How about a game of chess?" Delia asked. "Or backgammon?"

Oma shook her head. "Do you mind if I don't?"

Delia looked away and watched the purling brown waters of the river. "Of course not."

They sat in silence for a time as the boat sailed downstream. Wafts of perfume blew in from outsize flowers on the riverbank, scents so sweet they were almost sickly.

Delia ventured, "I know how you're feeling. It sometimes hits us hard, after an experience like that."

Oma stared ahead. "The conflict with the Skelt?"

Delia nodded. "It was a close thing. You can't help wondering 'what if?' You feel a kind of retrospective dread at the thought of what might have happened, but for a stroke of good fortune."

"Mmm. Perhaps that's it."

"It'll pass. We've got to look ahead." She stopped, for fear of sounding glib.

Oma looked at her and smiled. "Of course we have. Yes, you're right."

"You were pretty handy with the laser, back there."

"Before I trained to be a pilot and joined the ESO, I served five years in the South African Army."

Delia stared at the tiny woman, trying to imagine her in combat fatigues and hauling a fifty kilo backpack.

She was wondering what possessed people to join their country's army – it seemed an act of desperation to her – when Oma said, as if reading her thoughts, "I always wanted to be a pilot, and the army ran system integration courses." She tapped the spar of import jacks at the base of her skull. "It was one way to get wired up."

"I've often wondered what it's like to mesh with a ship."

Oma smiled, almost beatific with recollection. "Oh, it's wonderful, Delia. A complete negation of self and a union with this thing that's much bigger and more powerful than yourself." She shook her head. "I can't wait until Jav gets the shuttle up and running again, and..." She stopped.

Delia looked away. But to what end, she thought. Oma might be able to go joy-riding, might be able to indulge her desire to integrate with the shipboard matrix, with something bigger than herself, but that was all it would ever be – an indulgence that would serve no greater purpose.

She thought Oma realised this, too.

The South African sighed. "I'm tired. I think I'll lie down."

"Sure. Catch you later."

She watched the small woman climb to the higher deck and the rows of sleeping booths, hoping that Oma would be restored to her old, irrepressible self after a rest.

Mahn joined her a little later. "Var and I are about to eat. We wondered if you would like to join us?"

They ate under an awning at the prow of the ship. The meal consisted of a bowl of salad, a medley of fruit and vegetable that had no real Terran analogue, plus, for protein, something that resembled a carob pod but which tasted like raw meat. Mahn told her it was a delicacy of the south, a bean which grew on a tree for one month only during early summer.

They washed down the meal with a warm, milky fluid which Delia found unpalatable, salty and cloying.

Mahn, excited at the prospect of visiting the shrine at Larahama and the Rising of Chalto at journey's end, indicated the group of Fahran seated across the deck. "It is the first time my friends have made the pilgrimage also," he said. "They say that this Rising will be special."

"In what way?"

The Fahran turned his hand. "I do not know, specifically, but the High Priests at Mahkanda have communicated with Chalto, and He has announced that this Rising will be like no other."

She stared at the dregs of her drink, decided against finishing it, and asked, "Do you know how the High Priests communicate with Chalto?"

She had expected another negative, and was surprised when Mahn said, "Yes, they are mind-linked to our God."

"Mind-linked? You mean they're telepathic?"

"Or Chalto is able to communicate directly with their minds, telling them His thoughts, His wishes."

The more she heard about the strange Fahran religion surrounding Chalto, the more intrigued she became; she was anticipating witnessing the Rising almost as much as Mahn himself.

The afternoon progressed; the sun climbed and the temperature crept into the low forties. Since her arrival on Valinda, the sun had grown to fill a quarter of the sky, alive with slow motion fire spouts and crawling sunspots. It was uncomfortably hot and sticky on the deck, even in the shade of the awning.

She glanced up at the higher deck, her eye drawn by something. A light pulsed from the third booth along the row; Oma was evidently in contact with Javinder. She decided to join the South African and see how the engineer's work on the shuttle was progressing.

She left Mahn and Var slumbering under the awning and climbed to the upper deck.

She heard Oma's dialogue with Javinder before she reached the booth.

"I don't believe it!" the Indian said.

"It's true," Oma said. "Why the hell would I make up something like that?"

Delia stopped, her pulse racing, and listened.

"This changes things," Javinder said.

"You're telling me it does."

"Okay, okay. What should I do?"

"Sit tight," Oma said. "Work on the repairs. I'll be in contact once we've reached Larahama. I should know a lot more then."

"Very well," Javinder said. "What does Delia think?"

Oma hesitated, then said, "I haven't told her."

"You haven't? Why not?"

Another hesitation, then Oma said, "What do you think of Delia, Jav?"

Delia leaned against a timber partition, her heart racing. She felt dizzy.

Javinder said, "She's professional, ultra-competent, friendly. I don't know. She's fine. What do you think of her?"

Oma sighed. "I like her a lot, Jav. But I'm worried about her."

Delia blinked. This was news to her.

Oma went on, "Look, she strikes me as one of those highly-motivated, ambitious types who set their mind on one thing and get it done. I had my Imp access the shuttle's core cache and hacked her ESO personnel details. She sailed through med school and came out the other end with honours. She's served six missions with distinction."

"So, that's good, right?"

Oma sighed again. "I'm no psychologist... It just strikes me that she's a neurotic, highly-strung type who might go off the rails if anything disastrous happens."

Neurotic? Highly-strung? Oma was right – she was no psychologist. But what the hell was all this about?

"Have you noticed she never talks about her folks back home, lovers, friends?"

"So what?" the engineer replied.

"I think she's taken what's happened, our being stranded here, very hard – and she doesn't want to show it, or even perhaps admit it to herself. She finds it hard to talk about what she's lost."

"Ah, so you think if you told her about...?"

"That's right," Oma said. "I need more information, first – corroboration."

"Okay. As soon as you get to Larahama, get in touch."

"Will do."

Delia hesitated, torn between marching into Oma's booth and asking what the hell was going on, or retreating to the lower deck and quizzing Oma in her own good time, when she'd had time to think things through.

She made her way back down the steps to the front of the boat.

She sat under an awning, staring across to where Var and Mahn were sleeping; the Vo sat with her legs curled under her, while the Fahran curled up against her shell like a contended cat.

So Oma was in possession of some information she feared might destabilise her – Delia's – fragile psyche? She felt an odd gratification at her friend's concern, but at the same time irritation that Oma thought her unable to shoulder the mental burden.

It could only be something to do with the *Amsterdam*, she thought. Had Oma come across some package of information in the shuttle's core cache referring to the loss of the starship? But why had Oma contacted Javinder now? Had her Imp accessed the shuttle's core just recently – while sailing through the air last night, perhaps? – and discovered something she felt unable to share with Delia?

She sat up, wiped sweat from her forehead with the cuff of her onepiece, and said to Imp: *Can you access the shuttle's core cache?*

Imp replied, *Negative.*

Why not?

Access denied.

She sat back against the rail of the boat, frowning. *And who authorised the denial, Imp?*

Javinder.

Okay. She felt as if she were getting somewhere. *Do you know when this was?*

Six hours after the explosion aboard the Amsterdam.

Dammit. So Oma *couldn't* have accessed the files last night.

Do you have any suggestions why Jav might have authorised a denial? she asked.

As senior officer aboard the shuttle, he might have deemed the measure necessary for any number of reasons.

She thought about this, then said, *Imp, was it possible that the loss of the* Amsterdam *was brought about by sabotage, rather than an accident?*

It is impossible to ascertain what caused the ship's destruction.

But might Oma and Javinder have access to information suggesting that the Amsterdam *was deliberately destroyed?*

I have assessed all possibilities, and I conclude that Oma Massinga and Javinder Lal do not have the wherewithal to determine whether or not the loss of the Amsterdam *was occasioned by sabotage.*

Very well. She gazed into the white hot sky, perplexed.

She recalled something that Oma had said to Jav about knowing more when they reached Larahama, and a thought occurred to her.

Imp, is it possible that there was another life-raft or shuttle that managed to escape from the front-end wreckage of the Amsterdam?

I have had no contact with another vessel.

But do you know if another vessel, other than mine and Oma's, left the Amsterdam?

I know of no such occurrence, Delia. I would have notified you if this were the case.

She took a breath and asked, *But is it possible that a shuttle or life-raft from the* Amsterdam *managed to land on Valinda, near Larahama, without your knowledge?*

That is highly improbable, Delia. Any such ship would have left an ion signature in the atmosphere of Valinda, and I have issued constant scans since our arrival on Valinda.

Okay, so that's a definite no, then? Are you sure? What if it came down without power, glided to planetfall?

In which case, Delia, I suspect that any survivors would have achieved contact with us before now.

Ah, she thought – but what if survivors contacted the shuttle, and for some reason Oma was keeping it from her?

But why?

All this speculation was not only going around in circles but serving to make her paranoid.

The sun was setting, and the riverboat was an hour away from the port from which they would trek inland to Larahama, when Oma came down from the upper deck and crossed to Delia.

"Feeling better?" Delia asked.

"Much, thanks. I slept a little."

Delia asked, "And what did Jav have to say? I saw the light," she explained.

"Oh." The South African looked away, staring into the jungle. "I just asked him about how the repairs were going."

"And?"

Oma shrugged. "Progressing. The ship will be able to make short jumps in a day or so."

Delia nodded and sat back, watching the woman. She said, "I've been thinking about the *Amsterdam*."

"What about it?"

"The explosion. What might have caused it? An accident –?"

Oma flashed her big eyes at her. "What else might it have been?"

"I don't know. Sabotage? Europe has enemies, you know."

Oma shook her head. "That's not a nice thought. I took it to be just a catastrophic systems failure, a meltdown in the plasma core." She shrugged. "I don't know. I'm no physicist."

Delia nodded. "I tried to access the shuttle's core cache, to see if I might learn anything about the blow-out. But I found that access was denied."

Oma raised her head and regarded her calmly. "That would be Javinder. He cited special security circumstances and closed the core just after we left the *Amsterdam*."

Delia raised her eyebrows. "Rather excessive, don't you think? What did he think you were, a spy?"

Oma laughed. "Oh, you know Jav. All left brain and male imperatives. He was going by the book and I didn't stir the waters by quibbling."

Delia yawned. "I'm looking forward to arriving at the shrine at Larahama," she said, watching Oma closely, "seeing what we might find there."

Oma didn't react, other than to shrug and say, "It should be interesting."

"I was thinking, while I was hanging onto the yarm last night... I just wondered if we were the only survivors from the *Amsterdam*? What if other life-rafts got away?"

Oma shook her head. "I doubt it. I had my Imp run a search. Nothing doing."

"I did the same," Delia said. "Only, we didn't know of your shuttle until we saw the con-trail. Your chargers were down and you weren't broadcasting. What if the same applied to a third vessel? Or what if it located the shuttle and contacted the core direct, but as it's in 'access denied' mode it hasn't seen fit to inform us?"

Oma gave her an odd look.

"What?" Delia asked, mock-surprised. "Do you think I'm being neurotic or something?"

Oma's regard of her turned suspicious. She said, "Or something. You're fantasizing. I think you need to get some sleep, girl."

"Perhaps you're right."

She was about to say, "Look, enough of the games. I overheard you and Jav talking earlier," when a shout went up from the shore as the riverboat pulled into a ramshackle timber jetty – and the moment was over.

Oma jumped to her feet and moved towards the gangplank, joined by Mahn and Var. Delia crossed the deck and followed her friends from the boat.

THE SUN WAS going down over the jungle, but rather than stay the night in the tiny port town, Mahn suggested they press on.

"Larahama is less than six hours away," he said, indicating the foothills of the southern range, stark against the sunset, "and pilgrims process along the route with lighted torches. Our way will be illuminated."

"And as I slept during the day," Var put in, "I will happily carry you to Larahama."

They had a light meal at a stall selling spiced stew – the closest thing to curry Delia had tasted on Valinda – then climbed onto Var's back and set off along the track that rose through the jungle towards the foothills.

Fahran disciples with flaming torches created a river of fire stretching before them through the jungle. Within minutes Var, setting a good pace, came alongside the frontrunners leading the procession. She moved to the head of the column and slowed down, her bulking shadow sprawling before them in the torchlight of the following pilgrims.

Mahn told of how his hive ancestors, thirty summers ago, had progressed along this very track to investigate reports of fire falling from the sky. "They were hah growers and harvesters of jey, and they set off in torchlight procession during the night and joined their fellows at Larahama and proceeded towards the valley of Mahkanda to make the great discovery."

Delia listened, then lay down on Var's back and drifted off.

She awoke six hours later to find that they had arrived at the shrine town of Larahama. Var had paused at the ancient, pillared gates of the city, and in silence Vo, Fahran and the humans stared in wonder at what lay before them.

The town perched on a hilltop with the star-washed mountain range as a backdrop. Buildings hewn from what looked like pink marble glowed in the light, a series of minarets and towers connected by walkways made from jungle vines. These buildings were set out around a great central dome, coruscating in the starlight, which Mahn described proudly as the shrine. Unlike in the ancient city of Khalamb, which had been surrendered to the jungle, Larahama had been tended like a garden so that only prescribed growths were allowed to proliferate, giant flowers winding up and around obelisks and straining for the sun.

The pilgrims were met by the first Fahran Delia had seen wearing clothes: a line of elderly aliens, garbed in green robes, wandered among the tired pilgrims, bestowing what she assumed were blessings. Mahn said they were holy men, High Priests, whose touch conferred good luck in the pilgrimage ahead. He said they should dismount and continue on foot into the town, where they would be allocated dormitory accommodation and would sleep until daylight. Then, Mahn said, they would make their way to the shrine.

Delia, Oma and Mahn climbed down and joined the torchlight procession as it shuffled obediently forward. A High Priest came towards them through the crowd, then stopped and called to one of his fellows. He was joined, rapidly, by three other priests who stood regarding the humans in what looked to Delia like confusion, or even consternation.

The priests conferred, gestured, pointing at the tall interlopers, their eyes wide. A ripple of comment passed through the crowd, and Delia wondered why their presence had occasioned no such comment amongst Fahrans north of here.

Then, moving rapidly, the priests approached Oma, reached up and took her arms and led her, gently but persistently, towards a flower-garlanded tower. Mahn, in a flurry of concern, followed at speed. Soon, both were lost to sight in the crowd.

Delia stood with Var, a rock in the river of Fahran pilgrims who flowed around the obstruction with curious stares and comments.

"I think we'd better move so we don't block the road," Delia said.

Var joined her, chattering worriedly. "But what did the priests want with Oma?" she asked.

Delia shook her head. Yet another mystery surrounding the woman, to add to all the others.

Mahn returned minutes later, alone.

"Mahn?" she said. "What happened?"

He turned his hand and gestured towards one of the tall towers.

"The High Priests took her," he said, "and would not allow me to follow."

CHAPTER THIRTY-ONE

THEY WERE LED to a dormitory building and allocated a small room with a window-door opening on to a starlit garden. Var, too large to enter the room, accommodated herself on the verandah. Delia and Mahn joined her and discussed the situation.

"But why would they take Oma?" Delia asked. "What did the High Priests say?"

"When I asked why they were taking Oma away, they said merely that they must question her."

"They didn't say why?"

"They said no more."

The garden was bordered by a bed of luxurious blooms. In any other situation she would have been glad to relax and take in the beauty of the garden and the surrounding mountains. But Oma's arrest, coming on top of the woman's strange behaviour and her enigmatic conversation with Javinder aboard the riverboat, was unsettling.

For perhaps the fifth time since her arrest, Delia attempted to get through to Oma, without success.

Imp, what's the problem? Why isn't she replying?

I cannot tell, Delia.

Can you communicate directly with her implant?

Negative.

Might her charge be low?

I very much doubt that, as she charged her implant just this morning. My suggestion is that she has deliberately deactivated her implant.

But why would she do that? Delia wondered.

Very well, Imp. Tell me if you detect any activity from her implant, okay?

Affirmative.

"I have a suggestion," Mahn said.

"Go on."

"I think perhaps the High Priests are curious. It is the first time any humans have visited Valinda, and they wish to question Oma about why she came here, and from where she came. They might very well have selected you, but as Oma was closer when they approached..."

"Well, maybe," she said, but remained unconvinced. If that were the case, why might Oma have deactivated her implant?

Var said, "I think Mahn is right, Delia. I think we should not worry."

Delia looked around the garden. Within the ancient walls, a thousand translucent blooms glowed in the twilight. She imagined the little Fahran priests tending the garden every ten years in anticipation of the resurrection of their god.

She said, "I'm dead beat. How long to sunrise?"

"Eight hours," Mahn said.

"I'm going inside to get some sleep. I'll see you in the morning."

The room consisted of six small beds, and as there were no other occupants beside Delia and Mahn, she dragged two of the short mattresses on to the floor, lay them end to end, and attempted to sleep.

She was awake for a long time, wondering what tomorrow might bring.

In the event, she was awoken before the sun came up.

Delia, Imp said, *communication from Oma.*

She sat up quickly in the darkness, disoriented. She looked around, recognised the dormitory and saw the starlit shape of Mahn across the room, sleeping soundly. She rolled from her bed, eased through the door and stepped out into the garden. The night was preternaturally still, the air heavy with scent, and the stars seemed to pulse. She sat down on a small stone seat.

Delia: *Oma? What the hell's going on?*

Oma: *Delia, don't worry. Everything's okay.*

Delia: *I tried to reach you earlier. I couldn't. Why did you shut down your implant?*

Oma, after a hesitation: *I had to concentrate on what the Fahran were asking me.*

That sounded a pretty thin excuse.

Delia: *So why didn't you get in touch when the interrogation was over?*

Oma: *I have. I've been shut up with them all this time.*

Delia: *What did they want? Why did they arrest you?*

Oma: *I wouldn't call it an arrest. They were just curious.*

So, according to Oma, Mahn's supposition was correct.

Delia: *What did they say?*

Oma: *They questioned me about who we were, where we came from, what we were doing here. I told them the truth.*

Delia: *Where are you now?*

Oma: *In a comfortable room in the tower. I'm not sure they believed what I told them. They're keeping me for further questioning.*

On the face of it, Oma's story was entirely plausible. But taking into consideration her dialogue with Javinder, and her line about knowing more when they reached Larahama, Delia was suspicious.

She took a breath.

Delia: *Oma, will you tell me straight: what the hell is going on?*

Oma, after another hesitation: *What do you mean?*

Delia: *Look, I overheard some of what you and Jav were talking about back on the boat. You're keeping something from me. Why is this place, Larahama, so important? You said you'd know more when you reached here.*

There was no reply from the South African.

Delia: *Oma?*

Oma: *Look, I'll explain everything when I see you later, okay?*

Delia: *Why not explain now?*

Oma: *Because I still don't know the full situation here. I don't know if I'm right about what's happening.*

Delia: *But why can't you –?*

Oma: *Delia, please trust me. Please.*

Delia sighed, then nodded even though Oma could not see her.

Delia: *Okay, okay. I'll trust you. I just hope it's worth waiting for.*

Oma: *I think it will be, girl.*

Delia: *When do you think they'll release you?*

Oma: *I don't know. When are you going to the shrine?*

Delia: *Mahn said that as soon as we've had breakfast.*

Oma: *I think they'll still be questioning me then. Look, will you do something for me?*

Delia: *Go on.*

Oma: *When you get to the shrine, squirt the images of the holy 'vessel' or ship directly to my Imp, okay?*

Delia: *Of course, but why?*

Oma: *I'm interested, that's all.*

Delia: *Okay, I'll do that. But I wish you'd trust me enough to tell me what they hell's going on.*

Oma: *It's not that I don't trust you.*

Delia: *Just that you think I'm neurotic, right?*

Oma: *I'll explain everything soon enough, okay? Look, I'd better go. I can hear movement outside.*

Oma cut the connection.

Delia lay awake for a long time, going over what Oma had said and trying to make sense of her promises, requests, and maddening ambiguities.

She must have fallen asleep well before dawn because the next she knew, Mahn was gently shaking her awake, and she felt oddly rested. Dazzling sunlight filled the room, outlining the Fahran's tiny figure. "Will you join us for breakfast in the garden, Delia?"

They sat on the verandah and ate bowls of fruit salad and flat bread. Delia told them that she'd heard from Oma in the night, and that Mahn was correct: the High Priests were indeed curious about the aliens in their midst.

"She hopes to be released later today, and then we can continue on our way."

"First we will visit the shrine," Mahn said, "where Chalto's disciples fell in their brave stand against the Skelt."

After breakfast, dozens of other Fahran disciples milled into the garden in a visible, and audible, state of excitement: they intermingled and chattered in their high, fluting tongue, eager to be released to make their long-awaited obeisance. The presence of a human and a Var occasioned comment and curious stares, but they soon returned to their excited speculation concerning the imminent visit to the holy shrine.

In due course a pair of timber gates opened at the far end of the garden, and two green-robed High Priests appeared and ushered the disciples from the enclosure. Twittering with excitement, the Fahran filed out and passed through the roseate stonework of the ancient city.

The dome rose high above the surrounding buildings, visible from all points – a structure so large, Delia thought, that it was out of place amongst the more modest Fahran architecture. They approached it along a wide boulevard, three individuals amongst hundreds of disciples shuffling patiently towards the shrine.

Var murmured, "I wonder if I am the first Vo to visit the shrine, Mahn?"

"I have heard that others of your kind have made the pilgrimage."

"But I see no other Vo now," she said.

"And I will be the very first human to enter the shrine," Delia said.

"How do you feel?" Mahn asked as they queued to enter the dome. "Excited? Do you sense the feeling of... of exaltedness that fills the crowd?"

She smiled. "I do," she said. "And I too feel excitement." But perhaps, she added to herself, for altogether different reasons.

A short while later they approached the marmoreal portals of the dome, passed inside and found themselves in a vast open space filled with rose-tinted sunlight from a petal-like arrangement of transparent panels set into the apex of the structure. High Priests met them with murmured greetings and suggested they take in, first, the series of frescoes around the perimeter of the dome.

Delia's attention was taken, however, by what stood in the very centre of the floor – the stylised representation of the vessel that had brought Chalto and his disciples to Valinda, thirty summers ago, as depicted by a great Fahran artist at the time. The icon stood five metres high, and thirty long, a rust-coloured craft tapering from a blunt stern to a pointed prow; highly stylised, it was the paradigm of all space-going vessels.

She opened communications with Oma.

Delia: *You there, Oma?*

There was no reply.

Imp, she said, *squirt this to Oma. I'll be getting other, closer images once I've taken in the frescoes. Make sure she gets everything.*

Affirmative.

With Mahn and Var and a hundred other pilgrims, she processed around the perimeter of the dome. The frescoes were set on plinths at waist-height – eye-level for the Fahran – and carved into lozenges of the same roseate, marmoreal stone from which the dome and other buildings of Larahama were built. The first scene depicted Chalto's vessel nestling amid the mountains, the second a torchlight procession of Fahran winding through the foothills to greet the craft. Others showed the Fahran surrounded by what looked like asterisks.

Pointing to the floating starbursts, Mahn explained, "They are Chalto's disciples."

"Ah, I see. They cannot be depicted in their true forms, right?"

"Correct. The great Yarly, the artist who carved these frescoes and constructed the icon, depicted Chalto and his disciples as supernal beings of light."

They moved on. Other frescoes showed the will-o'-the-wisps making offerings to the Fahran, bows and crossbows and spears. Mahn explained that these offerings were given in thanks for the Fahran having nursed back to health certain disciples who had fallen ill.

"And we come now," Mahn said, "to the frescoes showing the terrible siege of Larahama. You see, Chalto's disciples saved the city from the Skelt, held the Skelt at bay while we Fahran escaped to our underground winter cities. But then..." Mahn gestured to the frescoes.

The frescoes showed hordes of Skelt – thousands of the locust-beings – descend on the city in wave after wave, eventually overcoming the limited ranks of the disciples.

"The history books say that there were just one hundred disciples holding back ten thousand Skelt," Mahn said in hushed tones. "Though the disciples were armed with superior weapons, they could not hold back the vast Skelt armies. But they were fearless, and brave, and fought for long enough to allow my kind to escape unharmed, before they fell."

"Impressive," Delia murmured, genuinely moved by the depicted sacrifice of the unknown alien race. She shivered, thinking back to her flight from the Skelt. What terror the disciples must have faced when confronted by the implacable alien onslaught.

They came to the last fresco, which showed a lone will-o'-the-wisp above the alien starship in the mountains. "And this is Chalto," Mahn said. "He was the only one of his kind to survive. He sleeps, to Rise each summer and bestow his blessings, before sleeping again until the next Rising."

"It is a wonderful story," Var said. "I cannot wait to see what kind of being this Chalto is."

"I'm more than a little intrigued myself," Delia admitted. An alien being that slept for ten years at a time, and had done so over a span of three hundred years...

"And now we move on to the ship itself," Mahn murmured, "the exalted holy icon."

He stared across the marble floor to the icon, wide-eyed.

Together the three crossed to the cone-shaped ship.

It really did, Delia thought, resemble a stylised pine-cone, with a series of overlapping scales that might have been radiation tiles, and here and there, dotted across its surface, the ports and blisters of fuel inlets and observation points.

"Yarly fashioned the icon from the trunk of a Lo tree which grew in Larahama; legend has it that some of the disciples sought sanctuary in its boughs before being hunted down and slaughtered by the Skelt. The words inscribed on the flank of the vessel are from Yarly's epic verse celebrating the sacrifice of Chalto's disciples."

Delia walked around the icon, taking in the flowing script and ensuring that she viewed the vessel from all angles. She ensured that her Imp was sending the images to Oma, then tried to reach her friend again, without success.

Imp, why isn't she answering? she asked in frustration.

It is my opinion that she is still being questioned by the Fahran priests.

Okay, I'll try later.

"We'll *know more when we reach Larahama,*" Oma had told Javinder.

Mahn was silent as they filed from the dome with the other pilgrims. Delia touched his shoulder. "That was truly impressive. Thank you for bringing me here, Mahn."

"And what excites me the most," said the Fahran, "is that this is but the start. It was impressive enough – I have read about the icon, and heard other pilgrims speak of its magnificence and wonder – but it is as nothing compared to what awaits us."

Delia smiled. The Rising. She could well believe it.

The majority of the pilgrims who had viewed the icon were now beginning the next stage of their journey: the trek through the foothills towards the valley of Mahkanda and Chalto's ship. They formed a straggling column that wound through the streets of the city and up the far hillside, disappearing into the folded hills.

Mahn suggested they return to the garden to await Oma's release and eat before they too embarked.

Once in the quiet of the enclosed garden, Delia moved to a low seat beneath the spreading bows of a scented fruit tree and attempted to reach Oma, again without success.

She looked across the garden to the low, vine-shrouded stone dwelling. Var was on the verandah, Mahn inside collecting food.

She told Imp to establish a connection with Javinder, and seconds later the engineer responded.

Javinder: *Delia?*

Delia: *Jav, how are the repairs coming along?*

Javinder: *Very well. Almost finished. I should have the ship up and running in a matter of hours.*

Delia: *Great. Well done.*

Javinder: *Is Oma there?*

Delia: *Not at the moment. She's... she's busy with the Fahran High Priests. I was wondering... What she told you earlier about Larahama and what she wanted here.*

Javinder: *She's told you?* He sounded suspicious.

Delia: *Yes, she thought it best.*

Javinder: *One moment.*

He broke the connection.

Dammit, Delia swore to herself. He doesn't believe me and he's trying to check with Oma.

He came back seconds later.

Javinder: *I can't reach Oma to corroborate that, Delia.*

Delia: *You think I'm lying?*

Javinder: *I don't know.*

Delia: *Look, I'd like to know what the hell's going on here. You're keeping something from me and I'd like to know what it is, okay?*

Five seconds elapsed.

Javinder: *I'm not sure that that would be wise.*

Delia: *Because Oma thinks I'm neurotic, right, and couldn't take whatever it is you're hiding from me?*

Javinder: *Look, I don't know. Have it out with Oma, okay? Leave me out of this.*

Delia: *Dammit, Jav – tell me!*

Javinder cut the connection and Delia hit the bench in frustration. She tried to get through to Oma again, in vain.

Imp, what the hell is going on, here?

If you could elucidate.

They're keeping something form me. About Larahama, about the situation here.

I'm afraid I don't have sufficient information to enlighten you. And all Oma and Javinder's communications to date have been encrypted.

"The bastards," she said to herself.

She sat in fuming silence for a while, then saw Mahn emerge from the dwelling with a tray of food and sit down at a table beside Var. He raised a hand and waved to her, and Delia left her seat and joined them.

The meal this time was cooked vegetables and an appetising, spicy meat.

"A substantial meal before we set off. We have a trek of some ten hours ahead of us."

Var took her plate in a claw and tipped the food into her slit mouth, masticating noisily. "As before, it will be my pleasure to carry you," she said.

Mahn gestured. "It is written that Fahran disciples must make the last leg of the journey on foot. All vehicles and other modes of transport are forbidden. I will walk, thank you."

"I take it that that proscription doesn't apply to humans, Mahn?" Delia asked.

"No precedent has ever been set on that matter," he replied.

"In that case I'll set it, and take up Var's kind offer of a ride."

"I am sure that will be acceptable to the High Priests," Mahn said. "I wonder when Oma will return? We need to be setting off soon if we are to reach Mahkanda by nightfall."

Delia finished her meal. "I'll try to reach her."

She strode off down the garden and attempted to communicate with the South African.

This time, to her surprise, she did get through.

Oma: *Thanks for the images, Delia.*

Delia: *What's happening? I've been trying to reach you all morning.*

Oma: *The High Priests have been keeping me busy.*

Delia: *Why did you want to see the images?*

Oma: *Later, okay? I need to check a few things.*

Delia: *This is getting beyond a joke, you know?*

Oma: *I know, and I'm sorry.*

The woman's tone mollified her somewhat.

Delia: *Okay. So you still can't tell me what's going on?*

Oma: *Soon.*

Delia sighed, watching her friends on the verandah as they sat face to face, chatting in their alien tongue.

Delia: *Look, Mahn's pretty itchy to be setting off. Have you any idea when they'll let you go?*

Oma: *Ah, there have been developments on that front.*

Delia: *That sounds ominous. What's happening?*

Oma: *Look, you set off for Mahkanda now –*

Delia: *Without you?*

Oma: *I'll see you there.*

Delia: *I don't understand.*

Oma: *You don't have to understand, just do as I say, right? Set off now and I'll see you in ten, twelve hours.*

Delia: *But we'll see you on the way..? Oma? Oma, will you answer, damn you? Answer me!*

But Oma had cut the connection.

She stared up at the mountains, which rose stark and silver against the whitening sky.

Imp, can you trace Oma? Is she still in the tower?

I have traced her, and no, she is no longer in the tower.

She's already set off? In that case we'll catch up with her.

That will be impossible, Delia.

For chrissake! Now you're talking in riddles! Okay, tell me, why will that be impossible?

Because Oma has not taken the road through the foothills to Mahkanda.

Delia felt as if she were stuck in a dream where logic was askew and no-one would give her a straight answer.

So how the hell is she getting there?

Tracing the trajectory of her implant, Imp told her, *I have ascertained that Oma is currently half a kilometre below ground and heading away from us into the foothills.*

Delia blinked, taking this in. *So presumably the High Priests took her underground?*

I would assume so, yes.

They're taking her to the valley of Mahkanda and Chalto's ship?

That is the obvious conclusion, Delia.

Very well. We'd better set off.

She tried to reach Oma, but was not in the least surprised to find that she couldn't establish a link.

She returned to the verandah. "I've just been talking to Oma. She's already on her way. The Priests are taking her to Mahkanda through underground passages."

Mahn stared at her. "But why are they doing this?"

"I wish I knew, Mahn. She didn't say."

"But –?"

Delia held up a hand. "Then I lost the connection – probably because she was so far underground. Okay, we're wasting time hanging around here."

She returned to the dorm, found her backpack, and joined Mahn and Var as they left the garden and moved through the busy streets, Delia electing to walk for a while before taking up Var's offer of a ride.

CHAPTER THIRTY-TWO

A LINE OF pilgrims followed the road winding from the city into the hills. The heat was punishing. Imp informed Delia that the temperature was forty-five and rising. She pulled up the hood of her thermal suit and ordered Imp to cool her down. As they left the last of the buildings in their wake and struck out into the hills, her suit's refrigeration nexus kicked in. She felt sorry for the furry Fahran at her side, who must be suffering beneath his heavy pelt.

An hour into the trek, she gave in and climbed onto Var's back, enjoying the elevated view. She looked back at Larahama, the city nestling in a wide valley, the huge ball of the fiery primary high above. She had taken the beauty of the city for granted: familiarity, she thought, breeds not contempt but apathy; six months ago, with only the cities of Earth and the newly constructed cities of the colony worlds as comparison, she would have found the alien magnificence of Larahama, with its ethereal towers and great central dome, breathtaking in its otherness. Now, the city was just one more wonder to add to all the others she had encountered on Valinda.

Despite herself, she wondered if she were becoming reconciled to thinking of the planet as home.

Ahead, the dusty track wound into the foothills, edged by the jungle falling away on one side and by a thick, green, tendrilly growth on the upper slopes. Even as she watched, the tendrils grew, writhing like snakes and transforming into jungle. Fahran workers were stationed in teams every twenty metres along the road, chopping away at the constant growth with sickle-bladed tools.

She looked ahead; the road skirted the side of the mountain for kilometres, a silver line like a geological stratum populated by the tiny figures of the Fahran. She wondered how many thousands of Fahran she would find at journey's end.

Three hours into the trek, they stopped beneath the spreading shade of a tree and drank from a canteen of water Mahn had brought along. They rested for half an hour, the little Fahran sitting against the bulk of one of Var's great forelegs.

She had noticed a change in Mahn over the course of the past day: usually talkative, he was more reflective and reserved now. It was as if the enormity of the pilgrimage was at last dawning on him.

"Do you know how close to Chalto we'll be able to get?" she asked him.

"There will be crowds of many, many thousands, Delia. Even if we were close to the front of the crowd, I have been told that the view is limited. It will be enough to view him at a distance, even if the spectacle is thus reduced."

Delia nodded. She would be able to assist him, there. She would have Imp record the moment when Chalto arose, then play it back and magnify it for Mahn's delight.

"Tell me about the Rising," she said. "Is there some kind of schedule?"

"Chalto will rise at the sunrise after next," he said. "Before that, starting tomorrow morning, the High Priest of Mahkanda will address the crowd, reminding the pilgrims of the importance of heeding

Chalto's wise words. Then our story-tellers, the Twelve, will take it in turn to recite the twelve stories of Chalto's Coming, the Meeting, the Bestowing of Gifts, the Salvation at Larahama, and others. They will hold the crowd spellbound with their words, and we will relive every minute of the events that took place thirty summers ago. At sunset tomorrow, the stories will cease and Fahran musicians will serenade the gathering with traditional songs and those bequeathed us by Chalto and his disciples. At midnight, all festivities will cease and the crowds will sleep until dawn and the Rising of Chalto." His huge dark eyes stared into the distance, in rapture.

"And where will we spend the night?" she asked.

Mahn turned his head to regard her. "Many years ago, with the swelling of the crowds at the Rising, Fahran farmers planted a hundred thousand haval seeds, and these seeds provide soft beds on which we Fahran repose on the eve of the Rising."

"A delightful image," she said.

"I find it hard to believe that I am but one day away from witnessing the Rising," Mahn said. "I have anticipated making a pilgrimage for so long." He looked from Delia to Var, "and I could hardly have dreamed that I would be joined by a Vo and a human."

"Would you rather be with your own kind?" Var asked.

Mahn tipped his head and considered the question. "Upon reflection, no," he said. "If I were among other Fahran, then the excitement would be great, yes, but perhaps not so great as I am feeling now – because being with you two friends, one a stranger to my planet, the other a member of another species, I am witnessing events through your eyes also, and I am feeling a certain pride in my religion. It is hard to explain, but your presence *enhances* the experience."

They set off again, Delia riding on Var while Mahn trotted alongside, seemingly indefatigable in his religious enthusiasm. The road switch-backed through the foothills, climbed a mountainside, and then cut through a pass to enter another valley. All the time they were climbing, and it felt as if they were moving closer to the sun as the temperature rose and Delia's thermal suit worked to compensate for the increased heat.

Fahran thronged the road, groups of thirty or more which Mahn explained were entire hives; and smaller groups of older Fahran who were making the pilgrimage for the second time, along with individuals. Although Var slowed to accommodate Mahn's slower pace, she was still moving much faster than the other pilgrims. They outpaced groups of Fahran who set up curious twitterings that a Vo and a strange biped should be making the pilgrimage.

Once or twice brave youngsters approached and asked Mahn about his travelling companions, and he replied that he had accompanied his friends on a long journey beginning in the northern hemisphere of Valinda and only now coming to its conclusion – a journey that involved imprisonment by the Skelt, battles with the same, and aerial escape thanks to the yarm. The youngsters listened with exclamations of wonder, then ran off to tell their parents of the strange trio and their tales.

Delia attempted to get through to Oma again, but Imp informed her that there was no signal: Oma was far underground, and incommunicable, and for perhaps the hundredth time that day she wondered why the Fahran High Priests had taken such an interest in the South African.

At one point, as the sun was dipping towards the serrated line of the mountains ahead, to bring premature twilight to the foothills, Imp informed her that she had a communication

She sat up, thinking Oma was at last responding, only to hear Javinder's sing-song Indian voice in her head.

Javinder: *Good news, Delia.*

Delia: *Go on.*

Javinder: *The shuttle's auxiliary drive is repaired and I'll be test-flying the ship first thing tomorrow.*

Delia: *Excellent. Good work, Javinder.*

Javinder: *All that remains is to locate your life-raft and cannibalise the drive, and with luck the shuttle will be space-worthy.*

Delia: *And then?*

Javinder: *And then we leave this hellish cauldron.*

Delia smiled, recalling that Alarah was equatorial and considerably hotter than at this southern latitude.

Delia: *It's hot up there?*

Javinder: *Delia, I am accustomed to the high summer temperatures of Chennai, but this is something else. Even the shuttle's cooling system is battling to combat the heat.*

Delia: *I'm sure you'll cope.*

Javinder: *I certainly will. As soon as I'm sure the shuttle is air-worthy, I'll be making the hop down to join you.*

Delia: *You will?*

Javinder: *Oma's orders. I'll pick you up in a couple of days, then we'll head north to Alkellion and locate your life-raft.*

Delia: *Thank you for informing me of that small detail, Javinder.*

Javinder: *Right, I'd better get back to it.*

He cut the connection.

Delia sat back against Var's haunch and thought that she had reason to tear Oma off a strip or two when they finally met up again.

The sun was disappearing over the mountain-rage ahead as they approached what Mahn informed them was the final pass. "Beyond lies the valley of Mahkanda, and Chalto's great ship. Prepare yourself, my friends!"

As they moved slowly through the pass, a bottleneck congested by thousands of pilgrims, Delia looked up and made out Fahran dotting the slopes like scree on either side. They wore bandoliers, and carried crossbows and spears, and looked down upon the crowds with a protective air. They were the first Fahran she had seen bearing arms.

Delia pointed, and Mahn looked up and said, "Elite Fahran guard."

"They expect trouble?"

"Very infrequently, Skelt raiding parties venture this way – but it has never been known to happen this far into summer. Down the centuries the Skelt have tried and tried again to gain admittance to Chalto's ship, usually at winter's end, or at the end of summer – all to no avail. The defences are strong, the Skelt's instruments puny. But occasionally they have killed pilgrims, out of sadistic malice." He indicated the armed Fahran. "Hence the elite guard."

"But in winter, when the Fahran are underground and the Skelt have the run of Valinda?"

Mahn looked up at her as he trotted alongside the Vo. He grimaced, in what might have been a smile. "Then nature's defences prove too much for the Skelt," he said. "The ship is entombed in a mantle of ice two kilometres thick."

She considered the extremes of weather endured by the planet, and the creatures which had adapted to the punishing routine, and the strange belief system which had grown up around the crashed starship.

Darkness descended while they were still in the pass, and the temperature dropped. Overhead the spread of pulsing stars took centre stage, as if attempting to outdo the effulgence of the swollen sun.

Suddenly, she was aware of a commotion up ahead. A swift murmur passed through the crowd, like the soughing of the wind through the branches of an oak. Delia sat up, alert for danger, and found her hand reaching for the laser in her belt.

Mahn explained. "The pilgrims ahead have come upon the valley, and for the first time cast their eyes on the hallowed site."

She relaxed, looking about her at the pilgrims. Where before she had seen the weariness of footsore travellers, now the Fahran were transformed; a spring had entered their step, and every last alien was atwitter with the wonder that awaited them at journey's end.

She looked ahead. All she could make out was a mass of tiny bodies in the narrow defile, their pelts as dark as ink in the starlight. Heads craned to see the valley, and arms waved in exultation. The murmur rose to cries, and the joy passed down the ranks to those, around her, who had yet to set eyes on the holy valley. Even Mahn was affected; trotting beside Var, he looked up at Delia and gave an uncharacteristic yelp of anticipatory delight.

Delia was affected too: she felt a tightness in her chest, a constriction in her throat. She found herself welling up, taken by a nameless emotion as she was carried along on a wave of alien joy.

They came to the crest of the pass, and those around her raised their arms and sang aloud, Mahn along with them. He danced along, a puppet in thrall to the hysteria; even Var moved with a lively jounce in her step, her eye-stalks waving this way and that to take in the sight ahead.

They came over the crest and down the other side, three pilgrims amongst perhaps a hundred thousand packed into the broad valley. Every pilgrim was staring ahead, towards the far end of the valley and the enclosing mountains. Delia searched for the pine-cone shape of Chalto's ship, but saw only a mass of vegetation in the distance – a bank of vines and leaves cocooning the hallowed vessel.

She climbed from Var's back and joined Mahn.

"Do you see them?" he breathed, transported. "The holy vines that enshroud and encapsulate Chalto's sleeping place?"

She could not give voice to her disappointment, that she had hoped to see the ship itself. It was enough for Mahn to glimpse even the foliage that concealed the vessel.

Before the banked vegetation she made out a raised roadway that terminated in a long esplanade; on this she could just about see the tiny figures of Fahran workers, wielding scythes with which they cut away the encroaching vines.

Delia indicated the workers and asked Mahn if they would in time work to reveal the ship.

He shook his head and said in a reverential whisper, "No, not the ship itself. They keep the platform clear for Chalto's eventual Rising, when He will step forth and address the crowds."

They passed down the incline, moving amongst pilgrims who had already staked claim to their sleeping berths. Mahn indicated the swollen, luminescent pods on which the Fahran rested or slept; they grew on vines, like marrows, and gave of a heady scent which Delia found soporific.

High Priests in green robes passed through the crowd, ushering newly-arrived pilgrims to vacant haval plants. Rising from the ground at intervals of a few hundred metres, Delia made out short stone towers with arched doorways in their sides.

She pointed them out to Mahn and asked what they might be.

"The twelve holy towers," he explained. "The entrances to the system of underground labyrinths that give the Priests access to the platform before the ship."

They were approached by a green-robed Fahran who led them to a haval plant. Var settled herself alongside, while Mahn lay upon a bloated pod.

Delia sat down on a neighbouring pod; it gave beneath her weight, moulding itself to her shape, and only then, as she lay back and gazed up at the stars and wondered what the day ahead might bring, did she realise how tired she was.

She tried to contact Oma; the South African had said they would meet her here at the valley, but as ever there was no signal.

She was engulfed in a mist of spores released from the pod by her weight, and she turned her head with the intention of telling Mahn that she thought the spores were a sedative – but the Fahran was already fast asleep.

She smiled, and felt herself drifting off, and the last thing she saw was the glow of massed stars overhead.

She slept.

CHAPTER THIRTY-THREE

WHEN SHE AWOKE it was daylight, and the sun was high in the sky.

A strange calm had settled over the gathering in the valley. Delia heard the lilting, fluting tone of a single Fahran voice. She struggled upright on her pod, staring around at the faithful. They sat very still, staring at the closest stone tower.

Mahn moved to her side. "You have slept through the Address of the High Priests," he whispered. "You were sleeping so soundly, I thought it wise not to wake you. Now the Twelve story-tellers are recounting the tale of Chalto's Coming."

Delia looked around the valley. A red-robed Fahran stood on the summit of each tower, intoning the same story. The crowd listened, spellbound.

She ordered her Imp to translate the story-teller's words.

"... And then silence. Far to the north, in the city of Larahama, farmers had seen the bright light descending, and a party of them decided to investigate. They were led by the venerable Rohm, and their party numbered fifty. For hours they trekked through uncleared jungle, through mountain passes and across ravines..."

She listened as the story-teller told of how the farmers entered the valley and beheld, for the first time, Chalto's ship.

"And that is the end of the first story in the cycle," the story-teller intoned. "Next, the Meeting."

An excited twitter passed through the crowd. Mahn said, "There will be a break before the next story. You must be hungry."

He opened his bag and passed fruit and flat bread to Delia and Var. She ate and gazed around the valley; in the distance, the Fahran lost individual identity and became one vast sweep of blue, interspersed with the stone towers manned by the story-tellers.

"I don't see any other Vo," Var said.

"I think you might be the only one present, this time," Mahn said.

Delia tried to contact Oma, but still there was no signal.

"When Chalto Rises," Var said, "he will be so far away that we will have difficulty seeing him."

Delia stared across the valley to the enshrouded ship and the cleared stone platform before it. Chalto, when he appeared, would be a tiny figure hardly observable at this distance.

"It will be enough to see him from afar, and hear his words," Mahn said.

Delia was about to tell him that she might be able to enhance the experience, with the aid of her Implant, when she noticed a High Priest making his way through the crowd. He was still some distance away, but from the direction of his gaze Delia guessed that he was heading towards them.

Mahn had seen him too, and stood in readiness to greet the holy Fahran.

The High Priest, silver-haired and of great age, paused and looked from Mahn to Delia, and then to Var. "You are Mahn, Delia, and Var?"

Mahn stuttered a reply. "Yes... yes, we are. My companions have come far indeed."

The High Priest spread his hands. "Welcome to the valley of Mahkanda," he said. "If you would care to follow me."

He turned and moved off, and Mahn gave Delia a startled glance and followed. Var climbed to her feet and scuttled after them.

They moved through the crowd, the passage of three such disparate beings, led by a High Priest, arousing comment. She asked Imp to translate the twitterings.

"A Fahran, a Vo, and a giant together. Strange indeed."

"And in the company of a High Priest."

"I wonder where they are being taken."

"Might they have transgressed some Holy code?"

They were being led, it appeared towards the closest stone tower.

Mahn came alongside Delia and whispered, "But what might he want with us?" He was caught between excitement and agitation as he hopped along between Delia and Var.

"I think it might have something to do with Oma's earlier 'arrest'," she said.

"Are we too being arrested?"

"I think not."

They came to the tower, and the High Priest opened a timber door in the stone flank and stood back, ushering in first Delia, then Mahn and Var. Aware of the rising wave of comment from the Fahran around the tower, Delia passed into the dark shadow of the interior.

It was a moment before her vision adjusted and she could take in the curving stone walls and, directly before her, a flight of steps set into the stone-slabbed floor.

Mahn was dancing from foot to foot. "If I might, with all humility, ask why we have been brought here?"

The priest turned to him. "You will learn of that in time, little one. Suffice to say that this might – indeed will – turn out to be the most momentous day of your life."

And with this, the priest turned and led the way down the steps, issuing instructions that they were to follow.

Mahn gripped Delia's arm and said, "But what can he mean? The 'most momentous day' of my life?"

"I have a feeling," she said as she followed the priest down the steps, "that his pronouncement might go for all of us."

Var came last, having to turn sideways and skitter down the steps on one set of legs in order to negotiate the narrow gap. The passage opened out at the bottom, and all three were able to walk side by side, hurrying along after the holy Fahran.

Delia tried to reach Oma again, and this time got through.

Oma: *Sorry about the delay.*

Delia: *What's going on, Oma? Where the hell are you?*

Oma: *Not too far away, Delia. You're with Garan, the priest? You'll soon be with us.*

Delia: *Why all the secrecy? What's going on?*

Oma: *I'll explain everything soon, Delia. Everything.*

She cut the connection before Delia could demand an explanation.

The corridor was wide and low, the slabbed ceiling a matter of centimetres above her head. The corridor receded into the distance, diminishing in perspective. Flaming torches set in sconces lighted the way. Their footsteps rang as they hurried along, Var's claws clicking on the stone slabs.

Mahn clutched Delia's arm again and hissed, "Delia! The direction we are taking! I have worked it out. *We are heading towards Chalto's ship!*"

Delia smiled to herself. "I think you're right."

"But why? What is happening? Why are we being taken to... to...?"

"I think we'll find out soon enough."

Var said, "Perhaps this is a privilege accorded to special guests, human and Vo?"

"I have never heard of such before," Mahn said. "And why was Oma taken earlier? And where is she now?"

They seemed to have been walking for an age. At least, Delia thought, they were no longer in the direct sunlight; it was cool down here, despite the flaming torches.

"Look," Mahn said, pointing ahead.

The corridor terminated in a timber door similar to the one in the side of the tower. The High Priest paused before it, pulled a huge wooden key from his robes, and inserted it into the lock. He pushed open the double doors and ushered them inside.

They entered a short corridor and soon came to a flight of steps.

"We must be in another tower," Var said. "I think, as special guests, we have been brought here so that we will have a better view of Chalto when he awakens!"

Mahn turned wide eyes on the Vo. "Perhaps you're right," he said. "Oh, I never dreamed..." and he fell silent as words failed him.

They climbed the steps, the flight wider this time so that Var was not compelled to turn herself edge-on. The stairway seemed to go on for ever, and at one point Mahn whispered, "We are in no tower, Delia, or we would have reached the top by now!"

"Then where are we?" Var asked.

They climbed on. The steps were small, made for Fahran feet, and Delia's thigh muscles were soon aching from the unaccustomed exertion.

Ahead, the old priest climbed with methodical stoicism, his head bobbing with every step.

Just as Delia was wondering if they would ever reach the top, she made out an increasingly bright source of light in the distance.

Mahn said excitedly, "We're coming to the end!"

The light brightened and the heat increased. The steps widened and emerged onto a wide stone platform, and Delia realised where they were. Ahead, across the esplanade, was the wall of vines and creepers that cocooned Chalto's ship.

They stepped into the bright sunlight and looked about them in wonder.

Delia turned, rocked by the sight of a hundred thousand Fahran faces turned up towards her. Seen from this elevation, the valley seemed even longer and wider, a vast amphitheatre filled with expectant alien pilgrims.

She watched Mahn, who seemed about to swoon in religious euphoria at the turn of events. He rushed forwards, towards the bank of vines enclosing the ship, then turned and approached the balustrade and stared down on the massed ranks of the faithful. Var was at his side, sharing his wonder in silence.

Delia heard the voices of the story-tellers drift across the valley, their words a mere susurrus at this distance as they told the tale of events enacted here almost three hundred Terran years ago.

Delia felt soft fingers on her arm. The High Priest gestured across the esplanade, and Delia turned and stared.

Oma, a small figure twenty metres away, smiled and raised a hand in greeting.

Delia swallowed, her heart thumping, and approached the South African.

"What the hell," she said, as she took the woman in a tight embrace, "is going on here?"

CHAPTER THIRTY-FOUR

OMA TOOK DELIA'S hand and led her across the esplanade to a bench under an awning of creepers, out of the sunlight and away from the staring eyes of the massed Fahran pilgrims.

Delia looked across at Mahn and Var; they were absorbed in the wonder of the moment, exchanging awed comments and waving down at the pilgrims.

"I have a lot to explain," Oma said, "and I apologise for the secrecy. I was thinking of you. I... I didn't want to shock you with my half-baked theories. I might have been wrong, very wrong. I had to make sure."

"Oma." Delia squeezed her hand. "You're not making much sense, to be honest."

"I'm sorry. It's hard to order my thoughts, present the events in an orderly, logical way. You can't imagine how I felt. At one point I honestly thought I was going mad."

"Oma?"

The woman laughed. "Okay, it was back at Khalamb, on the summit of the zig. When I relieved you in the seat of the super-weapon and looked at the control array..."

"Go on."

"I saw something."

Delia stared at her. "I wondered why you hesitated. But...?"

"I think you'd better look at this. That way you'll see it from my perspective."

Oma sub-vocced a command to her Imp, and an image sprang into the air before the women.

"I had my Imp record this," Oma said.

The moving image was hazy, jerky, and showed the control array of the Skelt weapon. "I don't know what I was expecting," she said, "but it wasn't a command console laid out and configured for use by a five-digit hand. The Skelt have four long, multi-articulated fingers. Didn't it strike you as odd?"

Delia shrugged, squinting at the grainy image dancing before her. "I... I don't know. In the heat of the battle..."

Oma froze the image, showing a section of the command console. She pointed. "When I saw this, I really thought I'd lost it."

"What?" Delia said, peering. "I don't see –"

Oma indicated the top right of the image. "There."

Delia leaned forward, and could just make out in the shadows the beginning of a line of letters. A word.

She turned to Oma, swallowed. "No wonder you thought you were going mad."

Oma smiled. "I had my Imp enhance the image, clean it up. This is the result."

The scene changed, zoomed in on the word, which became sharper, more focused.

"What do you see?" Oma asked.

Delia read: "*Fabriqué*..."

Oma nodded. "That's what I read, too, up there surrounded by hostile Skelt, on an alien world Christ knows how many light years from Earth."

Delia's heartbeat thundered in her head; she felt dizzy. "It's impossible."

Oma rocked her head from side to side. "That's what I thought. Later I squirted the image to Jav, along with images of the weapon, and asked him to look into it."

"And?"

"He got back to me during the night when we were being carried away by the yarm."

"And?" Delia said again, feeling faint.

"And Jav raided the shuttle's core cache and came up with the goods. The ground-to-air missile was a Rapier Mk IIa, *fabriqué en l'Union européenne*, way back in 2095."

Delia found Oma's hand and squeezed, speechless for the moment.

"So you see why I was so circumspect with you, when you overheard my conversation with Jav on the riverboat? I didn't want to get your hopes up. I mean..." She shrugged. "What if I were wrong? That's why, later, I wanted you to squirt me the images of the icon at Larahama, so I could compare it and see if I was right."

Delia nodded. "About?" she asked, though she knew full well what about.

"About," Oma said, "Chalto's ship."

Delia screwed her eyes tight shut, shook her head as if emerging from water, and stared at the South African. She felt dizzy. She gestured to the vine-covered bulk to her left and whispered, "It's from Earth, isn't it?"

Oma said, "I had Jav go through the shuttle's core, checking the history records. He got back to me while you were sleeping on the boat."

"And?"

"The ESO ship *Orpheus* was just the third starship to test the then-nascent quantum lattice wormhole technology. In May 2107 it passed through the lattice... and something went wrong. No one knows what. It was lost with all hands. The scientists back home didn't even know where in the galaxy it might have ended up – they couldn't even begin a search. The loss was hushed up at the time, the quantum lattice tech overhauled. Five years later the wormhole programme recommenced, and there wasn't another starship fatality until the *Amsterdam*."

Delia held her head in her hands. "I don't believe this." She couldn't stop her tears.

Oma put an arm around Delia's shoulders. "I had Jav look into the personnel records of the *Orpheus*, and he came up with the goods. The second officer aboard the starship was one Edward Charlton, an African American physicist born in Boston but a naturalised EU citizen."

"Charlton?" Delia said in a hush voice, "*Chalto?*"

Oma nodded. "Chalto," she said.

"Oh, my God!"

Oma laughed. "You can say that again, girl! So you see why those High Priests back at Larahama were in such a tizz when they saw me, why they whisked me off for questioning?"

"I wondered at the time, why you and not me?"

"Because I am the same colour as their god, Delia. You might have been the same shape, but I was the same shape *and* the same colour."

"What happened? I mean, when the High Priests questioned you? What the hell did you tell them?"

"I told them the truth, that I was from Earth, as was their god, Chalto. I realised I might have been making a mistake as soon as I opened my mouth. I mean, what if Charlton was stringing them along – what if he really was into playing the role of their god, and hadn't told them of his origins?"

"And?"

"And I needn't have worried. They knew he was from a world called Earth, a place they considered mythical. You know the rest."

Delia looked up, wondering how many more shocks she was in for as she realised something. She stared at Oma. "The Rising?" she said. "My God, the Rising..."

"Those early starships," Oma said, "were equipped with the first suspended animation capsules, mainly for any medical emergencies they might encounter out there amongst the stars which they couldn't deal with immediately. So imagine the situation here. The *Orpheus* crash-landed and the spacers find themselves on Valinda, caught in a conflict between the peaceable Fahran and the Skelt. They take sides – they even install a great laser in the Fahran city of Khalamb. But, as the Fahran stories tell, most of them fell at the siege of Larahama."

"And the others?" Hope clutched her heart. "That's another reason you didn't want to get my hopes up, wasn't it? There were other survivors, who used the suspension capsules?"

If there were other survivors, then she, Oma and Javinder were not alone on Valinda – they were not the only human beings here. They might set up a community, a like-minded, human colony.

But Oma was shaking her head. "There were no survivors, other than Edward Charlton. The High Priests told me that there were many fatalities when the *Orpheus* crash-landed, and many crew succumbed to their injuries. More than a dozen contracted diseases and perished – and the Skelt accounted for over a hundred, leaving just Charlton."

"So..." Delia shook her head, trying to put herself in the place of Second Officer Edward Charlton. "The poor man found himself all alone on an alien world, the only human being among the Fahran and the Skelt. Christ, I know how he must have felt. For a while back there, before I met you and Jav..." She recalled her desolation, the soul-destroying notion of the loneliness she would have to bear for years and years to come. "The poor, poor man. And he wouldn't even have had the consolation of an Implant."

"So Charlton took the option to suspend himself," Oma said. "Winter was approaching, and he really didn't want to spend ten years underground with an alien race, so he suspended himself for that long, but not before setting up a primitive distress beacon."

"A beacon?"

"I've been in long conversation with Jav about this, and he has a pet theory – nothing more, at this stage – that it was Charlton's quantum beacon that set up some kind of sympathetic gluon fold-in resonance with the Lunar quantum lattice just as it was bombarded by the plasma blast from the *Amsterdam*."

"Which resulted in the front end of the *Amsterdam* being shunted all the way out here?"

Oma nodded. "That's Jav's working hypothesis. But as I said, it's just a theory at the moment."

Delia felt excitement bubbling in her chest. "Hell, the look on Edward Charlton's face when we walk in." She looked at Oma. "You haven't already met him, have you?"

The South African shook her head. "He's being revived as we speak. Garan, the High Priest who brought you here, told me that Chalto was being readied for his speech."

"But this religion... how did that come about? Was it Charlton's doing?"

"I doubt it. The way I see it is this. The Fahran were so grateful to Charlton and his 'disciples' for fighting with them against the Skelt, and bequeathing the Fahran weapons, primitive though they were, that when Charlton suspended himself, programmed the capsule to reawaken him in ten years time, at winter's end... Well, the Fahran must have seen it as some kind of miracle, and the religion, the High Priests, the Shrine at Larahama, the Twelve Story-Tellers and everything else, just grew naturally over three hundred years."

"And they aren't at all put out to find that their God is a mere mortal?"

Oma frowned. "If you want my opinion, the priesthood knew that all along. Much can evolve in three hundred years – facts can takes on the stuff of myth and become embroidered with all manner of fantastic apocrypha. But as I see it, we humans – with our advanced science and technology – are seen as some kind of super-beings. The Fahran are beside themselves at the thought of our presence amongst them. I bet they're scheming right now – if these priests are anything like their Terran counterparts – as to how our arrival might benefit them in their fight against the Skelt. It can only be advantageous to their cause, as they see it."

"We might be able to help them, work with the Fahran to defend themselves, maybe even fight back."

Oma hesitated. "Delia, there's something else I haven't told you, but maybe that can wait till we've met Edward Charlton and discussed events with him, okay?"

"You really like to make a drama out of things, don't you?"

"Well, this is certainly the stuff of drama, isn't it?"

Delia looked across the esplanade to where Mahn and Var were staring down at the massed Fahran. Garan the High Priest was beside them, explaining something. She shook her head. "Look at them – they're like kids at a fair. All this – being allowed up here, so close to the ship... it's exceeded Mahn's expectations already. Wait till we tell him about Chalto. Wait until he realises that soon he'll meet his God."

Oma looked at her. "How do you think he'll take it?"

"It might be too much for him. He was beside himself at the thought of witnessing the Rising from afar, and hearing Chalto's pronouncements. How might he react when he actually meets Chalto?"

"And comes to the understanding that his friends, you and me and Jav, are of the same species as his God?"

Delia said, "Or that his God is merely human."

She looked across the esplanade, to a stone archway set into the banked vines covering the starship, as three Fahran priests emerged and crossed to the High Priest. They conferred, looking up from time to time and gesturing across to where Delia and Oma were sitting, and then Garan left them and crossed to the women.

He bowed his head reverentially to Oma. "Chalto is awakened, and prepared. We have informed him, as you instructed, that there are petitioners who require an audience."

Delia glanced at Oma. "Petitioners?" she smiled.

"Well, I didn't want to give the game away too soon."

They stood. Delia indicated Mahn and Var, who had turned from the balustrade and were watching Delia and Oma's meeting with the priest. "I would like my friends, Mahn and Var, to accompany us."

"They will be welcome," Garan said.

Delia beckoned to them, and the tiny Fahran, dwarfed by the black bulk of the Vo, hurried across the esplanade.

"But Delia!" Mahn gabbled, staring up at her with his massive eyes. "This is a miracle beyond my greatest dreams!"

"It is?"

"To be allowed upon the Holy Esplanade, so close to the ship itself..." He gazed at the vine-shrouded bulk in wonder. "Do you think, Delia, that I might be allowed to touch the skin of the ship itself?"

Delia frowned and turned to Oma. "What do you think, Oma? Would Chalto mind if Mahn the Fahran touched the ship itself?"

"Well..." Oma temporised – and Mahn stared at her, moving from foot to foot in anticipation – "why don't we go one better than that, and let Mahn and Var enter the ship?"

"Enter the ship?" Mahn echoed, incredulous.

"Not only enter the ship," Delia said, "but how about meeting Chalto?"

Mahn gasped and swayed. "Meet my God?"

Delia reached out and placed an arm around Mahn's shoulder, steadying him.

"Let's do that," she murmured, and they followed the High Priest across the esplanade and through the stone archway.

CHAPTER THIRTY-FIVE

THEY PASSED BENEATH the ancient stone arch, through the tended vines, and into a bright atrium that Delia recognised, with a nostalgic catch in her throat, as the hold of an old European starship.

Mahn looked around in wonder. "I am *inside* the holy ship," he breathed. "But will I *really* be allowed to meet Chalto?"

"Of course – a small repayment for all you have done for me." She hesitated. "You see, Mahn, Chalto is human."

He stopped and stared at her. "Human? Like you and Oma and Javinder?"

She stared at the alien, wondering at the thought processes going on behind those huge eyes. How might he take this demotion of the being he had thought, until now, as a deity?

She said, "He came from Earth, almost three hundred of our years ago, and crash-landed on Valinda. I've only just found out myself, from Oma. I'm as shocked as you are."

"And I will meet him," he said in a tiny voice.

The High Priest led the way across the vast hold to the triangular entrance of an elevator. Var danced along, her eyestalks waving. "A starship!" she sang. "But will we be able to take off and travel amongst the bright stars, Delia?"

She smiled and pointed up to the high, vaulted ceiling, to where a lateral rent let in a fall of vines and creepers. "The starship was damaged, probably before it crashed here. There is no way it can fly now, broken-backed."

"Which is why Chalto never left my planet," Mahn mused.

They shuffled into the lift and the High priest touched the controls. They were whisked upwards. Mahn cried, "What is this? A small room that moves?"

"It is called an elevator," Delia said. "It takes us to another, higher part of the starship."

"A miracle," he said.

The elevator bobbed to a halt and the doors slid open. The High Priest led the way down a long, wide corridor, illuminated by concealed lighting activated by their approach and dimming as they passed.

Delia felt a tight pressure in her chest at the thought of meeting Edward Charlton, and anticipated his reaction when he realised that he was no longer alone on Valinda.

She was about to meet a man born on Earth over three hundred years ago – a man from another time, another era. History was not her forte: what had life been like, back then? She had a dim recollection of the world being divided between competing, and warring, power blocs, of states divided by religious and ideological differences; it was a miracle, she thought, that Europe and China had formed, eventually, into a federated state and initiated an ambitious space programme in order to reach for the stars. The ill-fated flight of the *Orpheus*, nearly three hundred years ago, had been one of ESO's first forays into the vast galaxy.

So much had happened since then, and Second Officer Edward Charlton, revered God of Valinda, would want to know all about it.

They arrived at last at another triangular doorway. The priest turned and spoke. "This is called the Bridge, my friends; it is the holiest of holy sanctums on the ship. It is Chalto's especial resting place. Please enter in silence, and allow Chalto to speak first."

Delia placed an arm around Mahn's shoulders. The Fahran raised a long-fingered hand to his mouth in what struck her as a very human gesture of awe.

The priest touched a control panel and the door slid open.

The bridge was a great open space, banked like an amphitheatre, with raked seats where technicians and flight-controllers had sat at their consoles. Straight ahead was a long, wraparound viewscreen, showing only a dense wall of jungle now.

In pride of position, in the centre of the bridge, the Captain's swivel chair faced the viewscreen.

Without turning his seat, Edward Charlton spoke. "Very well, Garan, who are these people? I'll see them briefly, and then we'll get on with it." He spoke in strangely accented English, his voice deep-timbred, almost gruff. His translation device issued the fluting Fahran approximation of his words.

The High Priest stepped forward. "Your guests, Chalto," he intoned.

Charlton swivelled his chair and stared across the bridge at the little group.

Mahn slipped from beneath Delia's arm and fell to the floor in a dead faint, quickly attended to by Garan and Var.

Delia and Oma stepped forward until they were standing three metres before Edward Charlton.

He was a big-boned man in his fifties, with a thin face and grey curls and a look in his eyes that spoke of years of loneliness, of hope deferred. He stared at the women without the slightest flicker of emotion, his brown eyes intent first on Delia, and then Oma.

He swallowed, clearly searching for his words.

At last he said, "You've come."

Delia found her hand moving in an involuntary salute, deferring to his rank. "Dr Cordelia Kemp," she said, "Medical Officer, the ESO ship *Pride of Amsterdam*, sir."

Oma followed suit. "Oma Massinga, Pilot First Grade, also of the *Amsterdam*, sir."

His hands gripped the arms of his seat. "How long?" he said in barely a whisper, then answered his own question. "Almost three hundred years, right?"

"Two hundred and ninety-eight, sir," Oma said.

"And..." His eyes narrowed in calculation. "Help me out. What's the date back on Earth?"

Delia said, "2405, sir."

"Three hundred years, give or take..." he said. "I never thought it'd happen. I dreamed, of course. But I was realistic. I knew the chances were slim, even with the beacon. I'd long ago reconciled myself to what I had here, amongst these good people." He smiled, and the expression illuminated his craggy features. "And before you think me an ego-maniac who relished the godhood these people conferred on me... let me tell you that my suspension and reawakening began as a survival tactic. I thought I was losing my mind, in the early years after... after I lost my crew. We fought a great battle with an alien race called the Skelt."

Oma said, "We know all about the Skelt, and the battle at Larahama, sir."

"Then you'll know I was the sole survivor. Can you imagine that? I lost friends and colleagues in the initial crash-landing, then to disease, and finally to the Skelt. I thought I'd go mad with the loneliness, the terrible isolation. It was like..." His face crumpled as he sought a comparison. "It was very much like a feeling of claustrophobia, a despair that crushed me, took the breath from my body and robbed me of hope. So..."

He gestured across the bridge to where a suspension capsule stood like an ancient catafalque. "So I took refuge in that, programmed it to awake me at winter's end every ten years. After the second awakening, when I learned how the Fahran fight with the Skelt was going, and briefed them on what they might do, I found that I was attended by a priesthood, and that crowds had come to listen to my words, and as the decades progressed, so did their veneration of me. None of it, I hasten to add, of my doing. I suppose it gave the Fahran hope." He smiled. "I spoke of a time when I would be joined by my kind – when your coming would free Valinda, at last, of the scourge of the Skelt."

Delia said, "I was informed that you said this time would be special."

Edward Charlton smiled. "A fabrication of the priesthood," he said.

"And that the priests are in mind-contact with you...?"

He laughed. "That, also."

Delia smiled. "I thought so."

Charlton shook his head again, sadly. "Of course, all that seems such a short time ago, subjectively – since the siege at Larahama, when Captain Rossetti died in my arms. She was a brave woman, and a great leader. She would have made a far better godhead than myself. My grief... I think I was a little in love with her, you know? So in my grief and loneliness I slept for ten years, coming awake every decade for just a few days. It seems so short a time ago, and now this, you've come, salvation." He raised his head and smiled. "I'm sorry. I'm babbling. I have so much to tell you, and so much to learn, as well. Your starship – what did you call it, the *Pride of Amsterdam?* Hell, but the technology must have advanced so much in nearly three hundred years. And Earth, planet Earth... Oh, how I dreamed. It was a war-torn place, three hundred years ago. I saw the stars as our salvation, the place where we might start again, wipe the slate clean, build utopia. All nonsense, of course. The human race takes with it the seeds of its own raging conflicts. But tell me, what of Earth? The conflict between the US and China? Tell me!"

Oma smiled. "Resolved long ago, sir. The US is now a united state comprising Canada, old America and South America. China and Europe are one great nation."

"But there must be conflict?"

"A little, here and there, small nations wanting independence," Oma said, "but humankind's diaspora to the stars has defused the territorial land-grab mentality of rapacious nations and greedy politicians. We have settled over fifty planets along the arm in the last hundred years."

"Fifty planets?" Charlton shook his head. "And terrorism, the religious fundamentalists?"

"Quashed," Delia said, "though small-scale trouble raises its ugly head from time to time."

"I never thought I'd see the day," he whispered to himself. "Of course, I'll be an anachronism, back home. A man from the past. A museum piece. But I think I can live with that."

Delia glanced at Oma, who nodded minimally and said, "Sir, I'm sorry. We should have made it clear, earlier. We, too, crash-landed on Valinda." And as Oma talked him through the explosion aboard the *Amsterdam* and the subsequent events, Delia saw the light of hope die in Edward Charlton's eyes.

He sat forward when Oma finished. "But they'll send a search party? Earth will institute a rescue mission?"

"According to my Imp, sir, that would be impossible."

Charlton shook his head. "Your 'Imp'? And what, might I ask, is an Imp?"

He hailed from three hundred years ago, Delia reminded herself; from a time before cerebral integrated augmentation was *de rigueur*. She touched the raised ridge at her temple and said, "My implant, a nano-AI system wired into my cortex. We all have them, now."

He stared in wonder. "Of course, the technology was in its early stage back in my day," he said. "But I, personally, never thought it would get off the ground." He shook his head. "So... no rescue mission from Earth?"

"I'm afraid not, sir," Delia wondered whether to mention the shuttle and its possible space-worthiness, but elected to leave that until later. What point would there be in raising his hope with talk of a shuttle that could escape Valinda but go no further?

"Very well." He stared past the women to where the priest and Var were assisting Mahn to his feet. "Well, you don't know how good it is to be amongst friendly, human faces. We'll just have to make the most of it here, won't we? Be grateful that we have each other." He smiled. "And the first thing I'll do is mothball that damned thing." He pointed to the suspension capsule. "And live the life of a normal human being, not a damned god. We can make the lives of the Fahran better, between us. Sort out the scourge of the Skelt. In the early days we taught the Fahran how to manufacture weapons. Primitive stuff. I was loath to give them anything more sophisticated, lest it fell into the hands of the Skelt."

He stopped, a worried expression clouding his features. "They're out there, you know," he said in almost a whisper. "The Skelt, with their starships and weapons. This lot" – he waved –"the local Skelt are nothing, devolved savages. It's the star-faring Skelt we ought to be worried about. You see, sooner or later they'll come into contact with Earth and those colonies."

The High Priest moved from Var and Mahn, crossed to where Edward Charlton sat, enthroned, and whispered to him. Charlton replied, then said to Delia and Oma, "I'm afraid duty calls, my friends. A god," and he smiled ironically, "must serve his faithful." He stood, towering over the Fahran priest. "And I have a lot to tell the pilgrims, this time. That it is the end of an era, but the start of another. That my compatriots have at last arrived on Valinda, and that from now on we will work tirelessly to vanquish the scourge of the Skelt."

Behind Delia, Mahn stood beside Var. Hesitantly they joined Delia and Oma, Mahn staring up wordlessly at his god.

Delia said, "May I introduce Mahn and Var, whose courage and loyalty has helped Oma, Javinder and myself since our arrival on Valinda."

Charlton smiled, reached out and touched Mahn's shoulder, then Var's bulbous right claw. "I am honoured to know such brave beings," he said with touching humility, "and I will be even more honoured if you would accompany me to the esplanade and listen to my pronouncement."

Mahn found his tongue. "It would be a privilege," he stammered.

Charlton swept from the bridge, leading the way.

Delia made to follow, but felt Oma's restraining hand on her arm. "Delia, we'll stay here."

"Don't you want to...?" She indicated the departing group.

Oma shook her head. "We need to talk."

CHAPTER THIRTY-SIX

"YOU SAID THERE was something you hadn't told me," Delia said. "Should I be worried?"

Oma smiled. "I need to summon Jav and have him in on this."

She closed her eyes briefly, communing with her Imp. Almost instantly, Javinder's image flashed into life before them. He looked out, smiling. He was sitting in the shuttle's command chair, swivelling back and forth and looking pleased with himself.

"Good news?" Oma asked.

"The shuttle's up and running, Oma. The auxiliary's good for a planetary jump, but the main drive's still dysfunctional. I should be with you in about five hours."

"Excellent," she said. "Look, I'll route the visuals through my viewpoint."

Jav leaned forward, staring. "Hey, you're in the ship!"

Oma recounted their meeting with Edward Charlton.

"You were right all along," Javinder said to Oma, then glanced at Delia. "I hope you're not too upset about our keeping it from you?"

"I understand," she said. "I don't really mind being thought neurotic and unstable, you know?"

Oma cleared her throat. "There's still something I haven't told Delia yet," she said to the Indian.

Javinder opened his mouth in a silent, "Ah," and smiled. "Well, I suggest you take us through to the smartcore nexus and we'll see what the situation is."

Delia stared at Oma. "What?"

The South African smiled, and said to Javinder, "You've accessed the *Orpheus*'s schematics, Jav?"

"I have them here," Javinder said. "Take the elevator and you'll find the smartware nexus on the level below the bridge."

Delia followed Oma and took the elevator down to the next level, wondering what surprise might lie in store for her now.

The lift halted and the doors swished open. They stepped out and Javinder, his seated image bobbing before them, said, "Along the corridor."

They passed down a narrow corridor so stark and functional Delia guessed that few crew members had ever come this way, even when the *Orpheus* had been fully operational.

"Just where are we going?"

Oma said, "As Jav said, the smartcore nexus. It's in the nose cone of the ship."

They came to a sliding door, waited until it opened, and stepped through.

Delia looked around in amazement. She had expected a continuation of the corridor, a stark, girdered, functional space given over to ugly information cores never meant to see the light of day.

The reality, however, was very different. It was as if she were standing at the end of a narrowing funnel spun from spars of delicate crystal. A catwalk stretched ahead, diminishing in perspective. Globules of what looked like old-fashioned gelware hung between the glittering, crystalline spars; bottle green and brown, its biological appearance contrasted with the sparkling nexus of the crystal.

Oma turned in a slow circle, giving Javinder a comprehensive view. She waited, then said, "So, what do you think?"

"My God," he whispered. "It looks pretty much complete to me, Oma. Of course, you'll have to check with Charlton."

"I'll do that," Oma said.

"Would you mind," Delia said, "telling me what's going on here?"

Oma smiled, then said to Javinder. "You or me, Jav?"

The Indian smiled and raised a hand. "Be my guest."

"Hokay," Oma said. She paced along the catwalk, Delia following her. "The *Orpheus* was an early, experimental starship, Delia. Or rather the technology it carried was experimental. Quantum lattice tech was in its early stages. The scientists back then didn't have the knowledge to build free-floating lattices as vast as they're able to do now – this was three hundred years ago, remember. They tried, but the webs were too flimsy for the huge amounts of energy they were required to channel: they exploded, or imploded, with spectacular results. So they decide to work on much smaller scales. The idea behind the original quantum lattices was that they'd leach energy from a nearby star sufficient to keep a wormhole open for minutes, and so allow the transit of multiple exploration ships. When this failed, they looked into opening wormholes for seconds only – ten or twenty at the very most – allowing the passage of one ship at a time." She stared around her and smiled. "This, Delia, is what they came up with, a small-scale lattice carried and used by one starship only."

Delia leaned against a rail, following through the implications of what Oma was telling her.

"How it worked," Oma went on, "was that a ship, the *Orpheus* in this case, channelled vast amounts of energy for seconds only and this" – she gestured at the crystal funnel – "projected a wormhole portal into space a matter of kilometres before the ship which, seconds later, made the transit to its destination. It worked, though the tech was unstable – a case in point being the *Orpheus*, which due to a shunt anomaly ended up all the way out here."

Delia shook her head. "So you're saying...?"

Javinder took over. "We're saying, Delia, that if this rig is in full working order, and if we can decouple it from the *Orpheus* and jerry-rig it to the front-end of the shuttle, and of course if we can cannibalise the requisite part from your life-raft at Alkellion, then we *might*, just might, get ourselves back to Earth."

"But that," Oma said, "is a lot of ifs."

Delia felt faint. She tried not to allow herself to hope.

Javinder went on, "Unfortunately for Charlton, the *Orpheus* was irreparably damaged when it came down on Valinda, otherwise he might have been able to patch things up, get back into orbit and make the transit – if the lattice was working, of course."

Delia looked at the Indian. "And what do you think the chances are of the lattice functioning as required?"

Javinder tipped his head back and forth. "I'll have a better idea of that once I've spoken to Charlton. Then, of course, there's the nuts and bolts engineering of getting the rig fixed to the shuttle – though with the help of a hundred eager Fahran, I'm sure we'll manage."

"But we have to find your life-raft, and its ion-exchange unit, to make any of this achievable," Oma said.

Delia took a deep breath. "Well, I hope the Skelt have vacated Alkellion, and left the life-raft where it was."

"I have your co-ordinates," Javinder said. "I'll give the auxiliaries a test burn, and I reckon I'll be with you by noon."

He cut the connection and his image vanished.

"Shall we return to the esplanade and see how Chalto is wooing the masses?" Oma said. "And then tell him there's an outside chance that he'll yet see planet Earth?"

Still dazed, Delia followed the South African. They left the smartcore nexus and took the elevator to the cavernous hold, then passed through the archway onto the esplanade.

Edward Charlton stood on a raised dais at the front of the concourse, addressing his followers. The priesthood had rigged up a speaker system from the *Orpheus*, and Charlton's translation device – an external unit clipped to the lapel of his uniform – relayed his words in Fahranese out across the valley.

Mahn and Var stood to one side, staring up in awed silence as Charlton's words rang out.

Delia and Oma crossed to where they stood, and Delia placed a hand on Mahn's shoulder. He looked up at her, tears filling his huge eyes.

"And a time of change has come to Valinda," Charlton was saying. "The time I prophesied has come to pass. I have been joined by more of my kind, beings from the stars beyond – and with their help, and the hard work and faith of the Fahran, we will enter an age of peace for all Valinda, a time of peace between the races, though first we must deal with the Skelt. And this will be no easy undertaking; there will be days and weeks and months of hardship, and sacrifice, but I vow that I will do all within my power to aid the Fahran in the long fight against your oppressors."

A strange sound welled up from the watching crowd, a sigh like a tidal wave, a mass exhalation of approval and hope.

Charlton went on. "The time of change starts now, for unlike on earlier occasions when I have returned to the ship to sleep the winter out, that is no more. From now on I will remain awake, and active, and I will come among you – me and my kind – and instruct you in the way forward."

A ragged fluting came from the audience, a Fahranese cheer, and Mahn shook his head in wonder.

"There will follow a day of rest, and then I will come here again and make a further pronouncement, and then I exhort you to go among your people and spread the word, that Chalto has Risen, and that the time to fight against Skelt oppression is drawing close."

He turned to his right and left, and raised a hand, and a whispering cheer greeted his words as he stepped down from the dais and crossed to where Delia and the others stood.

He wiped sweat from his brow, then smiled and hugged first Oma, and then Delia – a god made very human by the simplicity of the heartfelt gesture.

"And now the hard work begins," he said. "We need to talk, to plan the way ahead. I'd value your opinion."

Delia glanced at Oma, who gestured for her to go ahead.

"There have been developments," Delia said. "Our engineer, Javinder, has examined the *Orpheus*'s quantum lattice, and there is a chance that we might be able to utilise it on our shuttle."

Charlton looked from Delia to Oma, and back to Delia, his eyes wide. He shook his head. "But... but I thought you said you were stranded here?"

"We thought we were," Oma said, "before we learned of the lattice."

"You see," Delia went on, "our shuttle was disabled, but Javinder has managed to repair its auxiliary drives. And if we can couple the lattice to the shuttle..."

Mahn looked up at her. He gripped her hand. "You mean that you might, after all, be able to return to Earth?"

Delia smiled. "Perhaps. It is a long-shot, with many hurdles in the way. But I promise you that, if we do return to Earth, then we'll be back to help your people in their struggle."

"But perhaps," Mahn said, his tone awed, "perhaps we – Var and myself – perhaps we could journey with you to the stars?"

Charlton reached out and touched the Fahran's shoulder. "If it is achievable," he said, "if we can indeed return to Earth... I could think of no more suitable travelling companions than yourselves."

Oma said, injecting a note of caution, "Of course, before then, there's the small matter of retrieving the requisite part from the life-raft at Alkellion."

CHAPTER THIRTY-SEVEN

Delia stood before the shuttle's viewscreen and stared out at the alien city.

The northern fastness of Alkellion had undergone a dramatic transformation since Delia and Mahn had escaped the clutches of the Skelt. Where just two weeks ago the city had been gripped by ice, surrounded by vast plains of tundra, its soaring architecture coated in frozen slabs which had added a frigid grandeur to the place, now the ice had melted with the onslaught of summer. The city was revealed as more ethereal than Delia recalled, the towers slighter and more delicate. All around, the plains were brilliant with a carpet of multi-coloured plant-life, and tenacious tendrils and vines were creeping up the foothills and the ramparts of the city itself.

Seen from the elevation of the approaching shuttle, the city appeared deserted.

Oma, jacked into the pilot's sling, guided the ship over the pit of Vo bones through which Delia and Mahn had fled, what seemed a lifetime ago now.

The city lay straight ahead, silhouetted against the fiery ball of the rising sun. Delia saw no movement on the approach roads rising like ramparts, and none on the narrow streets between the rearing buildings.

Mahn and Var stood beside her as the shuttle powered slowly over the pit.

Var stared down, her eyestalks rigid. "I've heard terrible stories of what the Skelt did to my people," she said. "I heard that we were enslaved, that the Skelt used us as pack animals, and sacrificed the weakest and the lame when we had come to the end of our usefulness. But, to be honest, I never really believed these stories..."

They stared down at the vast pit piled with its macabre collection of chitin, and the stone pier projecting out into this charnel sea, where the Skelt guards had brought the weakened Vo and despatched them, slicing off legs and pincers and eyestalks and pitching the pieces to their final resting place.

"Until now," Var finished.

Mahn said, "The deaths of all your people, the enslavement of your race and the subjugation of mine, will be avenged in time, my friend. As Chalto said, the time of change is here."

Javinder sat cross-legged on the deck, his occipital implant jacked into a diagnostic readout as he monitored the drive. He looked up and smiled at Delia. "Running smooth," he said.

Edward Charlton stood beside Delia; he had broken out a store of weapons held in the *Orpheus*, and they were armed with laser rifles and stun grenades. To the rear of the bridge, a dozen hand-picked Fahran guards chattered excitedly amongst themselves; Charlton had distributed the lasers before lift-off and instructed the aliens in their use.

"I know you said that the Skelt vacate the city in high summer," Charlton said to Delia, "but I must admit that a part of me is itching for a fight."

"We might have one yet," she said. "The city may be deserted, but the Skelt might have taken the life-raft with them. The difficulty, then, will be tracing it."

Mahn said, "The catacombs and caverns beneath Alkellion are vast and limitless. We could be searching them for days."

"But surely the Skelt can't have gone far, dragging the life-raft with them," Charlton said.

"They used a captive Vo to drag the raft to the city, from where we came down on the plain," Delia said. "They'll have used the same method to transport it underground. The thing is, how long ago did they set off, and how will we trace them?"

"Of course," Oma said from her sling, "they might have left the raft where it was."

"They intended to move it from a temporary garage to what they called a machine shop, on the day Mahn and I escaped," Delia said. "Fortunately, Mahn knows the location of the machine shop."

The Fahran looked up at Charlton, timidly, still in awe of his god. "I was taken by the Skelt and forced to work as an interpreter," he explained. "The Skelt used hundreds of my people as slaves in the city, and rather than learn our language they used interpreters."

"Your story of how you and Delia escaped from the Skelt and fled Alkellion will be told to the Twelve Story-Tellers," Charlton promised, "and disseminated far and wide across the face of Valinda. It did, after all, bring about what we are doing now."

Weak at the knees upon this pronouncement, and speechless, Mahn settled himself on the floor beside Javinder and stared up at Charlton in silence.

They left the grave pit in their wake and came in over the city, hovering. Delia peered down, pointing out the wide boulevard, clear of ice now, along which she had approached the city two weeks ago. "And beside that tall building, like a cathedral, is a square where we can land. The temporary hangar is nearby."

Mahn climbed to his feet and joined her, peering down. "And the machine shop is a little way off along a street that leads towards the Vo pit."

"Here goes," Oma said, and closed her eyes.

Delia noticed Charlton, watching Oma with an amazed expression. Technology had progressed exponentially in three hundred years, and gone was the hands-on approach to piloting. Oma, her cortex integrated with the shuttle's logic matrix, controlled its flight with the power of her mind alone. Delia could see the realisation, in Charlton's eyes, that the next few months would be a steep learning curve as he sought to understand the scientific advances that had outstripped his limited knowledge.

The pitch of the shuttle's auxiliary drive diminished as Oma turned the ship on its axis and brought it down between the buildings.

The craft settled on its ramrod landing legs and Oma cut the drive.

Charlton, as agreed before lift-off, took command. "We'll proceed with caution," he said. "The guard will alight first, secure the square and signal when the way is clear."

The Fahran guard came to attention, fingering their new weapons. Oma lowered the ramp and Delia watched as the Fahran moved circumspectly from the ship and fanned out across the square.

She scanned the buildings. They appeared very different, now. She had only seen them before in the twilight of winter, the steely-grey light lending the buildings a sombre aspect. Now the grey stone glittered with rouge highlights as the summer sun rose.

She made out the double-doored building where the Skelt had taken her life-raft, and hoped that their task would be made easy by finding the vessel still in situ.

A tiny Fahran guard hurried back to the shuttle and gestured that the square was safe.

Charlton led the way, followed by Delia, Javinder, Mahn and Var. Oma remained jacked into the shuttle in case a quick getaway was required.

Delia gripped her laser and gestured across the square to the double doors. The cobbles before the doors were excoriated, but whether that indicated the passage of the raft as it was brought here – or taken away – she could not say.

The door was locked, but a brief pulse of laser fire shattered the mechanism. Charlton applied a boot to the door and it swung slowly open to reveal a yawning, empty space where once the life-raft had stood.

He turned to Mahn. "Very well, if you could lead the way to the machine shop..."

Charlton detailed six Fahran guards to remain in the square with the shuttle, and the remaining six to accompany the foray to the machine shop.

Flanked by two guards, Mahn led the way through the streets.

Delia found herself advancing in a circumspect crouch, half expecting to be ambushed by a Skelt hunting party. The streets were unnaturally quiet, the only sound her breathing and the skitter of Var's claws on the cobbles.

Delia said to Var, "You can see where the raft was dragged along the street." She pointed to the gouges and scuff marks engraved in the cobbles.

"It will give me great satisfaction," Var said, "to liberate my fellow Vo who was coerced into dragging the craft."

Delia wasn't sure whether she shared the Vo's sentiments. She would be quite content to locate the life-raft without encountering a single Skelt.

Minutes later the party stopped, Mahn pointing to a pair of timber doors similar to the last. The scuff marks approached the doors. Again they were locked, and everyone stood back while Charlton aimed his laser at the lock and turned the metal to dripping slag.

Delia advanced, holding her breath, as Charlton pushed open the door. So much rode on what they might find in the machine shop... or not find.

She swore as the door swung open. The chamber was empty.

Charlton said, "Are you sure this is the only machine shop?"

Mahn gestured, turning his hand. "I am certain." He moved off along the street, peering at the ground. He turned quickly and called, "Here! The tracks continue this way."

They moved along the street and examined the excoriated cobbles.

Charlton urged caution. "We need to consider our options before we give chase. It would appear that the Skelt have indeed taken the life-raft with them underground. Fortunately," he said, indicating the gouges, "they've obligingly left a trail." He thought about it. "Very well. It would appear that the city is deserted, rendering the guards back at the shuttle pretty much redundant." He looked at Delia. "How about we leave two guards with the shuttle and have the rest come with us?"

She agreed. "That makes sense."

Charlton issued orders to a Fahran to return to the square and fetch four guards.

As the Fahran hurried off, Delia's Imp informed her that Oma was calling.

Oma: *Any luck?*

Delia: *We've found the machine shop. It's empty.*

Oma: *Damn it. What now?*

Delia: *We're following marks where they dragged the raft. I'll keep you posted.*

She cut the connection.

The Fahran returned with four guards.

Charlton said, "Six guards will lead the way, following the tracks. You four, bring up the rear." He looked up, eyeing the towers and their high window openings. "And keep a wary eye out for Skelt. I suspect they've left the city, but we don't want to be surprised by stragglers. Very well, let's go."

They hurried through the brightening streets. The sun was climbing, blasting its light into the caverns between the buildings. Delia wondered how fresh the scrapes on the cobbles might be; clearly they'd been made since the melting of the ice, but that might have been a week or so ago. The Skelt might have transported the raft far underground in that time, and they would be unwilling to give up the vessel without a fight. They were armed only with crossbows and spears, but what the Skelt lacked in weaponry they more than made up for in numbers and hive-mind tenacity.

They came to an archway, into whose stygian gloom the street descended. Mahn said, "An entrance to the underground caverns. The tunnel will drop steeply after a short distance, and soon we will be travelling along corridors chiselled through solid rock by our ancestors many years ago."

Charlton regarded the Fahran. "Do you have any idea how far down the Skelt have their summer dwelling? What is it down there – a city, a vast chamber?"

"I was taken there once, soon after my capture," Mahn said. "It is a series of great, interconnected chambers, the largest the size of Alkellion itself. I would estimate that it is perhaps two kilometres deep."

"And crawling with Skelt." Charlton nodded. "Very well, lead the way, but be wary."

They activated headlamps, brought along for this very contingency, and set off again. They passed from the dazzling sunlight into cool shadow, following the bobbing cones of their headlights.

Delia contacted Oma.

Delia: *We've come to the start of the caverns and we're descending.*

Oma: *Hokay. Good luck. Take care, Delia.*

Delia: *Will do, and I'll be in touch when I have news.*

She hurried along beside Var, following Charlton's commanding bulk as he, in his turn, followed the Fahran guards.

The floor and walls were squared off to begin with, the ceiling arched, but after a hundred metres the ground inclined steeply and the finished stonework gave way to natural rock.

They had been descending for thirty minutes when Charlton called a halt. "We must have come almost a kilometre by now," he said. "We can't be far away from the first chamber."

"And when we reach it?" Delia asked.

Mahn said, "There will be lights visible ahead, giving warning that we are approaching the cavern."

"I just hope we find the raft before we come to the Skelt's lair," Javinder said. "I don't like the idea of attacking them on home territory."

"We won't," Charlton replied. "If they've taken the raft all the way, then we'll beat a tactical retreat and come back in greater numbers. Don't worry, we'll get what we want."

Javinder nodded, his headlight bobbing. "I just hope the Skelt haven't taken the ship apart and damaged the unit we need."

"Don't say things like that," Delia said. "There's enough standing between us and getting back to Earth. I'm trying to stay positive."

They set off again.

The tunnel widened, and Delia wondered if this were significant and signalled the proximity of the cavern.

She was startled, then, by a cry from behind her.

"Stop!" Var said.

Charlton called ahead to the vanguard of Fahran, then returned with the others to where Var had come to a halt. Her chitin threw off a hundred highlights from the focused headlamps.

"Var?" Delia said.

"I scent Skelt – close by and recent! They passed this way just minutes ago. They cannot be far ahead."

Charlton ordered everyone to extinguish their headlamps. Delia deactivated hers, pitching the tunnel into absolute darkness. She crouched, hearing only her heartbeat at first and then, very faintly, as if coming from far, far away, the sound of Skelt conversation – the multiple clacking of mandibles.

Charlton called the Fahran guards to him and whispered, "Two of you scout ahead, see what the situation is. On no account engage with the Skelt."

Delia heard scurrying in the tunnel, and silence descended.

"Var?" Charlton whispered.

She said, "The Skelt were moving in the same direction as ourselves, towards the cavern."

"Do you know how many there were?" Delia asked.

"No more than six."

"Accompanied by a Vo?"

"No. They were alone."

"In that case," she said, "it can't have been the team with the life-boat."

"It's my guess," Charlton said, "that they brought it down here days ago."

"That's what I was fearing," Javinder said.

Delia heard a rustling further along the tunnel, the guards returning. A Fahran voice piped up, "We came upon a party of Skelt guards. We are two hundred metres from the main entrance to the Skelt lair. We advanced to the entrance and we saw the life-raft we seek."

Charlton said, "How far away?"

"They have taken it far into the cavern and are taking it apart."

Charlton swore. "Just what we need. We should retreat, come back with reinforcements. But that risks the unit being damaged, or lost."

The Fahran said, "There is a branch corridor not far away, leading to a gallery which looks down on the cavern. We could hurry there and observe."

"Good work. We'd better remain in darkness. The only way to do this is to link hands and move ahead slowly."

For a minute they fumbled in the darkness until they were assured that everyone was linked. Delia grasped Javinder's hand and that of a Fahran guard, the latter's hairless palm dry and leathery in her grip.

They edged forward slowly, step by step. Var brought up the rear, murmuring to Delia that she would keep track of her friends by dint of their scent.

Delia sensed they were veering right, and then the ground underfoot inclined upwards; they were traversing the tributary corridor. She saw dim light ahead, and the shapes of the Fahran guards cautiously advancing. She released Javinder's hand and that of the Fahran and crept forward.

The tunnel emerged high up on the sloping side of the cavern, fifty metres above and to the right of where the original tunnel entered the Skelt lair. They crouched in the entrance and peered down.

The sight that greeted her eyes was at once breathtaking and shocking. Never before had she seen so many Skelt in one place and she was reminded of an ants' nest, the insect-creatures scurrying back and forth in a ferment of industrious activity that seemed without purpose. She heard a constant clatter of mandibles, a percussive cacophony that rose and fell, eerie in its alienness.

Then she saw the life-raft far below, surrounded by Skelt. Many swarmed across its surface, employed in taking the ship apart panel by panel; enslaved Vo, burdened with machine parts, moved to and from the vessel in orderly lines.

Charlton, crouching beside her, said grimly, "They're destroying it."

"With luck," Javinder said, "they haven't reached the ion-exchange unit yet. It's deep to the rear of the craft."

She watched as a team of Skelt removed a section of the life-raft's outer tegument, attached it to ropes slung around the rear haunches of a Vo, and ordered the creature to advance. Other Vo were hauling smaller components, and there were even a line of captive Fahran down there carrying ship parts under the watchful gaze of Skelt slave masters. The workers threaded their way across the cavern floor to a clearing where a team of Skelt was examining the components one by one.

"There must be thousands of them," Charlton murmured. "I could lead a well armed Fahran army down here, but at what risk? I'd be consigning many Fahran to their deaths. The Skelt might not possess sophisticated weaponry, but they fight with little care for individual safety."

Mahn crept alongside and whispered, "I have an idea."

Charlton regarded the Fahran. "Go on."

"There are Fahran down there, going in and out of the vessel. I could enter the cavern by way of the main tunnel, go amongst them and search for the unit."

Delia objected, "And how will you get away? If you haven't noticed, there are thousands of Skelt down there."

"But none of them are expecting an errant Fahran to abscond with a part. They are exhorting their slaves to work faster, not ensuring that none of them try to escape."

"And when you get into the ship?" Delia pointed out. "Do you know what you're looking for, exactly?"

Javinder said, "I can describe the unit in detail, Delia."

"But what if it's too big for him to carry?"

"It isn't. It's only about this big, a cylinder ten centimetres by three, at most."

She shot him a look. "Thanks for that, Jav."

Mahn turned to Charlton, who was staring down into the cavern as if considering the Fahran's plan. "Let's assess the risks," he said.

"There's bound to be a Skelt aboard the ship," Delia said, "supervising the removal of parts. Mahn can't simply waltz in there, select the part he wants, and skedaddle without arousing suspicion."

Mahn touched her arm. "But I will take great care inside the ship," he said. "I will take no risks. But if I get the opportunity, I will take the part and return."

Charlton said, "I think the risk is worth taking, Delia. The alternative is to come down here in force, risking many Fahran lives."

He looked at Mahn. "But listen to me, and take heed. If you can't find the unit without arousing suspicion, abandon the mission. If you are in any doubt at all, do not proceed. If you try, and fail and are caught, then the consequences for all of us are catastrophic. I'd rather you failed honourably, and allowed us to come back another day, than be captured and alert the Skelt to what we want. Do you understand, Mahn?"

The Fahran regarded Charlton with his big eyes. "I understand. I will take great care."

Delia gripped Mahn's arm, not letting him go. She stared at him. "You make damned sure you take care, do you hear? I don't want to lose you, you little monkey."

He blinked at her. "Monkey?"

"A term of affection," she said.

Javinder drew Mahn into the shadow of the cave mouth and started a whispered conversation, describing the ion-exchange unit, and where to find it, in great detail.

From where she crouched further back in the tunnel, Var said, "I could go with Mahn in case he needs assistance. Look, some Vo are steered by Fahran riders."

"You'll do nothing of the kind," Delia said. "You're staying here, and that's an order. I'm not risking both of you down there."

"And anyway," Charlton put in, "we might have to rely on your speed if we need to make a quick escape."

This mollified the Vo, and she fell silent.

Mahn finished his consultation with Javinder and looked around the expectant group. Delia took his hand. "Good luck," she said. "And remember, take no risks."

He inclined his head gravely, indicating his understanding, and retreated into the tunnel. Delia watched him go, wishing that a Fahran other than Mahn had volunteered for the mission.

They moved further back into the tunnel, lest an attentive Skelt look up and spot them. Delia crouched behind a rock and peered down at the ship.

"To me," Charlton said, at her side, "the Fahran are identical. How will we be able to tell Mahn from all the others down there?"

"I'll have my Imp track him and place a marker on him," Delia said. "Of course, only I'll be able to see it."

"Your implant can do that?"

"It can overlay visuals, project images, broadcast sounds and a hundred other things."

Charlton shook his head. "I really want to get back to Earth, to catch up with all the tech, if for no other reason."

Delia looked down into the cavern, ordered Imp to slap a sigil on Mahn's head when he appeared, then glanced at Charlton. "But do you know something? I think I'd be able to tell Mahn apart, even without help from Imp. He has a certain jauntiness to his gait, and upright posture I think I'd recognise."

"You're close to the little critter, aren't you?"

"He saved my life, Edward. He's been selfless on the trek south. Of course we're close." She peered down at the line of Fahran and Vo moving back and forth between the life-raft and the clearing at the centre of the cavern. "I just hope to hell he doesn't do anything foolhardy, thinking he has to play the hero."

"Well, we're armed to the teeth and despite the Skelt numbers, we'd put up quite a fight if anything did go wrong."

"I hope it doesn't come to that."

Imp said, *Mahn is approaching the mouth of the entrance tunnel and should be coming into sight in ten seconds, nine, eight...*

Delia relayed the message to Charlton and leaned forward, her mouth suddenly dry.

"There he is!" She pointed to the figure of a tiny Fahran dodging between boulders far below; Imp had obligingly hung a glowing letter M above his head.

"I see him," Charlton said.

Keeping in the cover of rocks, Mahn crept towards a line of Fahran making their way to the life-raft. Skelt overseers with whips supervised the line, calling out orders and occasionally lashing out at unfortunate Fahran.

Delia bit her lip, willing Mahn to make it to the line without being detected. Just as she thought he would make it, a Skelt turned, lightning fast, and saw him. The Skelt vanished, only to reappear a second later towering over Mahn.

"He's been caught," Charlton said, raising his laser.

Delia stayed his hand. "Wait. Look."

The Skelt was reprimanding Mahn for some perceived misdemeanour, and the Fahran was explaining himself. Whatever he said managed to convince the Skelt, who with a flick of its whip directed Mahn to the line filing towards the life-raft.

Delia let out a fluttery breath and smiled at Charlton.

"That was a close call," he said.

"The Skelt can't have had any real suspicions," Delia said. "I think the difficulty will come when he has the part – if he can find it – and tries to get away."

She returned her attention to the cavern and watched Mahn take on the gait of the enslaved Fahran in the line with him. Gone was his jaunty step; now he trudged along, shoulders hunched.

Beside her, Charlton said, "I've lost him. Where is he?"

"Sixth in line, passing the stalagmite on the right. He's about twenty metres from the ship."

"Got him."

Passing Mahn's line in the other direction, emerging from the life-raft, was a file of Fahran bearing machine parts. Soon, she thought, Mahn would be among them.

"The problem might be," Delia whispered, "how much freedom he has within the ship. If he's closely supervised..."

Charlton nodded. "Also, he'll be stymied if the unit's been removed already."

Mahn approached the ship's ramp, the dancing white M above his head. He climbed the ramp and passed inside. Delia held her breath.

He seemed to be within the ship for a long time. A minute elapsed, then two. "What's he doing in there?"

"Perhaps the Skelt are removing parts as the Fahran wait," Charlton surmised.

She eyed the line of departing Fahran, and then she saw the tiny blue creature beneath the letter M. "There he is!" she said, then swore. "Dammit!"

"Where?"

"Coming down the ramp, but that isn't the drive unit he's carrying. He's the Fahran struggling with a bulky box thing, leaking gelware."

"I see him," Charlton said. "Don't worry. He'll get another chance."

Delia watched as Mahn laboured under the weight of the box, staggering in line towards the clearing where the slaves were depositing machinery, panels, and com consoles.

Under the watchful eye of Skelt guards, Mahn lowered the gelware unit to the ground and set off back towards the ship.

"Second time lucky," Charlton said under his breath.

Delia considered the captive Fahran, and the life they must lead down here – working for overbearing taskmasters without hope of escape. She'd make it her first job, at some point in the future, to free these Fahran from the yoke of the Skelt.

Mahn approached the life-raft, climbed the ramp and passed inside.

The ship was a sorry sight now; panels had been removed, along with the viewscreen. Its exo-skeleton was revealed, and between the spars she made out silver gelware dripping like syrupy ichor.

Mahn emerged a minute later, and the renewed spring of his gait told Delia that he'd been successful.

Charlton said, "Damn. That isn't the ion-exchange unit."

Mahn was clutching a mass of cortical leads to his chest, wires trailing. Delia glanced at Charlton. "I think he's been clever."

"What?"

"See that silver cylinder just showing behind the leads? That's the unit. He's brought out the leads as camouflage."

Charlton smiled. "Clever indeed. I just hope he's clever enough to evade the Skelt."

Mahn stepped from the ramp and followed the line of Fahran away from the life-raft and across the cavern. He would be forced to deposit the mass of leads with the other mechanical detritus, and somehow conceal the cylindrical unit at the same time.

Her stomach clenched. She watched him approach the clearing, bend down and place the tangle of leads on the ground. With commendable legerdemain, he slipped the unit under his left arm, concealing it beneath his long fur.

He turned casually and rejoined the line of Fahran moving back to the life-raft.

Delia whispered, "This is where it gets dangerous."

The line passed boulders and stalagmites – as well as a number of vigilant Skelt guards. Mahn's only hope was to evade the attention of the guards and slip into the cover of a natural feature, and then make his way, dodging guards, all the way back to the tunnel entrance.

She found her hand clutching the butt of her laser, slick with sweat.

Mahn came alongside a stalagmite; he was at midpoint between two guards. He ducked, easing himself below the line of sight of the Skelt and using the Fahran slaves before and after him as cover. Then he quickly rolled across the rocky floor until he came to the crystal-encrusted torus of the stalagmite. He scrambled around the feature and hunkered down. Delia could only imagine the fear he must be experiencing now as he crouched behind the calcified tower and waited for the Skelt to raise the alarm.

It never came and, as the seconds elapsed, Delia breathed a little easier.

She estimated that Mahn was a couple of hundred metres from the tunnel entrance, with a dozen rock formations between him and safety. On the debit side, Skelt guards came and went between the main entrance and the life-raft – silver blurs streaking back and forth.

"Time's on his side," Charlton whispered to her. "There's no need to rush things. Just take it easy, buddy. Take your time. Easy does it."

Delia glanced at Charlton. Concern was etched into the lines of his face as he gazed down at the Fahran with yellowed, bloodshot eyes.

Mahn looked around him, waited another half minute, then made a move. He ran, doubled-up, from one stalagmite to another, ten metres away. Delia held her breath until he reached it, then released it in a rush.

"Made it! Now sit tight, pal. There's no rush." Charlton kept up a running commentary under his breath. "Absolutely no rush at all..."

Mahn was a hundred metres from the main tunnel entrance in the wall of the cavern. Delia watched the Skelt streaking back and forth, leaving Doppler images of themselves on her retina. Mahn peered out from his hiding place, watching the passing guards.

She could see him eyeing up his next place of concealment, a great boulder five metres away. To reach it, he would be in view from a pathway used by the Skelt. If a guard should pass just as he was negotiating the gap...

She watched him, crouching like a sprinter in the blocks, biding his time.

He took off, moving at speed from the base of the stalagmite.

Delia saw the Skelt before Mahn had any awareness of the guard's presence. The silver blur moved from the Fahran's left and stopped before him. To Mahn, it would seem as if the Skelt had appeared out of thin air. Mahn stopped short, cowering.

Charlton swore. Delia felt something like ice fill her belly with fear.

The Skelt advanced, drew its sickle sword and moved it towards Mahn's chin. The insect applied upward pressure, lifting Mahn's head as it interrogated him.

The Skelt reached out, its claw going for whatever Mahn was concealing under his arm.

Mahn danced away, backing himself up against the boulder.

Delia saw the Skelt's mandibles clack loosely, and a second later two more Skelt appeared on the scene.

Charlton swore again and raised his laser.

"Don't fire!" Delia hissed.

"You have a better idea?"

"I said my Imp can project images. Get back into the tunnel – take the others and make your way to the shuttle. Once I've created a diversion, there's nothing further we can do here."

"Apart from laser a few insects –"

"And in so doing risk Mahn's life, and our own."

She glanced back down into the cavern. The Skelt were quizzing Mahn, swords drawn.

Delia lost no time. She commanded Imp to project three images, spaced well apart, stationary to begin with but then moving off in different directions.

Instantly, images of her mother and father and Timothy Greene appeared beyond the Skelt, clearly startling them. Beside her, Charlton spoke under his breath. "So lifelike."

The human images moved off, her mother scurrying in a way that, under any other circumstances, would have been comical. Timothy Greene turned and ran, followed by the avatar of her elderly father.

She hissed to Charlton, "Get back to the ship!"

He ran into the tunnel and ordered Javinder and the others to follow him. They vanished in an instant, and Delia suddenly felt very much alone.

Down below, the three Skelt forgot about the Fahran and moved off – three silver blurs – in the direction of the phantom humans.

Mahn lost no time. He ran, dodging boulders and stalagmites, towards the tunnel entrance. One of the Skelt stopped, change direction and went after Mahn. Instinctively, Delia raised her laser. The Skelt was a hundred metres away, and she knew that her aim wasn't that good. But an accurate shot was not necessary in order to bring down a target. She set her weapon to constant beam, aimed it across the path of the Skelt, and depressed the firing stud.

The Skelt ran into the beam, through it, and stopped suddenly – the momentum of its halt sliding its upper torso from its pelvis and legs. For a grotesque second, its legs remained standing while its upper half hit the ground with a messy thud.

The disadvantage of using a laser in the cavern, of course, was that it attracted undue attention. She heard a welter of alarmed clacks from down below, then turned and sprinted into the tunnel, activating her headlamp.

She only hoped that Mahn had managed to evade the other Skelt and escape into the main tunnel. With luck, he would be ahead of her and racing back to the shuttle. She would fight a rearguard action, holding off the advancing Skelt with a hail of laser fire.

She came to the junction where the branch tunnel met the main tunnel, and turned left. She expected to see the running form of Mahn up ahead in the light cast by her headlamp, but all she did see was the empty tunnel. What, she asked herself, if she were running away from Mahn, leaving him to the mercy of the Skelt?

She heard a sound from up ahead, the skittering of multiple claws on rock. Var's jet black bulk filled the tunnel, coming towards her.

"I told you to get back to the ship!" she screamed.

"And leave you and Mahn here?"

So Mahn was not ahead of her...

"There's nothing you can do –" she began.

"Where is Mahn?"

"I don't know," she admitted. "Presumably back there."

She looked back, frozen with indecision.

"We've got to save him!"

"Of course," Delia said. "I'll go first. Hang back. You aren't armed, and I am. And get ready to run."

She readied her laser and ran back along the tunnel towards the cavern.

She heard a sound from up ahead, a ragged breath followed by multiple Skelt voices. A slight, dark figure appeared in the illuminated cone of her headlamp, running towards her.

"Mahn!" she cried.

"Run!" he yelled.

To Var she said, "You heard him – run!"

She knelt and took aim. Beyond the careering figure of the Fahran, she made out half a dozen tall, loping Skelt. She aimed past Mahn and fired, a brilliant lance of laser light drilling through the chest of the leading alien. Mahn passed her at a sprint and now she could wield the laser with greater abandon. She swept the beam across the tunnel, slicing through two further Skelt. More appeared behind them, clattering over the bodies of their fallen comrades. There must have been a dozen or more; the tunnel was full of the creatures, swarming towards her. She heard the whistle of something fly past her head – a crossbow bolt. She ducked, swept her laser right and left, and backed off.

Spears clattered around her. Another bolt narrowly missed her head. She heard it crack into something hard and was startled by a cry. She turned to see Var pulling the bolt from its bulging brow with a great pincer.

"I told you to run!" she said.

"And leave you alone? There are hundreds of Skelt –"

"And what the hell can you do?" she said, and immediately regretted the question.

"This!" Var said, pushing Delia aside with a great pincer.

Var scuttled up the tunnel towards the advancing Skelt, ignoring Delia's frenzied cries of protest.

She fired around the Vo, cursing the creature as it barrelled into the leading Skelt. For long seconds all was confusion, a shadow play of Skelt arms and legs as Var attacked with her pincers, cutting the aliens in half and removing limbs at random – and receiving heavy blows herself. Delia watched impotently, unable to fire for fear of hitting Var.

She jumped as she felt a hand on her shoulder.

"There's nothing we can do!" Mahn cried. "Come!"

In a last, futile act of defiance, Var had reared up on her back legs and wedged her shell across the tunnel. Delia ran, weeping as she went. She cast one final look over her shoulder and would never forget what she saw in the fitful light of her headlamp.

Var had succeeded in blocking the tunnel with her upended bulk, but only for so long. Her body rocked, and Delia thought the Skelt were attempting to push past it – then she saw the glint of a blade slice through the chitin, and great rents appear in the carapace, and a second later the shell exploded and three Skelt burst through.

"You murdering bastards!" she yelled, and decapitated the charging aliens with a swift sweep of her laser.

She turned and sprinted, gratified to see Mahn well ahead of her, as more Skelt burst through Var's shell in pursuit.

She felt something thump into her right shoulder – and knew that, this time, she had been hit. She staggered on, then stumbled and fell to her knees as the pain lanced though her. Dimly she made out the lights of half a dozen Fahran guards rushing towards her.

They knelt around her, crosshatching the tunnel with laser fire, and she felt tiny hands grab her arms and legs and bear her aloft. She was carried with surprising speed and she cried aloud as the pain increased, becoming unbearable.

Then they were no longer in the tunnel. The heat of the sun burned the back of her neck. She opened her eyes and saw a blur of cobbles passing centimetres beneath her. She heard laser fire, heard spears and crossbow bolts striking stone around them.

Then the cobbles were no longer rushing along beneath her, but the smooth grey surface of the shuttle's ramp. The pain mounted, and with it a crazed euphoria, and then she felt nothing as she passed into oblivion.

SHE CAME AWAKE and blinked up at a point of light.

She was lying on her back. The pain in her shoulder had abated, replaced by a dull ache. She turned her head. She was on a bunk in the shuttle.

Imp, how long since...?

Since you fled the Skelt cavern? Imp replied. *A little over a day, Delia.*

One day?

Where are we?

In the valley of Mahkanda.

She closed her eyes, relieved but at the same time obscurely troubled.

Mahn? Were was Mahn? Had he survived? And what of the drive unit?

She felt herself drifting off.

She opened her eyes. She had the vague impression that she had lost consciousness since speaking to her Imp.

Oma smiled down at her. "Delia, you're fine. Relax."

"But..."

"Don't worry. You'll be fine."

"Mahn!" she cried.

A small, blue face appeared, staring at her with huge eyes. "Here I am, Delia."

Oma held her hand.

"Don't ever again," the South African said, "make me perform an operation to remove a crossbow bolt from your shoulder, instructed only by my Imp and using the shuttle's limited surgical resources."

Delia smiled. "It's a promise. I won't."

"Fortunately the bolt didn't hit anything vital. Shattered your collar bone, but we managed to patch that up."

"Thank you." She squeezed the woman's hand. "How long have I...?"

Another voice said, "You've been out for over a day, Delia."

She turned her head and smiled up at Edward Charlton.

"Var..." she said, tears pricking her eyes.

Charlton murmured, "She'll never be forgotten, Delia. I've arranged for a statue to grace the esplanade, along with the three Fahran guards who perished. Also, their stories will join the Twelve."

"The ion-exchange unit?"

Javinder said, "Done. I slaved it to the shuttle's drive and ran preliminary tests yesterday. All the gelware has integrated and it's running without a hitch."

She reached out and took Mahn's long-fingered hand. "Good work, Monkey." She turned to the Indian. "So we can escape Valinda's gravity well and get into space?"

"Just as soon as the work on the *Orpheus*'s quantum lattice is completed. We removed it yesterday, with the help of a hundred Fahran, and attached it to the shuttle's nose-cone this morning. Not pretty, but if it survives the lift-off..."

"Yes?"

He smiled. "Then all we've got to worry about is whether the lattice will work and generate a wormhole long enough for us to transit."

She shook her head in wonder. "You have Earth's co-ordinates?"

Charlton said, "Stored in the memory cache of the *Orpheus*."

"So... when do we lift-off?" she asked.

"Twelve hours from now," Javinder said, "at sunset."

CHAPTER THIRTY-EIGHT

VALINDA FELL AWAY beneath the shuttle.

The tiny planet turned imperceptibly, striated with chiffon clouds above green landmasses and blues seas. Delia stared at the alien world and felt a strange pressure in her chest. She was leaving a place she had come to love, heading hopefully for a planet and a people she loved even more.

Mahn leaned against the console and stared at the viewscreen. "My world," he murmured, "as I've never seen it before. It's beautiful. And..."

"Yes?"

"It looks so peaceful from up here. It is hard to believe that the Skelt dwell down there, enslaving my people. It is hard to believe, Delia, that everything I have ever known could be contained on a thing so tiny."

Delia massaged her shoulder, easing the ache.

Edward Charlton came to her side. "How do you feel?"

"Never better."

"Modern surgery and medicine," he said. "Three hundred years ago you'd still be laid up, unable to move your shoulder."

Oma lay in the shuttle's command sling, jacked into the drive. Beside her, in the co-pilot's sling, Javinder monitored the core's performance.

The shuttle climbed into space, heading for the huge primary dead ahead.

Mahn said, "I wish Var had lived to see this, and accompany us on our journey."

Delia smiled. "She always wanted to travel, to see the world."

"I will miss her," Mahn said. "Never would I have thought I would become so close to a Vo."

Delia reached out and touched his arm.

She stared through the viewscreen at the quantum lattice that Javinder, Charlton and a team of Fahran workers had welded to the shuttle's nose cone. The construct – which resembled the Eiffel tower made of ice – made the shuttle look like a mechanical swordfish. Not pretty, Javinder had said, but functional, or hopefully so. They would find out in the next hour.

"It's very strange," Charlton said.

She looked at him, this calm, quiet, eminently reassuring man who had once been a god. "What is?"

"I have dreamed of this moment for three hundred years – well, subjectively for about two months – and I'm surprised I'm feeling so... so accepting of what might lie ahead, the three possibilities."

"That we might succeed, and pass through the wormhole to Earth; that we might fail, and spend the rest of our lives on Valinda, or that...?"

"Or that the whole process might blow-up spectacularly and kill us all."

Delia said, "But if it doesn't blow up, but we don't get back to Earth?"

"Then we'll face the rest of our lives on Valinda," he said, "which isn't the travail it might have been. Alone, I might have found it hard to cope; with you three, the job ahead – of aiding the Fahran against the Skelt – will be made that much easier."

"I can think of worse things than a life amongst the Fahran," she said.

Charlton stared ahead at the fulminating sun. He set his jaw and said, "But we must succeed, Delia. We must reach Earth, if for nothing else than to warn the world that there's a ruthless alien race out there – to warn our fellows that we must face the Skelt and defeat them, or face extinction."

He turned to Javinder. "How long?"

"I'm priming the core, Ed. The lattice is charging. Perhaps as soon as fifteen minutes."

Delia felt a tightness in her chest.

"The transition might be rough," she said to Charlton and Mahn. "I suggest we fasten ourselves in."

They crossed to a line of seats to the rear of the bridge. Delia sat between Charlton and the Fahran. She assisted Mahn with his strap, noticing as she did so that his feet hung inches above the deck.

The quantum lattice projecting from the shuttle's nose-cone glowed white as a charge stuttered along its length. The vessel vibrated; Oma and Javinder swung in the their slings. Delia gripped the armrests and smiled reassuringly at Mahn.

Javinder called out, "Channelling energy. Fifty-five per cent and rising. Optimum through-put. It's looking good."

"We've achieved transit speed," Oma said. "Looking good here, too."

"Eighty-five per cent," Javinder said. "The rig's holding up." He turned and smiled at Charlton. "Scratch that fifteen minutes, Ed. We could go for transition in five."

Charlton nodded. "Let's do it."

Delia found her hand moving to clutch Mahn's.

The swordfish projection glowed white hot, filling the bridge with blinding light.

Javinder yelled, "This is it."

She saw a beam of pure white light lance from the lattice and expand before the ship, a shimmering oval with all the fragility of a soap bubble. Oma's head hung back and her eyes rolled as she accelerated the ship towards the wormhole.

The ellipse swelled to fill the screen.

Delia gripped Mahn's hand and closed her eyes, unable to watch.

Javinder called out, "Three... Two... One!"

A pulverising pain hit Delia, slammed into her chest and flattened her, and a nausea worse than any she had experienced swelled in her, hot and intolerable. She heard the cries of her fellow humans, and the fluting agony of Mahn beside her.

The shuttle twisted with a scream of stressed metal. She felt herself spin head over heel. She waited for the pain, the inevitable break up of the shuttle and the airlessness of the vacuum.

It never came.

Instead, the spinning ceased and the squeal of metal was replaced by silence – a silence more absolute than anything she had ever experienced. She could not bring herself to open her eyes as the pain abated and the sickness passed.

She was still alive, so they had either succeed in passing though the wormhole to Earth, or not.

Would the latter, she wondered, be so intolerable? A life among a peaceable alien race, assisting them against an implacable alien foe? She would not be lonely, with friends like Oma and Charlton, Javinder and Mahn.

The silence stretched, and she knew from the stunned disappointment of her friends that they had failed.

Oma was the first to speak, "Oh, how *beautiful*..." and an emotion like joy kicked in Delia's chest as she opened her eyes.

Charlton was already out of his seat and standing before the viewscreen beside Javinder. Oma hung in her sling, but strained forward to stare out.

Beside Delia, Mahn leaned forward, tugging against the strap in his impatience. Delia unfastened him, and then herself, and joined the others at the viewscreen.

She wept.

Planet Earth, silent and majestic, hung before them like a jewel in the immensity of space.

Oma pointed, too stunned to speak, and Delia saw three sleek silver shapes streaking through space to intercept the shuttle

Javinder opened a com channel and a female voice filled the bridge. "I repeat, please identify yourself. This is Captain Elli Navarre, ESO jumpship *Barcelona*, requesting your identification."

Delia turned to Edward Charlton, to see tears tracking down his cheeks. He shook his head, unable to speak, and gestured Delia towards the microphone. She glanced at Javinder and Oma, who both nodded.

She leaned forward and said, "This is Dr Cordelia Kemp, of the ESO ship the *Pride of Amsterdam*."

"Ah, please repeat."

"This is Dr Cordelia Kemp, of the ESO ship the *Pride of Amsterdam*," she said, her voice catching.

"The *Pride of Amsterdam*?" The pilot sounded stunned.

"That what I said," Delia said, "and I have with me First Officer Edward Charlton of the ESO starship *Orpheus*, Pilot Oma Massinga of the *Amsterdam*, and Engineer Javinder Lal, also of the *Amsterdam*." She turned to Mahn. "And also..." she went on, "we have with us Ambassador Mahn an Ahntan, of the extraterrestrial species known as the Fahran, from the world of Valinda. Do you copy?"

After a second, the pilot murmured, "I copy, Dr Kemp, but... please forgive me if I don't believe a word you say."

Delia straightened up and stared through the viewscreen at her homeworld.

"Believe it or not," she said, "we're coming home."

EPILOGUE

Delia and Mahn stood before the viewscreen of the quarantine station, orbiting a thousand kilometres above Earth. Far below, the planet turned slowly, vast and blue. The sight brought tears to her eyes.

For the past three days they'd undergone medical check-ups and metabolic analyses from medics in bio-hazard suits, before being given the all clear. In less than an hour they were due to take a shuttle down to Orly spaceport, Paris.

A media screen hung in the air to their right, beaming breaking news across the chamber. The big event, of course, was the miraculous arrival from another world of survivors of the *Amsterdam* blow-out. A talking head said, "... as well as unconfirmed reports that accompanying the three survivors is a member of a sentient alien race know as the Fahran. According to ESO pilot Elli Navarre, who spoke to one of the crew of the Amsterdam on Tuesday..."

Delia smiled at Mahn. "You're famous, Mahn. Everyone will be wanting to talk to you when we land."

He stared down at the slowly turning planet. "Little did I know, when I first saw you, that day in the Skelt chamber..."

She touched his hand and pointed. "Look, that great landmass down there... That's Canada, where I was born. And see that lighted mass beside the inky area? Toronto, a great city on the shore of a vast lake. My parents will be down there."

She looked over her shoulder to the far end of the chamber, where Javinder was seated before a floating screen, talking to his fiancée. In just five minutes Delia was due to be patched through to her parents.

Edward Charlton and Oma joined them at the rail.

Charlton shook his head and smiled. "I find it almost impossible to believe, Delia. Earth... after so long." He stared down at the planet. "I don't even know what kind of world I'll find down there."

"You might be surprised at how little has changed," Delia said. "Human beings are still human beings, you know."

His gaze was far way. "I had a son. He was twenty when the *Orpheus* was lost. I... I'll be able to read about his life, consider his existence as if he were an ancestor. And I'll have family, perhaps, descendants who thought me long dead, if they considered me at all."

Delia smiled to herself as she anticipated the reunion with her mother and father.

Charlton said, "We've brought to Earth the most momentous news, the greatest discovery, perhaps, since the development of wormhole technology."

Delia looked at Mahn. "And the miracle of sentient alien life."

"This will change our lives," Charlton said. "We'll be in demand; the media will be in a furore; nothing will ever be the same again."

"For us individually," Oma said, "and for our respective worlds."

Charlton laid a hand on Mahn's shoulder. "Oma is right. Your world will change out of all recognition. On the plus side, we will rid you of the scourge of the Skelt."

Mahn looked up. "And on the minus?" he asked.

Charlton shrugged. "We will do our best to spare you from the depredations of our kind. There are charters in place for this eventuality – the coming together of humans and sentient aliens for the first time. I will work selflessly to ensure that your world remains unspoilt, sovereign."

Oma said, "We all will, Mahn." She looked at Charlton and Delia. "I want to go back to Valinda as soon as I can, you know? Just as soon as I've seen a few friends on Earth, I want to get back there and help the Fahran and the Vo."

Delia laughed. "You know something? I think I'm missing Valinda already."

Javinder joined them. "Delia, your turn."

She caught her breath as she turned to the screen. "Mahn, I'd like you to meet my parents."

She led the tiny alien across the chamber and sat down. Mahn stood before the chair, staring with huge eyes at the screen as the picture flickered and the scene switched to an empty studio. She saw movement, then her mother and father entered the shot and seated themselves. They looked so small, so old and small.

Her mother gasped, and Delia saw tears in her father's grey eyes. "Cordelia!" her mother said. "You don't know how... when we heard the news about the *Amsterdam*... And then, just three days ago. Oh, our joy..." She broke down and wept, and Delia's father placed a protective arm around her shoulders.

"We celebrated, Cordelia," he said. "The whole town did. We had all the neighbours round. My word, the party lasted till this morning."

"We're so proud of you," her mother said. "You don't know how proud..."

Delia fought back the tears. "I have so much to tell you. You'll hardly believe the half of it. And..." She reached out and touched Mahn's arm. "And I'd like you to meet my great friend, Mahn an Ahntan, who saved my life."

Her father stared at the alien. "We're indebted to you, sir."

Mahn spoke in his fluting tongue, and her Imp translated: "It was an honour to help Delia..."

"Mom, Dad, get the spare room ready, will you? Mahn is staying a few days as out guest."

Her mother beamed. "I'll do that, Cordelia. And I'll bake one of my special blueberry pies, okay?"

Across the chamber, a hatch irised open and an official in the uniform of the European Space Organisation stepped through. "If you'd care to accompany me..." she said.

"Mom, Dad, that's the shuttle. See you in around ten hours, okay? I love you."

Her parents raised their hands in farewell and the picture broke up.

She climbed to her feet and stared across the chamber to the blue world far below. At last, the final leg of her long, long journey home was about to commence.

Taking Mahn's hand, Delia joined her friends as they made their way through the hatch to the waiting shuttle.